D0255245

HEARTLESS 2:
STILL GRIMY

CACHET

HEARTLESS 2: STILL GRIMY

Copyright 2014 Cachet Johnson

Published by:
G Street Chronicles

All rights reserved. No part of this book may be used or reproduced in any manner whatsoever without written permission from the publisher, except where permitted by law.

This is a work of fiction. Any resemblance to actual persons living or dead is purely coincidental.

First Trade Paperback Edition Printing 2015

ISBN-13: 978-1511996853
ISBN-10: 10: 1511996854

Dedication

This book is dedicated to all of the readers who have ever picked up one of my books. Your support and input makes this thing worth wold, and I appreciate you all, more than you'll ever know.

PRELUDE

When I finally open my eyes, I'm dazed and confused. I look around, trying to figure out where I am, but it's too dark to see anything. It seems like I'm sitting in a chair of some sort. *But...how?* I wonder. Trying to move my arms gets me nowhere, because they seem to be bound tightly by something; the same goes for my legs. Panic shoots through my body when I remember that I am in my own house, and I think someone is still inside with me. I recall making my way to the front door, but just as I reached out to grab the knob, I was hit over the head with something hard; I don't remember anything after that. My mind is racing, I'm trying to figure out what the hell is going on and what whoever is in my house plans to do to me. I kind of figure they must not want me dead, because if they did, they could have already made it so I'd never wake up. *What else could they possibly want?* I'm scared to ask the question and even more scared of the answer.

The back of my head is throbbing, and I smell the stench of blood in the air. Again I try to move my arms and legs, but nothing happens; I'm still stuck. Minutes pass as I'm tied to this chair, and I still don't hear anything—nothing at all. I want to scream for help, but I'm worried that the person who did this to me is still inside. *What will I do then? I guess the same thing I'm gonna do whenever that bastard decides to come back and do whatever he or she has planned to do all along. Fuck it,* I decide. *It ain't like I have anything to lose at*

1

this point anyway. "Help! Help!"" I scream at the top of my lungs.

Suddenly, the lights come back on, causing my eyes to sting a bit. My head instantly begins to pulsate from the pain of being drunk, as well as from the blow I received. I try my best to squint, trying to regain focus in my vision; that's pretty hard to do since I've been in the dark for so long. When I'm finally able to see clearly, I notice that I'm in the center of my master bathroom. Duct tape is around my wrists, and I'm tied to one of my dining room chairs. I'm still dressed in my panties and bra, so I kinda figure I haven't been sexually assaulted. There are small stains of blood on my left breast and my shoulder, but I've got no idea where it came from. I tilt my head toward the mirror over by the sink; my hair has dried blood caked in it, and it's on my face as well. I cringe at the sight of my reflection. *Who in the hell could've done this? And why?*

"So Sleeping Beauty's finally awake, huh?" a female voice says.

I snap my head in the direction of the voice, which is coming from right outside my door, but I don't see anything.

"You thought you were untouchable, didn't you?"

Still, I can't seem to make out the bitch's voice. "Wh-who the hell is that?" I ask.

"You've done a lot of shit to a lot of people, Miss Lady, and now it's time for you to pay."

"Who the fuck are you? Why don't you show your face, bitch?" I boldly yell, even though I'm scared shitless.

When she rounds the corner and enters the bedroom, I find myself in utter shock. *Wait...what the hell is she doing here?*

CHAPTER ONE

A beeping sound wakens me from my slumber. My eyes dart open, and I look around frantically, trying to figure out where I am. My head is pounding, and my body aches terribly. An IV bag is hanging from a skinny pole beside me, and the beeping continues. I realize that I'm in a hospital, but I have no idea which one. The last thing I remember is being shot at by somebody in that Cadillac Seville, my chest bleeding, and crashing my truck. I'm sure one of the onlookers must have called 911. Whoever it was, I'm extremely grateful.

"Ugh!" I scream when a sharp, stabbing pain moves from my back to my armpit. "What the fuck!?"

A young black girl, dressed in scrubs, comes into my room. "How are you today, Ms. Wilson?" she asks, walking over to the bed with a clipboard in her hand. As she gets closer, I catch a glimpse at her nametag. Her name is Yvette, and I'm at Metro Health.

"Not so good. Am I gonna be all right?"

"Sure. You just need to—"

"When can I go home?" I ask, cutting her off. There's no need to bullshit; I'm ready to get the fuck out of here.

"Well, I'll have the doctor talk to you about that, but between me and you, I'm pretty sure you can leave as early as tomorrow."

"Cool. Can you do me a favor and go get the doctor so I can see what I need to do to get the hell outta here?"

3

"One sec'. Just let me get your vitals and check your wound," Yvette tells me with a smile.

She takes my temperature and makes sure my blood pressure is all right. When she asks me to pull my gown down, I stare at the bandage taped to my chest. I cringe as she slowly pulls back the adhesive and reveals an opening just above my right breast. It doesn't look as bad as I expected. I thought surely I'd be staring down at a huge, gaping hole.

"All set. I'll go get the doctor for you right now," she says, then leaves the room.

Moments later, a balding white doctor comes in and introduces himself as Dr. Morgan. "You're a lucky lady," he says.

"I don't feel so damn lucky right now."

"Well, things could have been a whole lot worse. The two bullets that struck you didn't do any real damage. The one that hit you in the back went in just under the skin and passed right through. The other one will likely cause the most pain, as it entered via your armpit and came out on the right of your chest. Neither are life-threatening, and should heal with barely any visible scarring. Still, you're going to be in quite bit of pain for the next few weeks, Ms. Wilson, so you'll have to take it easy."

I thank him when he informs me that I'll be discharged in the early morning, and he goes on his way.

Right after he leaves, two police officers step into my room and ask me a hundred questions I can't answer. They seem to get angry when I don't have answers and can't tell them much. They keep on saying, "We're trying to help you," and asking me who I'm protecting, but that's a crock of bullshit, because I ain't protecting nobody. I'm not one of these dumb muthafuckas who lies based on that no-snitching rule. Fuck that rule! If I knew who did this to me, I'd sure as hell let the police in on it, and I wouldn't give a damn about who feels some kind of way about it. When they're done interrogating me, they wrap up their grilling session by passing me their cards and telling me to call them if I remember any more information.

After they leave, I just lie there thinking, while the hours tick away. Truth is, I've fucked so many people over in such a short amount of time, and any one of them coulda tried to take me out. *Maybe Osha found out I drugged and taped her. Hell, Meka, Sade's dumb-ass cousin, coulda followed me from the mall. Maybe it was Angel or, hell, even Rodger. I've got no fucking clue! All I do know is that nothing's gonna stop me from getting every dollar I can before I get the hell out of Dodge—or at least out of the damn Buckeye State. Ohio ain't for me anymore. If those fuckers want me, they better find me quick, because I'm taking everything when I go!*

***

The ringing phone awakens me from my midday nap. After tossing the covers off, I grunt from the small sting in my arm. It's been a little over a week since I was released from the hospital, and my body is slowly starting to feel better. Sitting up, I reach for the cordless phone on the nightstand, only to realize it isn't there. I remember dropping it somewhere in the covers, so I begin to search for it. "Hello?" I answer groggily when I finally find it, without looking at the caller ID.

"Hey, Brandy. It's me, Osha. Are you sleeping?" she asks.

What the hell does this bitch want? I haven't talked to her in weeks, and now she wants to call and wake my ass up? "Naw, I just woke up. What's up?" I ask, still wondering why in the world she's calling me.

"I really need somebody to talk to." She sniffles. "I know it's been a while, but I also wanted to call and apologize about the way I acted on the trip. I know it wasn't

5

your fault, but I didn't know what else to do."

"It's cool. I ain't even thinking about it anymore," I lie, biting my tongue to keep from cussing her ass out like I want to.

"That's good, because I don't want our friendship to end over something so stupid and small."

Stupid, yes, but small? I shake my head. It wasn't such a small thing back in Vegas, when she flipped the fuck out. See, that's exactly why I don't fuck with bitches, because of shit like this. Like I said, that was a few weeks ago, and now that her dumb ass needs somebody to talk to, I'm the first one she calls.

"Yeah, I feel you. Brandy, let me call you right back in a few minutes. I'm about to get up outta this bed and get myself together."

"Okay." I hang up the phone and climb out of my bed.

In the bathroom, I get myself situated, then take a quick shower. After washing my hair and body, I dry off and step over to one of the mirrors. Not in the mood for blow-drying, I comb my wet hair into a ponytail and secure it with a scrunchie. Back in my room, sitting on my bed, I dial Osha back.

"Hello?" she answers on the first ring.

God, her ass must be thirsty as hell to talk. "So…what's up? You said you need to talk."

"Right. Well, I wanna talk to you because I've been over here going through it since Taz left."

"Hold up. What?"

"Yeah, girl, you heard right. Taz left me, and I have no clue why." She breaks down and sobs into the phone.

"What happened?" I ask, faking concern.

"I don't know. He left a few days after we came back from Vegas. I was just lying in bed, and he came in the room and told me I ain't shit and that we were through. When I asked him why, he said he doesn't hit women, but he wanted to knock the fuck out of a hoe like me. He even told me not

6

to call his phone no more!" she wails. "I haven't seen him since, Brandy, and I don't know what's going on."

"What he mean, you ain't shit? What did you do? Did he say anything else?" I want to know exactly what happened so I know where I should go from here.

"Girl, no. He just left. Hold on..." Even though she takes the phone away from her mouth, I still hear her yell, "TJ, keep yo' damn hands to yourself! I don't care if she hit you first. You hear me?"

"Yeah, Mom," Terrence Jr. says meekly in the background.

"Damn, Brandy, I don't know what's going on, and these kids are driving me insane over here."

"Sounds like you need a break. Let's go out and have dinner and maybe a few drinks. We can go to the Olive Garden. I've got a craving for some chicken Alfredo anyway."

"Hmm. That doesn't sound bad. Matter of fact, yeah, I'm down. Hold on..." She yells to her sister, "Ash, can you watch the kids for me while I go out with Brandy?" There's a small pause while she waits for an answer. "She said yeah, so do you want to go the one on Bagley?"

"Yeah, that's fine, since it's between the both of us. Let me get dressed, and I'll meet you there in an hour and a half."

"Works for me. See ya in a minute," she says, and we hang up.

Still in shock from the new information, I sit on the edge of the bed, just shaking my head. *I can't believe Taz left her weeks ago and has yet to call me and say shit! He was all in my ear, blowing up my fucking phone when he was with her, but now that they ain't together anymore, the nigga ain't got no holla? Nah, it's cool. He'll call me sooner or later, and when he does, I've got something for his ass!*

Twenty minutes later, I'm dressed and standing in front of the mirror, fixing my hair. It's kind of thick from air-

7

drying, so I decide on a messy bun with my bangs out. I check my bag to make sure the .22 I bought the other day is inside and loaded, then make my way out the door. *I'm still not sure if Osha is behind that shit with me being shot, but if she is, I ain't taking no chances.*

As soon as the elevator opens, I hit the remote start for the fire-red Chevy Camaro I've been renting since I've been back home. Since my truck was destroyed, and I had full coverage, I got a nice chunk of change for it. I haven't figured out what I want just yet, but for now, I figure this bad bitch will do.

My ass sinks into the soft leather bucket seats as I adjust my review mirror. I drop the top as I pull out of the parking lot and take in the beautiful evening. The wind feels good as it blows around inside the car while I drive toward the freeway. The ride is smooth, and I can barely feel the bumps and potholes, even though the car sits so low to the ground. *Hmm. I might just by one of these, because this shit's fly as hell and a lot better on gas than my truck was.* Fifteen minutes later, I'm pulling up at the restaurant and strutting my way over the entrance.

As soon as I walk into the door, I run into Osha, who is standing in the front, speaking to the greeter. She turns around when she hears my heels clicking loudly on the floor and walks over to give me a friendly hug. I return it, but in the back of my mind it kills me; I still want to fuck her up over that smart shit she said in Vegas. The hostess seats us at a table near the front, before a young-looking male waiter takes our orders and disappears.

"I'm happy you asked me to come out," Osha says as soon as he's out of earshot.

"No problem, girl. So, tell me, what the hell is going on with you and Taz?" I ask, getting back to the subject at hand. *I don't have time to chitchat with this bitch. I'm only here for the 411.*

"Well, the day that we got home from Vegas, he and the

kids greeted me at the door. Once the kids gave me their hugs and kisses, he tells me how much he missed me and how he couldn't wait for me to get home. I didn't say too much to him because I was still upset about the fact that he basically ignored the hell out of me while I was gone. He must have felt that I wasn't really paying him any attention, because he went on to explain that he was sorry for being so distant and that he hoped I'd accept his apology." She stopped and took a sip of her water. "Anyway, the next two days were almost perfect. We did the whole family thing and spent almost all of our time together. We took the kids to the movies, out to eat, and even to the park. It was like I had my old Taz back. For the first time in a long while, I was actually happy to be with him."

This bitch is sounding like Charlie Brown's teacher with all this "Mwa-mwa-mwa-mwa-mwa..." that I'm hearing. I want to tell her, *"Damn, bitch, skip to the good part,"* but I don't. Instead, I just sit back and hope she'll hurry the hell up with her boring-ass story.

"The third day, I was in bed, and heard him call my name. I figured he must have wanted some more of this goodness, but when he came upstairs, the look on his face scared the shit out of me. I asked him what was wrong, and he didn't say anything at first. He just continued to stare. Finally, Taz said, 'You ain't shit.' When he said that, I jumped up out of bed and asked him to repeat what he said. He did, and I just stood there all confused. I didn't know what the hell he was talking about...or why he looked at me with disgust in his eyes." Tears slowly roll down her face, and I can tell it's killing her to tell me about it, but I love every minute of it.

"Calm down, Osha. It's gonna be okay," I lie, consoling her like the friend she thinks I am.

"Thanks, girl. When he said we're through, I walked over toward him, but he took a step back. He gave me a cold glare and said he doesn't hit women, but he'd knock the fuck out of a hoe like me. I was baffled. As he was walking down the stairs, he told me not to ever call his phone, that I'm just dead to him."

"Girl, I'm sorry," I tell her, patting her hand as if I give a damn.

"Brandy, what could I have done that was so bad that he would say some shit like that to me?" By now, the tears have soaked her face, and people are starting to look over at her, wondering why she's such a mess.

"It's okay, Osha. It's gonna be okay, one way or another." I hand her a napkin for her face and rub small circles in her back.

"I haven't seen him since, and I still don't know what's going on."

"What about Dan? Did he say anything to Zema?"

"Nope. He only told her it ain't her business to know what's going on in my household." She sniffles.

"That's fucked up," I say, knowing she really has no clue why he's acting the way he is.

When the food arrives, we eat while making small talk. After a few glasses of Moscato, Osha totally forgets about being upset over Taz and begins acting like her old self. When it's time to go, she gives me a big hug and tells me she's grateful to have a friend like me on her side. *Little does that bitch know!* She also continues to apologize about the Vegas thing and tells me she loves me. I walk her to her car, before getting in my own, and heading home. She's pretty tipsy to be driving herself, but I really don't give a damn.

As soon as I step inside the house, the phone rings. It's Osha, calling to let me know she made it home safely, as if I care. I tell her I'm glad, then disconnect the call in a hurry, as I've had my fill of listening to her bullshit for one day. After removing my clothes, I pull back the comforter on my bed and slide inside, clad in nothing but my panties and bra. My mind wanders to Taz. *What the hell is his deal anyway? Honestly, I don't know, and I really don't give two shits, but if he thinks for one fucking minute that I'm not taking what's mine, that fool's got another thing coming! I've already staked claim on that paper, and I'll be damned if I don't get my hands on it just 'cause he's sniffing some other bitch's pussy like the horny-ass dog he is. He can do whatever the hell he wants after I get mine, but till then, his ass belongs to me.*

My cell phone chimes from the living room, and I race in there to pick it up. Rummaging inside my purse, I locate it, and I answer without looking at the caller ID. "Hello?" I say, out of breath.

"Damn, bitch, what you doin'? You all out of breath and shit. Did I catch you mid-fuck or something?" the caller asks before laughing loudly in my ear.

"Who the fuck is this?"

"The person who's gonna fuck you up again on sight!"

"Meka?" I say, finally catching on to her boyish voice. "Don't call my phone with that corny shit! Yeah, you saw me, and we got it in, but you got that ass tapped. What else do you want?"

"Bitch, please! I'm gonna tag that ass every time I see you, so don't get it twisted."

"I ain't worried about you or anybody you bring with you. You've already seen that your bitch wasn't no kinda help." I chuckle. "Like I said, I ain't scared, so come on and bring whatever you've got."

"I don't want you to be scared, ho. I want—"

"I don't give a shit what you want. Please believe me when I tell you that my heart don't pump Kool-Aid, bitch! Don't let the pretty face and these fly-ass clothes fool you, boo-boo, because I'm far from a punk bitch. I fucks up butches *and* bitches, so you just think about that and let yo' next move be ya best one!" I yell before hitting end and hanging up on her dumb ass.

Irritated, I drop my phone back in my purse, but not before turning the power off. *I don't have time for her corny shit. If she wanna see me, that's what's gonna happen. Who still plays on people's phones nowadays anyway? That's some adolescent, 1990s bullshit. Sade gave that bitch my number and she started all this shit. She better pray like hell that I never see her, or her ass is surely mine. Ugh! I knew I shoulda just let that bitch go to voicemail, but naw, I had to sprint my fine ass in there and answer it. This pisses me off. I was so relaxed just a minute ago, and now my nerves are shot and I'm tense as hell.*

It doesn't make it any better that I haven't had any good dick in a while. I'm sure that would relax me just right. I don't really have nobody to call neither, 'cause I'll be damned if I call Taz, with his funny-acting ass. Xavier is almost a distant memory, so you know I ain't trying to reach out to him. I guess I'm gonna have to do what I have to do. I reach into my nightstand and pull out my butterfly vibrator and my eight-inch black dildo that I call Doc Johnson. I unclasp my bra and roll my panties down my legs, then kick them off the side of the bed.

Anxiously, I slide my legs into the straps of the butterfly, then pull them up and around my waist. I grab a few pillows and prop them up behind my head and lie back. I click the button on the remote in my hand, and the butterfly comes to life. The vibration is strong against my throbbing clit. I lie still for a while, not moving at all, before inserting Doc Johnson into my wet, awaiting hole. The combination of the two takes me to another world.

"Mmmmmm…" I moan as I begin to rock my body back in forth. Picking up speed, I push Doc Johnson deeper and deeper, until it's hitting my back walls. "Fuck!" My eyes close and roll into the back of my head. *This shit feels so damn good!*

My body begins to tingle, from my toes, up my calves, and to my thighs. I spread my legs a little bit wider for a better angle. My pussy muscles involuntarily tighten around the thick shaft of my bedtime buddy, and I know I'm coming closer to the nut I so desperately need. The rocking of the bed knocks the remote control onto the floor, but I don't even bother picking it up; I'm concentrating too hard on the task at hand, trying to satisfy this fire inside of me.

"Shit! Shit! Shit!" I scream as I cum hard as hell, still ramming Doc Johnson into my pussy relentlessly. "Ah!" I jump, because the butterfly is still on and working the hell out of my sensitive clit. I reach down to the floor and pick up the remote so I can turn it off.

Spent and out of breath, I lie back and collect myself. *That shit felt good as fuck, but it still doesn't take the place of the real thing. I'ma have to get me something new, because fucking myself is not gonna be a nightly thing. I'll be damned!* I pick up my toys and take them into the bathroom to clean them up, before putting them back in their place. Back in my bed, I pull the covers up to my chin and close my eyes; sleep welcomes me instantly.

CHAPTER TWO

*I*t's been a little over three months since I started living at the hotel. Harold, the hotel manager, has kept up his end of the bargain and allowed me to stay, as long as I sexually please him on demand. What turned into a few times a week has revolved into an everyday thing! It's gotten so bad that I had to make his ass leave yesterday because he'd been here for almost three days, laid up in my place like it's his room or something. Those were the hardest three days I've had since I've been here. I finally got tired and reminded him that our deal was for me to have my own room, and I'm not sharing shit! Of course he had an attitude about that, but I reminded him that a deal's a deal.

I still haven't heard anything from Trixie. Part of me is scared that my father, Pitch, got a hold of her and killed her for taking me away from him and stealing his money. Another very small part believes she just got tired of playing the mommy role and left me. That's unlikely, but you never know. I've learned from my background that anything is possible, and even mamas don't owe their babies shit. Either way, I've had to suck it up—and I mean that literally too—and put on my big girl panties, because I have to eat somehow.

I still don't leave the room much. In fact, I almost never do. When I want something, I just pick up the phone and call Harold, and he'll get anything I ask for, unless he's too busy. If he is, then I'm forced to head out into the world alone.

The last time I went out, I stopped at the convenience store for a snack. I was in the back grabbing a pop, when I felt someone staring at me. When I looked up, I locked eyes with a guy who just kept on staring. As the guy at the register rang my things up, the guy just kept looking at me, never breaking his gaze. When I had to walk past him to leave, I held my breath, 'cause I didn't know if he was going to try to grab me or not. Thankfully, he didn't, but I almost peed on myself when I heard him call out after I was about two feet from him.

"Hey!" he yelled.

I kept walking, picking up my pace.

"Hey, you in the black coat!"

I turned around slowly, scared of what he was going to say.

"Don't I know you from somewhere?" he asked, peering at me like he was trying to put a name to my face.

"Sorry, but I'm not from around here," I replied. Before he got a chance to contest my answer, I turned around and headed back to the hotel at record speed.

I haven't been out since. That guy scared the hell out of me. Even though I didn't tell him so, I'm sure I've seen him before too. It might have been just from walking to the store or from somewhere else, but either way, I'm not about to take the chance of running into him again.

I step out of the shower, with the towel wrapped tightly around my waist. I'm startled to see Harold, sitting on my bed and watching an old-ass rerun of Sanford and Son. *My pillows are propped behind his head, and he's chilling like it's his room—again. Who in the hell told him that it'd be okay to just waltz into my personal space anytime he wants? I sure as hell didn't.*

"What the hell are you doing?" I ask, clearly agitated.

He doesn't say anything, because he's all into the show.

"Excuse me!" I yell.

"Hey, what's up, baby?" His eyes roam my body. Even

*though he's had almost every piece of me, I still feel
awkward as I stand almost naked in front of him.*

"I'm not your damn baby." I grit my teeth.

*"Yeah, whatever! What you got plans to do today,
besides hiding in this damn room?"*

*"The same thing I do every day—just sitting here and
watching TV." I attempt to walk past him so I can get into the
drawer of the cheap-ass fiber-board dresser and find
something to throw on.*

*As soon as I move close enough to him, he reaches out
and grabs hold of my waist, then pulls me down on top of
him.*

*"Get the hell off me, Harold!" I scream, trying to get out
of his tight grasp.*

"Come on, baby. Give me some," he begs.

*"I just got out of the shower, and I don't feel like taking
another one," I whine, knowing it won't do a damn bit of
good; he never leaves until he gets his. When he lets me go, I
stand and hurry to fix my towel that came undone. I pray
he'll just give up and leave, but that'd be too much like right.*

"At least give me some head."

I roll my eyes.

*"I'm not gonna be able to come by later on because I've
gotta work the front desk all night, so come on, baby." Not
even waiting for a reply, he kicks off the white and yellow
Jordan's and unbuckles his belt, allowing his pants to fall
down and around his ankles.*

*While I don't want to do it, I have an agreed-upon duty,
so I hesitatingly drop to my knees while he removes his
boxers. I open my mouth wide so I can receive him. He
caresses my face with his right hand, moving it from my
cheek to the bottom of my chin. With that same hand, he takes
a hold of his hard member and traces circles around my lips,
as if it's some kind of lip gloss. I swear I hate when he does
that, because it feels like he's tryin'a let me know I'm nothing
but a ho and that he can do whatever the hell he wants with*

me.

"Stick out yo; tongue," he orders, and I obey because I don't figure I've got any other choice. "Go 'head, baby. Lick that dick like you love it." He moans, and in the reflection on the TV screen, I see a mask of pleasure plastered on his face, the fucking pervert!

A few minutes pass before he grabs the back of my head and slowly slides himself into my warm mouth. I open it as wide as I can so I can take all of him in. The first time I had to do it, I swore that the sides of my mouth were going to rip because he's so wide in girth. Problem is, he's just as long. I've gagged plenty of times trying to take all of him in, and believe me when I tell you he always tries. He seems to find it funny or some shit when he almost chokes me to death.

"Ooh shit! Suck that dick, baby. Deep-throat that dick." Both hands are on the back of my head as he pumps in and out of my mouth. I just close my eyes and let him do what he wants, praying that it will be over soon. "Get up on the bed."

"What?" I ask, as that wasn't a part of the plan.

"Get up on the bed. I want some pussy," he orders while removing his shirt.

"But I-I said I just got out of the shower, and—" I whine again, hoping he'll just drop it.

"Shower still works. You can take another one after. Now come on. I ain't got all fucking day."

I climb up on the bed with my booty tooted out; I know that's how he likes it. Doggy-style is his favorite position, and he wants to do it every time. I hate it, because my stomach always cramps up afterward; I swear he's probably messing up something in my insides. When I complain about it, he just tells me he loves to watch my ass jiggle when our bodies collide, and I should just take the dick and stop acting like a baby. Of course I bite my tongue, 'cause what I really wanna say is "Bitch, that's because I am a fucking baby! I'm only fourteen!"

As soon as he's finished and takes his nasty ass out the

door, I sit on the bed and cry, with my head in my hands. I get up to run some bath water, hoping it will soothe my aching body and help me feel a little better. That's all I can hope for, because there aren't enough showers and baths in the world to make me feel clean after what I've been through.

I rub my face roughly with both hands, furious as I wipe my falling tears away. I hate that I have to abuse and use my body like this, and I despise everyone who has ever put me in situations like the one I'm in right now. Reaching out, I begin to twist the knob for the hot water, but a knock at the door stops me in my tracks.

I curse under my breath; I know it's Harold, coming back with some excuse as to why I owe him more. I don't give a damn how late he has to work today; I'm not doing anything else. If he doesn't want to take no for an answer, tough titties! With the towel tied very tightly around me, I march over to the door and yell, "Who is it?"

"It's Harold, baby."

"What do you want? I'm about to take a bath," I tell him, not even bothering to open the door.

"Just open the door. I promise I won't be long. I just...I think I might have left my wallet in the room when I was here earlier."

"I don't see anything," I reply after glancing over at the bed, the nightstand, and the dresser.

"Come on, Brandy. Just open the damn door. I'll only be in there for a fucking minute!" he says, raising his voice.

Even though I don't wanna be bothered again—especially by him—I figure he'll just get his wallet and leave. Besides that, since he works here, I know he could find a way into the room if he really wanted with the spare key that I'm sure he has. I mean, how else has he been getting into my room? I'm also pretty sure he wouldn't force himself on me—or at least I hope not. I reach up and unlock the door, then snatch it open with attitude. "Make it quick, Harold. I'm just about to get in the tub and..." I stop mid-sentence when I look up and realize the devil himself is standing on the other side of my door. I'm so scared I don't know what to do or say, and in the next heartbeat, everything does black...

***

"No!" I bolt upright in my bed and frantically look around before realizing that I'm safe inside my own home. My heart is beating a mile a minute, and it's almost impossible to breathe. Since I can't catch my breath, I pull my legs up and place my head between them. After a minute or two, I finally stop panicking and am finally able to calm down. Without warning, tears burst out of my eyes like water through a broken dam, and my whole body trembles as I cry uncontrollably. I sob and wail from deep within the core of my soul, letting it all out. *I hate these fucking dreams! What the hell is wrong with me, and why do I have to keep reliving this shit night after night? Why can't I just go to sleep and dream about good shit like normal people do—fairies and rainbows and fucking happy memories?* Then again, I know my nightmares are nothing in comparison to the hell I've actually been through.

What scares me the most is that this shit seems so real. When I wake up from these horrible dreams, the hairs on the back of my neck are actually standing up. I remember how scared I was that night. I haven't asked this question in a long time, but I wonder why God has allowed me to go through all this shit. I don't understand why I had to be born to two of the sickest individuals to ever walk the Earth. I don't even know why I bother with questions, though, because nobody—not even God Himself—seems to wanna come forward with any fucking answers about why I deserve any of this nightmarish shit I've had to call my life.

After eating a bowl of cereal, I walk over to my purse and pick up my phone. I power it on and see the little mailbox icon on the top of the screen, flashing to alert me that there's a voicemail waiting for me. I tap the symbol quickly, and my voicemail dials, then prompts me to enter my password. There are nine messages in total, and the first six are from Meka, talking shit about what she's going to do to me. I don't listen to them entirely and just deleted them as soon as I hear her voice. *That ho seriously needs a hobby, and like I said, who the fuck plays these games on phones anymore anyway? She needs to grow the fuck up.*

The eighth message is from Angel, telling me how lucky I am to be alive and letting me know he'll finish the job next time. *At least I now know who shot up my truck and tried to kill me.* I save that message, prepared to call the detectives as soon as I'm done. Like I said, I ain't all about that no-snitching bullshit. After all, the man tried to kill me, and he deserves whatever the fucking police do to him and then some.

The final message is from McKenzie, the booster who is cold as fuck when it comes to getting that five finger discount. She's just calling to let me know she's taken care of my shopping list from the last time we were together. *Damn, I forgot all about ol' girl. Come to think of it, I was with her the day I got shot. I wonder if...nah.* I save her message as well and move on to the last and final one.

"Hey, baby, I see yo' phone off, which probably means you're busy. I was just calling to tell you I'm sorry about the way I acted a while ago. I just...well, I had a lot of shit on my mind. Some shit went down, so I've been staying at my other crib. Look, I'd really love to see you soon, so call me when you get a chance,"

Even though Taz's message pisses me off, and even though the nigga's got a lot of damn nerve I still manage to smile. I knew he'd eventually come around. I decide I'm not gonna call his ass for a few days, just because I wanna see him sweat. *That nigga needs to learn who he's fucking with!* I take a seat on the couch, sit back, and prop my feet up on the coffee table.

My phone rings in my hand, and McKenzie's name shows on the screen.

"Hello?" I answer.

"You a'ight over there?" she asks.

"Yeah, I'm good…now."

"What you mean, 'now'? What the hell happened?" she asks.

I fill her in on what went down after I left her at the mall that day.

"Girl, get the fuck outta here!" she yells after I finish.

"I swear."

"You mean to tell me that big gay chick tried to *kill* you?"

"Yep. Sho nuff, that bitch tried to take my ass out," I lie. I figure there's no need to tell her about Angel, because if I do, she might start wondering why everybody's out to get me.

"Damn, girl, that's fucked up! I knew something was wrong, because I knew you wanted yo' shit."

We both laugh.

"I was in my guestroom last night and saw your bag and thought about you. I'm glad you're all right though. Sounds like it coulda been real bad."

"Thanks, and you're right about that," I tell her, recalling how close I came to death. "On a lighter note, I still want my shit, so what's up with that?" I chuckle.

"Yo' ass is crazy. Do you wanna meet me today or some other time?"

"Today sounds good. Where will you be?" I ask, getting up from the couch to find something to wear.

"Well, I'm about to go to the Strongsville Mall with my daughter. You wanna meet me there?"

"Yeah, that's cool, and it ain't too far from me. By the way, how much do I owe you?"

"It's gonna be $3,000."

"Ok. Well, it's 12:30 now. Let's say we meet around

2:00. I have to run by the bank to get some cash."

"Sounds like a plan. I'll see you there."

I hang up the phone, tripping over how much this shit is gonna cost. *This ho is trying to run up in me for real! How in the hell she think she gon' charge me $3,000 for some shit she stole? This ho acting like I'm buying the shit out the store or something. I mean, isn't that why I got a booster anyway, so I wouldn't have to spend as much as I would in the actual stores? I've already made up my mind that I ain't paying her slick, connivin' ass nothing but what I got in my purse—and trust me when I tell you, that ain't three stacks.*

"I'm about to pull up. Where are you?"

McKenzie tells me she's sitting in the back of the parking lot.

When I see her car, I maneuver into an available parking space beside her.

"Hey!" she says as I step out of the car.

"Hey. Who's this little lady?" I ask, referring to the adorably cute toddler in her arms.

"This is McKayla, Mommy's little princess."

I smile. I can't help it because I love cute babies. McKayla grins, showing me a set of the deepest dimples I've ever seen in my life. She's so damn cute, with her little chubby face. There are colorful barrettes at the end of each one of her thick ponytails, matched perfectly to her plaid and denim Juicy Couture dress. On her feet is a pair of Prada, red patent leather Mary Janes. "How old is she?" I ask, sure the child can't be any older than two.

"She just turned eighteen months."

"Hello, McKayla." I bend down so my face is close to hers.

The baby grins again.

"Can you hold her for a second while I get yo' bag out the trunk?"

"Sure," I say, and then reach out my arms for the baby.

Little McKayla looks up at me, as if she's trying to figure out who I am. She then runs her plump little hand across my face, landing on my earring. My body tenses up because I fear that at any moment, the little girl's gonna rip a hole in my ear, but she does nothing but smile, still holding on to my earring.

McKenzie pops the trunk and pulls out a huge black bag. After dragging it over to the back of my car, she begins to pull things out one by one. I don't really pay her any attention because I'm too busy making funny faces at her kid, trying to make the baby laugh. Minutes past before she places everything back inside the bag. Popping my trunk, I allow her to place it inside, and slam it shut.

"Oh shit! I went to the bank, but they closed at noon, so I had to go to the ATM. My daily limit is only $500, but I've got $600 in my purse. Can I give you $1,100 and pay you the rest on Monday, when the bank reopens?" I lie, knowing damn well I don't have to go to no damn bank.

"Yeah, I guess that's cool," she replies hesitantly. It's clear that she's pissed, but there's not much she can do since I've already locked the goods in my trunk. "Fine, but I'm gonna need that on the early side, because I'm supposed to be going out of town with my dude, and I was counting on that as spending money.

"I got you. I'll be there as soon as they open on Monday, and then I'll catch up with you," I say, continuing my lie. Before I hand McKayla back, I plant a big kiss on her chubby cheek. Walking over to my truck, I speak over my shoulder and let McKenzie know I will call her on Monday, even though I know damn well I won't. As I pull off, I have to laugh at how dumb she is. *There's no way in hell I'd ever let a bitch take anything with paying me first. She's gonna have to eat that $1,900, 'cause I got no plans to give her a damn cent of it.*

Faintly, I hear my cell phone ringing from inside my purse. I pull to a stop at the red light and fish around for it, hoping to find it before it stops ringing. Once I have it, I see that Taz is calling once again. Since I don't have any plans to listen to his shit or call him back, I set my phone on top of my purse and accelerate when the light turns green. I make it back to my apartment in no time, only to be greeted by the ring of my home phone. I drop the bag on the floor and dash over to it, picking it up from the base. "Hello?"

"Hello. Is Ms. Wilson available?" the unfamiliar caller asks.

"This is she."

"Ms. Wilson, this is Sergeant Andres. I'm calling to inform you that we picked up Angel Rodriguez a little while ago. He will be charged for attempted murder, among a few other things."

"Oh my God! Thank you so much!" I exclaim, happy that I wouldn't have to look over my shoulder anymore—at least not for him.

"You're more than welcome, ma'am. We'll let you know when the case goes to trial, but until then, Mr. Rodriguez won't be going anywhere." He wraps up the call, and we disconnect.

Before I left to meet with McKenzie, I contacted the detectives that were at the hospital. After speaking to them, they advised me to forward the voicemail that Angel left to the station, and that was that. It amazes me at how fast they were able to pick him up, and I'm extremely grateful, and hop that they prosecute him to the fullest extent of the law.

After I put the phone back in its place, I drag my bag of goodies into my bedroom with plans to go through it later. I stopped at Popeye's on 105th on my way home, so my first plan of action is to eat. From the hall closet, I grab the tray I use when I'm eating in my bed and kick off my Giuseppe Zanotti flip-flops. I remove my Donna Karan cashmere leggings and lay them at the foot of my bed until a later time. I hate being dressed in the house; it's unnecessary and uncomfortable as hell. Tearing into my food, I turn on the television and see that there's a marathon on BET of *The Game.* I don't have plans to move from this spot for the rest of the day.

CHAPTER THREE

I t's been almost a week, and McKenzie has been calling nonstop. I've given her every excuse in the book as to why I can't give her the money I supposedly owe her, but she's persistent. When I went to the shop the other day, I was glad she wasn't there, because I'm sure I would have flipped on her ass for bugging me—especially after I went through my bag and saw that a bunch of shit's missing, shit I specifically asked for. *Not only is the li'l bitch trying to juice me for extra money, but she didn't even get me everything I pointed out.*

Thinking about it gets me even madder, and I know she really ain't got shit coming now. Suddenly, an idea hits me: *I'm gonna have her meet me at the mall to get the rest of my stuff, and I'll act like I'm ready to pay her. Soon as she gets all my shit, I'll spin her ass again.*

"What's up, Brandy?" she says with attitude when she answers, with McKayla in the background, baby babbling.

"I have your money, but I don't see that dress I wanted in the bag. A few other things are missing too," I inform her.

"Oh? My bad. What did I miss?"

"That dress I was dying for, the jacket I wanted and a few pairs of jeans."

"Damn. Well, I'll get them for you tomorrow."

"That won't work. I'm going on a date tonight, and I planned to wear that dress. Can we go get it right now? I'll be happy to pay extra for your trouble."

"I can't right now, Brandy. I've got McKayla, her daddy doesn't get off till later, and I ain't got no babysitter. I'm also about to get my hair done by Ze—"

"Damn it, McKenzie, I really needed that dress." I sigh into the phone, cutting her off.

"I'm sorry," she apologizes.

Still, baby or no baby, I refuse to let her ass off the hook that easy. "What if I watch McKayla while you're in the store?"

"I don't think that's a good idea, Brandy. Besides, I have a hair appointment at 4:00, and it's already 2:00 now."

"Please, McKenzie? I really need that dress, and I'm sure it'll only take you a few minutes," I say, trying to persuade her. "Like I said, I'll pay."

"Damn." She pauses. "Okay, but I'm gonna have to charge you $500 for getting you more stuff. That price I already gave you, the $3,000 less the $1,100 you already gave me, is only for what I got for you that day."

What!? This bitch is tripping for real! How the fuck she gon' charge me more for something she forgot in the first place? What kind of swindling shit is that? "Uh…that's not a problem. So my new total that I owe you is $2,400, right?"

"Right."

"All right. I'll have it for you when I get there."

She agrees, and we hang up.

I was just going to play her out her money, but after that, I had to think up something better for her funky ass. I take a quick shower and throw on a pair of dark blue, cut-off True Religion denim shorts and a white wife-beater. My hair is done in a tight straw set, something like a curly afro. I was worried it wouldn't turn out right, but Zema proved to be the bad bitch she is when she spun my chair around and revealed it to me. The blonde at the top really makes it pop, and I'm loving the whole big hair thing I've got going on. Before I walk out the door, I slide on my Gucci thong wedges, fluff out my hair, and grab my purse.

It's 3 o'clock, and I'm just five minutes from the mall when McKenzie calls me to let me know she's already there. I let her know I'm about to pull up in a minute, and she tells me to park in the back, the same place we were the other day. As I pull up, I see her holding McKayla's car seat; the little girl's inside it, sleeping like the baby she is. McKenzie walks over to the Camaro and opens the door, then sets her precious cargo on my front seat. After closing it back, she then walks around to the driver side, and taps on the window.

"I gotta make this quick so I can hurry back home. My god-sister's gonna be at my house in less than an hour, so I need to be there," she says. "The baby should be fine till I get back. She'll probably sleep the whole time. What size did you want again?" she asks, pulling her hair back into a ponytail.

"A seven will be fine," I say, then pull out the money I owe her. I take my time counting it, laying the bills on my lap slowly.

"I'll get that when I come back," she says, walking off toward the mall.

As soon as she's out of sight, I put the money back in my purse; I've got no plans of giving her one damn dollar. I just wanted to make her feel secure. I counted it slowly so she'd be in even more of a rush. *She's got less than an hour before her hair appointment, so she'll really have to hurry her ass up now.*

I glance over at a sleeping McKayla and can't help but smile. She looks so peaceful, and I just want to kiss her little fat cheeks.

When I'm sure McKenzie is inside the store, I reach into my purse and grab my cell phone. I dial the number, speak quickly to the person on the other end, then hang up. I then pull out of the parking space and move closer to the front of the mall to make sure I have a clear view. It takes about an hour, but I finally see a Beachwood police cruiser pull up and park directly in front of the double-doors. In no time, the officer is walking out of the mall with McKenzie in handcuffs, two of those fat-fuck mall security guards picking up the rear. Her hair is all over her head, and even from where I'm sitting, I can tell she's been crying. After he places her in the back seat, he turns and begins to speak to the guards.

Moments later, I slouch down as the cruiser drives by, just enough so McKenzie won't see me. I wait a while before driving back to where we met. I climb out of my rented Camaro, walk over to McKenzie's car, and am relieved to find it unlocked. I open my door, grab McKayla's car seat, and strap it in the back seat of her mom's car. I kiss her softly on her chubby cheek before closing the door, because I know I'll more than likely never see her again.

I pick up my phone again and call 911 to let them know I just drove by a car in the mall parking lot with an unattended baby inside. The operator asks me for my location, a description of the car, and if I know how long the baby's been alone. I answer all the questions, then disconnect the call and pull into a parking space not far from where McKayla is; I don't want to be too far from her, just in case the police take their damn sweet time coming to check on her. The last thing I want is for a baby to die in that hot-ass car. Yeah, I'm a bitch, but I'm not a totally heartless one—at least not all the time. The shit that happened to Sade's son from the poisoned pasta was an accident; I didn't plan for it to go down like that, and things just went a bit too far. I wasn't trying to kill the little nigga. I figured the bleach would just make him sick, nothing major. His death was way outta my control. *Hell, it musta been li'l dude's time to go, Maybe God was tryin'a save him from the shitty life he was gonna have to live with his triflin' mama.*

When the police show up and remove McKayla from the car, I finally pull off. Bobbing my head to the sounds of Rick Ross, I weave in and out of traffic. My cell phone rings, and when I see the number, I turn up the volume of the radio before answering. "Hello?"

"You ain't get my message?" Taz asks.

"Who this?" I ask, playing dumb, just to piss him off.

"Brandy…" He exhales unnecessarily loud in my ear. "Don't play with me."

"I ain't playing. Who is this?"

"Who you think?"

"If I knew, I wouldn't be asking who it is, now would I?"

"Okay, fine. I'll play this little game with you if that's what it takes. It's Taz. If you'd turn the damn music down, you'd recognize my voice. Plus, ain't you ever heard of caller ID?"

"Oh, Taz, huh? What's up? Sorry, but I deleted your number off my phone a while ago, and I haven't heard your voice in a while," I say ignoring his request to lower the volume of the music.

"Yeah, I'm sorry about that. Did you get my message?"

"Yep."

"Then why ain't you call me back?"

"Busy," I say flatly, hitting him with the same cold, one-word-answer shit he hit me with the last time I talked to him weeks ago.

"What you doing now?"

"Lying down"

"Well, do you feel like having company?"

"Naw, not really. Hey, let me call you back in a minute," I tell him and hang up in his ear.

The phone rings again; it's Taz.

"Hello?" I answer, agitated.

"Don't you ever fucking hang up on me like that again!" he barks in my ear.

"Excuse me?"

"You heard me. Don't you ever fucking hang up on me like that again!"

Huh? This nigga got a lot of damn nerve talking to me

30

like that. "Whatever, Taz. Is there something you want?"

"I want you to stop acting childish as fuck and talk to me like a grown woman. I don't have time for your little games today, Brandy," he snaps.

"For one muthafucking thing, I *always* act like a grown woman. Just because I don't kiss your ass like these other hoes, you accuse me of bein' childish? How the fuck do you figure that?"

"I call you, and you acting all funny and shit."

"What about when I called you a few weeks ago?" I ask, turning that accusatory shit back on him.

"I wasn't doing that on purpose. I just had a lot of shit on my mind."

"Good. Then you'll understand that I got a bunch of shit on my mind now, and I ain't got time to talk."

"See? That's what the fuck I mean. You like to play this tit-for-tat shit, and I ain't down with that. That's some little-kid bullshit, Brandy. Grow the fuck up!"

"How the hell do you know I ain't going through my own shit? Everything is not about yo' punk ass, Taz! Get over yourself!" I say, then quickly press the end key.

I can't believe how much this nigga just done pissed me the fuck off. My phone continues to ring, but I ignore the shit out of it. I know it ain't nobody but Taz calling back, and I don't have time to argue with him today. *It's a good thing I have a session today at the shooting range, because it'll help me blow off some of this steam.* I signed up after I was released from the hospital and have been going ever since. I have a private instructor, because I like one-on-one training. It's $45 an hour, but it's well worth it. I've already completed the twelve hours of the concealed carry weapons permit program, so I can carry with no problems, but I still like to practice.

Three hours later, I'm at home, showered and making myself something to eat. The range did help me blow off some steam like I hoped. I'm really glad I went, because I needed it. I stopped at the GFS in Mentor on my way home and bought a bag of Spicy Wing Zings. I've been craving them for a few days now, and I can't wait until they get done. Reaching into the cabinet, I grab the seasoning salt and sprinkle a small amount onto the fries I cut, sizzling in the pot on the stove. I open the fridge to get the pitcher of iced tea and see there's only a swallow left; I smack my lips in frustration, but I'm the only one who lives here, so I can't blame anyone but myself.

Thirty minutes later, my stomach is full, and I'm in a lazy mood. I walk over to the door to make sure my house is locked up before cutting off all the lights. I take a seat on my bed, prop my feet up, and channel-surf, looking for something to watch. *My Wife and Kids* will have to do.

When my cell phone startles me, I press pause on my DVR; I don't want to miss a minute of the show. I don't recognize the 216 number that's showing up on the caller ID, so I let it go to voicemail. I pick the DVR remote up again and prepare to play the show, but the phone rings again—the same number calling back. "Hello?" I answer, against my better judgment.

"Why the hell are they trying to charge me with child endangerment? What the fuck did you do with my daughter?" McKenzie asks.

"I don't know what you're talking about," I lie. I know she's in jail, so I'm not sure if the conversation is being recorded or not.

"All jokes aside, Brandy, where is my daughter?"

"I'm sorry, but who is this?" I continue playing the fuck out of crazy.

"Oh what? You don't know me now? It's McKenzie, bitch! Now were the fuck is my baby?"

"Like I said, I don't know what you're talking about, and I think you have the wrong number," I tell her before hanging up. *Damn. Maybe it's time I change my number if all these angry people are gonna be callin' me every day.*

I set my phone on my bed, and it rings again. This time, I don't bother answering and just let it go to voicemail. *I'm not gonna waste any time thinking about that ho. It's her fault she's in the position she's in anyway, with her thieving ass!* The chime lets me know I have a voicemail, so I pick my phone to see what's been said; I know it's her talking shit.

"It's cool, Brandy. Keep playin' that role like you don't know what the fuck I'm talking about. But remember, I'll see you sooner or later, bitch. They can't keep me in here forever. When I do touch down, it ain't gone be nothing pretty, baby girl. You played yo' hand all wrong when you fucked with my baby. Why the fuck would you put her in a hot-ass car though? And to think, I actually helped yo' ass when those girls was trying to fuck you up. I should've let them stomp yo' ass out. Maybe then I wouldn't be where I am today."

In the background, I hear someone whom I assume to be a corrections officer tell her that her time is up.

"I now understand why bitches be trying to come for your neck, shooting at you and shit. Like I said, it's cool, Brandy. You best just keep your eyes and ears open to the streets. You never know who I might know."

I delete the message, but now I'm pissed off. *That ho thinks I'm soft! McKenzie better watch herself before she let her mouth get her into something her ass can't get her out of. She's mad because I left her daughter in her car? Well, what the hell else was I supposed to do with her? Surely she ain't think I was gonna babysit the little bitch. She's the fucking dummy for leaving her with a perfect stranger anyway, but money makes people do crazy things. Now she's gotta pay for being a bad mother. In the end, I came out on top. Why? Because not only did I get to keep my money, but I also got everything I wanted out of her—except that damn dress, that jacket, and those jeans.*

When my phone rings again, I snatch it up and

answer it without looking at the caller ID. "Stop calling my damn phone!" I immediately yell.

"Damn. So it's like that, huh?" Taz asks on the other end of the line.

"Oh. I thought you were somebody else. What's up?"

"Well, I'm happy I ain't whoever that is." He chuckles. "I ain't want nothing. Just calling to tell you that thing earlier was all my bad. Baby, I been going through some real shit, but I didn't mean to take it out on you."

"What kind of shit?" I ask, as if I don't know.

"Man, you wouldn't believe it if I told you. What you doing now?"

"Nothing but lying in the bed, watching some TV."

"How about you come over here?"

"I don't know, Taz. It's getting late, and I don't feel like going out," I tell him truthfully.

"Then I'll come over there."

I know that's not about to happen, because I don't want him knowing where I live.

"Please, baby? I really need to talk to you," he pleads when I don't say anything right away.

I blow air out of my lungs. I really don't feel like driving, but I really ain't got a choice in this situation. "Okay. I'll come over your house. I'll see you in half."

I pull the covers back and climb out of the bed. Standing in my closet room, I slide out one of the custom drawers that hold a few of my shoes and scan each row. My t-strap suede Giambattista Valli platforms will be perfect for the evening, and I'm pairing them with 7 For All Mankind boot-cut skinny jeans. The top of my black La Perla bodysuit resembles a bra and is made of cotton, but the bottom half, down to the crotch, is see-through. After spraying a light mist of oil sheen evenly around my hair, I just stand there staring at myself. Even though I'm going over there to talk, I'm also planning to get some dick, because I'm well overdue. It takes me twenty minutes to get dressed, but since he's only fifteen minutes away, I'll be there before he knows it.

I pull up at the apartment complex and am glad to see that there's a parking space directly in front of his building. I take the elevator to the ninth floor and knock on his door. It takes him a couple seconds, but when the door opens, he greets me with a smile. I almost fall when he pulls me into a big huge, something I wasn't expecting.

"Bring your sexy ass in here," he tells me, looking at me lustfully.

I walk over and take a seat on the cream and chocolate sectional. The view is amazing; I can see all of downtown from this spot. I look over at him as he stands in the kitchen, pouring a drink for each of us. *Damn, that man is fine!* His hair is done up in small braids connected with two French braids in the back that hang just past his shoulder blade. The wife-beater he's wearing fits him snugly, and I can see his six-pack through it. He walks over and hands me a glass of my favorite drink: Absolut with orange and cranberry juice.

"Thank you. So…what's been going on with you?" I ask as I take a sip of my drink.

"Well, first I wanna apologize for the way I've been treating you. I just—"

I start to interrupt him, but he holds up his hand to stop me and continues.

"I know I've done it already, but I wanna say it face to face." He then goes on to tell me about everything that's transpired over these past few weeks. He explains what he saw on the tape and says he's got no idea who sent it to him, but he really wants to find out. Of course I sit here, looking like I've got no clue what he's talking about. He tells me he hasn't mentioned the tape to Osha because it'd probably be pointless. "She'll just deny it anyway," he said, "even though she was caught on tape."

When he almost breaks down because he hasn't seen his kids since he left, I put my arm around him. "Go on," I coax, loving every minute of it.

"I-I don't wanna go back over there to see 'em because I swear, Brandy, I'ma do something to that bitch Osha if I set eyes on her again. I don't know when I'm gonna see my kids again, man." He shakes his head back and forth for a minute and actually looks like he might cry. "I can't be mad at her for fuckin' around, I guess, since I been doing it since we met. What pisses me the fuck off is the fact that she's all playing around, spendin' my money while she's fuckin' another nigga. Sure, I mighta cheated on her many times, but I still take care of home first. What the hell is she bringin' to the table?"

I don't give him an answer because I don't have one, so I just shrug my shoulders.

"Nothing? That's exactly my point."

"So what're you gonna do?"

"Honestly, I don't got a clue, but it's over between me an' her. I can tell you that for damn sure. I fell out of love with her a long time ago anyway, and I'm ready to move on. So what do ya say?" he asks me.

"About?"

"About making this shit official—you and me. I want you to be my woman, Brandy."

I don't say a word at first because I'm shocked that he's asking me so soon. I thought I'd at least have to wait a month, but I guess my plan worked quicker than I hoped. "Why you wanna be with me now, Taz? Just 'cause she cheated on you?"

"You know that's not the reason. I been trying to be your man all this time, practically since I met you, but you kept pushing me away."

"I don't know, Taz. You just got out of this relationship, and I ain't tryin'a get hurt," I tell him with the best sad face I can muster.

"Aw, baby, I'd never hurt you. Osha and I haven't been happy in a long time, so I wouldn't call that a relationship. I've wanted you since the first day I met you. Please just give

36

me a chance," he begs, batting those puppy-dog eyes at me.

"You better not break my heart, Taz. I've been hurt before, and like I told you, I'm not trying to go down that road again," I said, giving him an Oscar-worthy performance. I squeeze my eyes shut and push a few tears out. "And you better never cheat on me, because I don't think I'd be able to take it," I warn as the tears roll down my face slowly.

Using his thumbs, he wipes them away before kissing me softly on the lips. "I love you, Brandy," I hear him whisper.

I look him right in the eyes and say what any nigga in this world would say without even blinking: "I love you too."

That seals the deal. We're now officially a couple, Taz and Brandy, and I'm ready to cash in.

CHAPTER FOUR

I *jump up and gasp for air when I feel a cold splash of what I assume to be water hitting my face. I look up and see that I'm lying on the bed naked, so I grab the blanket and cover my body quickly. I turned to my left and see Harold sitting in the chair in the corner with a bruised and bloody face; he looks at me with hate-filled eyes. To my right, the creepy, dark-skinned guy I saw at the store a little while ago looks as if he's guarding the door. Even though I see him, my attention is on the person standing beside me, because he's the one I'm afraid of. He smiles a wicked grin, and that's when I realize my worst fears have come true.*

"You don't look happy to see me, baby girl," he says as he walks over to me, causing every muscle in my body to tense up. "What, you not happy to see yo' daddy?"

I don't say anything. For one, I don't wanna tell him how I really feel. And two, I'm too scared to do anything other than just sit here.

My silence must have made him mad, because next he hauls off and slaps me hard in the face with the back of his hand. "I asked you a mu'fucking question, bitch! Now... did you miss yo' daddy or not?"

"Yes," I lie quietly, cradling my stinging face in my hand.

"I can't hear you. Speak the fuck up."

"Yes, Daddy, I've missed you," I tell him, scared of what's gonna happen next.

38

"That's good...very good. So, tell me, what have you been doing since you left?" he asks, keeping his eyes are fixed on Harold.

"Nothing," I reply.

"It looks to me like you've been doing something."

"Not really—just sittin' in this room watching TV."

He turns around quickly and grabs hold of my neck, lifting me up and off the bed. When he begins to apply pressure, I fight to catch my breath, but it's a fight I can't win; he quickly cuts off my oxygen supply. "Don't fucking lie to me, you little whore. We both know that ain't all you been doing! How have you managed to stay in this hotel for so long? You and Trixie ain't get that much money off me, and ain't shit in this world free, so how have you been taking care of yourself? Hold on though. Before you even think about lying to me, just know that I'll choke the fucking life out of you right here in this cheap-ass hotel room if you don't tell me the damn truth" He opens up his hand, and I bounce on the bed, gripping my crushed neck.

"Harold and I had...a deal." The next words are extremely difficult to admit. "He said as long as I slept with him, he'd let me stay here and pay for all my food."

"She's lying, man. I've never touched that girl!" Harold jumps up but slows his roll when Pitch takes a couple steps and stops right in front of his face.

"You mean to tell me you haven't been fucking my fourteen-year-old daughter in exchange for this room and food?"

"Naw, man. I'm married, and I'd never do no sick shit like that to a child," Harold lies.

"So she's lying on you, huh?" My heart starts beating a mile a minute, because I've got no idea what Pitch has in store for me.

"Yeah, she's lying." Pitch hits him so hard that the chair he's sitting in flips backward; the only thing that stops it from falling is the gaudy old radiator. Now the chair is sitting at an angle, with Harold looking over at me, terrified; little does he know that he's got good reason to be.

"Naw, you the lying one, bitch!" Pitch hits him again and again in the face, splattering blood all over the front of his shirt. "Who the fuck you think you fooling, trying to get over? This ho belongs to me, and whether you know it or not, yo' ass owes me a bunch of money!" he says between smacks. Harold isn't moving anymore, but that doesn't stop Pitch from his assault. "Get this mu'fucka outta here!" he tells the guy standing by the door.

The guy doesn't say anything and only walks over to Harold's bruised and broken body. Lifting him up, he places his dead weight over his shoulder with ease. After he's done, he turns around, looks over at Pitch, who nods his head. He then walks out of the room and closes the door behind him.

I wonder what he's going to do with Harold, and what I come up with isn't good. Even though Harold's some kind of pervert who forced me to have sex with him, he still doesn't deserve what Pitch will do to him. I sit on the bed and watch as Pitch goes into the bathroom to clean himself up. I try my best to breathe as quietly as possible; I figure he won't bother me if I don't make my presence known. All kinds of things run through my mind, but not one of them give me any thought that he might possibly let me go. I know that isn't going to happen. I'm scared to death, but I figure if he kills me, at least I'll be free from all this pain.

Minutes later, he walks back into the room and takes a seat on the bed, directly behind me. I brace myself for whatever he's planning to do, but instead of being hit, I'm surprised when I hear him speak.

"What I'm trying to understand is this. You fight and run away from me because you think you're too good to be a whore, but you ho yo'self out for him. Explain that one to me."

I don't know what to say, but I know I have to say something, or else he's going to get angry and put his hands on me—or worse. *"I-I didn't know what else to do, Daddy,"* I tell him timidly.

"You didn't know what else to do? Ain't that 'bout a bitch?" He stands up, grabs a huge chunk of my hair, and slings me clear across the room.

My naked body hits the wall so hard that it knocks the two pictures of a beach down; one of them shatters as it hits the nightstand. His shoes crunch the glass into the carpet as he walks over to me. I scoot as far into the corner as I can, but I know there's no getting away from him. He grabs my hair once again and stands me up before smacking me down with such force that I do a full 360. My head is spinning, and I'm dizzy. I can't see much, but I can hear him coming toward me again, which scares me even more. My first thought is that I have to get away somehow, but there isn't anywhere for me to go. Out the corner of my eye, I see the bed, so I get up on my knees and crawl quickly to it, then attempt to scurry under it. *"Ah!"* I scream when I feel Pitch deliver a solid kick to my backside. Since my butt is in the air, his big boot also connects roughly with my private parts. The pain from that sensitive area shoots through me, and I ball into a fetal position, holding my hands tightly between my legs.

"Where the fuck you going, huh?" he demands, then snatches up my left leg and begins dragging me back into the middle of the floor.

I look up at him in horror when I see his foot coming toward my face. Next, everything goes black.

I wake up disoriented, with no idea where I am or how I got here. I'm still naked, but on top of that, I have a headache that's out of this world. The last thing I remember is Pitch beating on me in the hotel room and seeing his foot coming toward me. It's dark, but I feel myself in motion. My body is in motion, and I can faintly hear music playing. It takes a minute, but it finally hits me, and I realize I'm in the trunk of a car. Fear engulfs me because I don't know where

I'm being taken, and it feels like I'm losing air. I can't think of anything else to do, so I start to bang on the car with my fists, hoping someone will hear me and call the police. I give up on that when music blares even louder from the car; I know he turned it up louder to drown out my screams and pounding.

I'm not sure how long the ride is, but eventually the car stops. The doors open and shut, but nobody comes back to let me out. I lie in the cramped space until the darkness turns to daylight. There isn't much else to do but stay in that balled-up position, because there's a bunch of stuff in the trunk along with me, and I can't move around. Time creeps by, and it gets hotter and hotter, as if I'm enclosed in a baking oven. I start to freak out because it feels like something is crawling all over me, but I calm down when I realize it's only beads of sweat rolling down my body. I'm faced with the task of trying to stay still, but that's impossible because it's so muggy inside. The more I move, the hotter I get, and the harder it is for me to breathe.

I assume I dozed off again, because when I open my eyes, I'm still in the same place, even though the sun is clearly going down. till in the same place, but the sun is going down. It's still cramped, but I thank God that it's not as hot in here as it was before. I don't know if this is where I'll take my last breath or not, but if it is, I'm ready for it. Truthfully, I'm tired of living anyway. I want nothing more than to be free of all the pain inflicted upon me by the people who are supposed to love me. They've hurt my mind and body so much.

I put my hands together and close my eyes, then say a prayer. "God, I don't know if You're up there listening to me or not, but I've got a lot on my mind. I don't know why I was born into this life, but I'm ready for it to be over. Please bring me home to you so I can finally be at peace. Not only is my mind tired, but my body is all used up and worn out, and I just wanna be free. I want to be free of pain, free of

*heartache. Nobody loves me down here, and no one will
actually miss me when I'm gone, so what do I have to lose?
The answer to that is nothing—absolutely nothing. I don't
want to live anymore. I'm just...I'm so tired of this." Tears
spill from the corners of my eyes and roll rapidly down my
face; I don't even bother to wipe them away. "My mother
never loved me. She just pimped me out for money to feed her
drug habit. When the father I never knew finally came into
my life, he wasn't any better than her. At the present moment,
he has me locked in a trunk, naked, because I won't agree to
work as a whore for him. I'm sorry for using foul language,
God, but it is what it is...and it's the absolute truth. What I
don't understand is why I'm being punished. What have I
done that was so bad that I have to go through all this?
Wait...You don't even have to answer that, because it doesn't
even matter right now. I'm ready to give up the fight and
come home—whenever you're ready to take me. Amen."*

*I open my eyes and just stare into the dark, limited space
of my tiny prison. Nothing goes through my mind except the
fact that I'm indeed ready to die. I'm not the least bit scared
and would actually welcome it. I wouldn't care if Pitch
leaves me out here in this trunk for a week. I hope he does,
because I don't wanna go anywhere else with him. I can't
deal with him torturing me again, treating me like some kind
of animal. He's already caused me enough pain. He's sick,
and I don't want any part of it. I'm better off out here, and
I'm ready to meet my Maker.*

*The sound of gravel crunching under someone's feet
wakes me up from my slumber, and I'm instantly alert. My
eyes dart from side to side as I struggle to hear something,
anything. I don't even realize I'm holding my breath until I
finally exhale. I'm glad no one is out there. I laugh out loud,
not sure if it was all my imagination, or if maybe I was just
hallucinating. Until I hear it again, I'm sure it's all in my
head. This time, it's closer. When I hear a key enter the lock,
I brace myself for whatever Pitch is planning to do to me.*

Cachet

The trunk opens, and the light outside is so bright that it hurts my eyes. I squint and try to look up at the person standing before me, but I can't make out who it is. When I'm finally able to get a clear view, I realize it's the guy from the store...

***

I feel a hand on my shoulder, and my eyes pop open. When they connect with Taz's, I recall that I'm at his apartment. He wouldn't let me go home last night and insisted that I stay the night with him. I didn't complain because I didn't really want to be alone; I just couldn't let him know that. I lie in the same spot for a few before sitting up, then reach down and pull the blanket up so it covers my exposed breast.

"Don't be shy now. Yo' ass wasn't shy last night when you was getting buck wild," he jokes. "Girl, yo' ass is something else." He laughs, shaking his head.

"What's that supposed to mean?"

"I mean yo' ass is a freak! You almost gave me a heart attack last night with yo' rowdy ass."

"Boy, please! I didn't do anything you didn't want me to do." I smirk. "You loved every minute of it. Tell me you didn't."

He doesn't answer and just sits there with a goofy grin on his face.

"That's what I thought." I flip back the cover and scoot to the edge of the bed, then climb out. Completely naked, I sashay over to the connected master bath, but not before grabbing my cosmetic bag with all my overnight stuff inside.

"Damn! You know you got a fat ass on you, girl," he says with his eyes planted on my behind.

I shoot him a quick smirk and continue my stride, on my way to take a shower. I reach into the linen closet and pull out a towel set and an extra washcloth for my face. I step into the glass-enclosed shower, and turn two of the many handles inside. I don't make the water too hot, because I know that'll only make my hair fall; for some reason, my extra shower cap isn't inside my bag. I step inside and close my eyes and allow the warm water to sprinkle over my naked body. I reach for the soap, then frown when I realize I can't use that kind of bar on my sensitive skin. "Taz!" I scream.

"What's up?" I hear him reply through the door.

"I need some better soap, because I'm not using this shit in here." I exhale impatiently when I don't hear him say anything for a full minute. When the shower door opens, I turn with attitude but come face to face with his chiseled, bare chest. In one hand is a gold bottle of Victoria's Secret Vanilla Lace body wash and in the other he's holding a bright pink loofah. Involuntarily, my eyes drop, and I see that he's naked. When I look up, I notice a slight smile covering his face. "I don't know what you smiling for, because I'm not using some other bitch's soap." I roll my eyes and take a step back.

"This ain't some other bitch's. I bought this for *you,* girl." He looks at me, confused. "It's brand new. Open it up."

"There ain't no damn way for me to tell if it's brand new, Taz. It don't come with a seal or anything."

"Well, I guess you gon' have to take my word for it then." He smiles.

I don't smile back at him.

"Come on now, baby. I wouldn't even play you like that. You know me." He moves further into the shower until he's standing right in front of me.

I bring my lips up to his and kiss him tenderly. "You're lucky I believe you," I tell him after I break the kiss.

"Do you need help washing up?"

"No. I can do that myself."

"Come on, baby. I've missed you so much. Let me wash you up. Let me cater to you," he begs.

"Okay, but that's all you're gonna do. I don't want to get

my

  hair wet in this damn shower."

"I'm only going to wash you up...nothing else," he promises.

For some reason, I still don't believe him; maybe it's that devious look on his face.

He removes the top from the bottle and pours a small amount onto the loofah. He holds it under the stream of water for a while, then rubs it between his hands and it creates a foamy lather. When I see him coming toward my neck, I lift my head so I can give him better access. I close my eyes as he moves down to my titties; he stops when he sees the small scar over my breast. "What happened to you?" he asks.

"I got into a fight a few weeks ago, and the chick tried to stab me," I lie. I haven't told him about my near-death experience, and I don't have plans to. "It ain't shit but a flesh wound."

"I don't want you out there fighting and shit!" he scolds. "You're too beautiful for that, you hear me?"

"I hear you, baby," I whisper, happily dropping it.

Using the loofah, he washes over that spot in small circles, covering both breasts with suds. I close my eyes, as he goes past my belly button, down to my love canal. He bends down and gently cleanses my short, trimmed pubic hair, then gestures me to open my legs a bit, just so he can clean my kitty.

Instead of the loofah, I feel one of his fingers enter me slowly. My eyes pop open, and I stare down at him. "Uh-uh! You said you were only gonna wash me up. Yo' ass ain't slick!"

"I'm sorry, baby, but you're just so damn sexy."

"Give it here. I'll do it myself." I hold my hand out, expecting to receive the sponge.

Instead, he stands up, grabs hold of my hand, and pulls me closer to him.

"What are you doing?" I sigh, even though I already

know the answer.

"I'm about to make love to my woman," he says with lust in his voice.

"Hold on, baby. Can't we wait a minute—or at least until I get out of the shower. I don't want to mess up my hair," I whine.

"I'll pay for you to get it done again. I just need you right now."

I don't get a chance to argue because he covers my lips with his. Instinctively and hungrily, I kiss him back; when our tongues connect, my pussy begins to pulsate.

He turns the hot knob a bit more and makes the temperature rise. Almost instantly, the glass walls steam up, making it impossible to see anything outside. Taz twists some of the other knobs, and water begins to pour from the other sprouts all around us. It feels like we're standing beneath a tropical waterfall, water raining down on us from every direction, even the ceiling. The suds slowly slide off my body and mix in with the water swirling around and down the drain.

Since my hair is already ruined, I step into the stream and allow the water to soak it entirely. Taz nudges me a few steps back, and I grab a hold of the steel bar that's placed conveniently in the middle of the wall. He lifts my leg up slightly and maneuvers his way between them, then rubs his dick up against my swollen clit. We continue to kiss each other passionately, as if there is no tomorrow. My body tenses, and I grunt when he begins to push himself inside of me. When he's all the way in, my body conforms around his manhood as he pumps in and out of my wetness. I moan every time his shaft rubs against my clit; it feels so damn good. Using the steadiness of the bar, I lower myself down to meet every thrust he sends my way. It feels as if he's all the way up in my stomach, but I don't mind because I love it deep.

"Put your arms around my neck," he orders. When both

my arms are wrapped tightly around him, he reaches down and picks up my other leg and starts going to work.

"Aw, shit! Ooh, damn...get this pussy, baby," I chant over and over as I feel my first orgasm coming.

"You like that shit, don't you?" he asks, watching his glistening dick as he moves it in and out of my tight opening.

"You know I do, baby. Give me that dick!" I shout when the orgasm comes on full force. The water, combined with the way he's grinding into me is driving me insane.

We fuck hard up against the wall, and he gives me everything he's got. He complies when I tell him to put me down, and I drop to my knees. With his dick in my hand, I lick the head and savor the taste of my own juices. When I'm satisfied that I've gotten every drop, I devour that muthafucka like my life depends on it. I alternate from bobbing my head up and down to jerking him off with my right hand, as the water rains down on my hair, making it stick to my face. I lightly massage his balls with my left hand, and when he attempts to pull away because he can't take it, I lock down on it with a death grip. Over the sound of the water, I hear a strange noise come from his mouth, and I know I've got him right where I want him. Relaxing my throat muscles, I push his rod back until I can damn near feel it hit my tonsils.

"Fuck! Damn, girl, what the hell are you doing to me?" he asks with his eyes pinched tight.

I don't say anything and just keep working hard to help him get his nut.

"Ah!" he screams as the salty liquid fills my mouth.

I don't even bother spitting it out. I just swallow every drop and lick my lips for effect, just to show him just how good I think it is. I don't stop stroking him until he's fully erect again, then push him backward until he's seated on the stone-lined seating area. I slowly mount him, grabbing hold of the step bar behind him. Bracing myself, I begin to bounce up and down. I go slow at first, but before long, I feel my second nut building, so I increase my speed. Each time I come up, I tighten my pussy muscles and squeeze the life out of his dick on my way back down. This lasts for about ten minutes before my toes begin to curl and my body shakes. I'm taken over the edge when he places both hands on each side of my hips and pushes himself into me all the way to the base.

"Are you cumming?" he asks when he feels my muscles start to pulsate.

I want to tell him I am, but it feels so good that I can't even respond verbally. All I can do is nod my head, which is good enough for him, because he smiles.

When my body comes down from my orgasm high, Taz lifts me up and lays my body back in the same area where he'd just been seated, then dives into my pussy, face first. I push my wet hair from my face and sit up on my elbows so I can see his face between my legs. He licks my clit a few times while staring up at me, before pushing his tongue so far up in my shit that his nose is sitting right on my pubic hair. A whine comes from deep in my throat when his soft but firm tongue slides in and out. Around and around I grind my hips on his tongue, allowing him to fuck me with his mouth.

My legs rest comfortably on his shoulder when he lifts up and locks his lips around my pink pearl. When he starts to beat on it like a drum, I reach down and spread my pussy lips to give him better access as he orally pleases me.

"Right there, baby. Ooh…yeah. Don't stop doing that." I sit my head back against the wall and begin to play with my breast. "Shit…ahhhh, shit! Eat this pussy, baby. It feels so fucking good." I feel that familiar tingle that starts from my toes and moves slowly up my body. My legs begin to shake, and I can hardly contain myself. "Ah, shit! Don't stop, baby! Please don't stop!" I scream as I rock my hips faster and faster against his face. My clit starts to jump, and my pussy begins to pulsate rapidly.

He reaches around and grabs hold of my hips and locks

on. By now, I'm rocking my hips so fast it's a wonder he doesn't fall back and bust his ass. The tingling feeling reaches my clit, and I cum hard, squirting my fluids in his mouth and down his throat. He happily swallows everything I give him and continues to assault my sensitive clit with his tongue. I wiggle and move, trying to unlock the hold he has on me, but he won't give up for anything. Instead, he carries on, thumping my shit repeatedly.

"What you running for?" he asks, after he removes his mouth from between my legs.

"I'm not running," I lie, out of breath.

He doesn't say anything back to me and just puts his head back between my legs.

It only takes one lick to get me jumping, trying to scoot closer to the wall. "Okay, okay! I can't take it!"

He smiles, stands up, and grabs hold of my hand.

After turning off the water, he opens the shower door and pulls me onto the warm floor. He then takes my towel and wraps it around my body, drying me off just enough so I'm not dripping wet. Dropping the towel on the floor, he leans down and scoops me up, then holds me in his arms. We move toward the bedroom and closer to the bed. I look up at him as he lays me down on top of the covers and climbs in behind me. His mouth opens, and he leans over to cover my hard nipples with it. At a snail's pace, he slides his hand past my stomach and parts my legs. I feel one of his fingers slide into me slowly. He pulls it out, brings it to his mouth, and licks it clean. "Damn, your pussy even taste good," he says with lust-filled eyes.

I don't reply. I just place my hands behind his head and pull him in for a kiss. I know for a fact that I don't love him, but I love how he makes my body feel.

CHAPTER FIVE

It's been a week since I came to Taz's apartment, and I'm about ready to go home. I tried to leave the next day, but he begged and pleaded for me to stay. When I came up with the excuse that I needed to go home to grab a few outfits, but he shot that muthafucka down. He had the outfit that I came over in dry-cleaned and took me to the mall, where he bought me enough stuff to last me for a month; I guess that's how long he *thought* I was going to stay. Everywhere he's gone for the past week, he wanted my ass planted in the passenger seat. *This shit's getting old though. I don't know if he thinks I'm gonna run away or what, but today's the day I'm getting the fuck out of here.*

"Where you going?" Taz asks when I climb up out of bed.

"Home," I state plainly as I walk over to the closet to pick out something to wear for the day.

"What for?" He sits up, wiping sleep from his eyes.

"Because I want to. I've been here with you for the past week, and I need to go home and check on my house," I lie.

"A'ight. Lemme ride with you." He begins to climb out of the bed.

"Naw, that's cool. I got a lot of stuff to do today, but I'll call you later."

"Oh. What time are you coming back here?"

Damn! Can't a bitch breathe or something? He's clingy as hell! "I'm not coming back here tonight. I'll be back tomorrow."

"Look, Brandy, don't make me have to fuck you up. You are acting all funny and shit, like you about to do something you ain't got no business doing."

I stop pulling clothes out and turned around to look at him. "Why I gotta be doing something sneaky? Why the hell can't I just want to go home and sleep in my own damn bed for one night?" I say, getting pissed because he's really tripping.

"Because I want you to sleep with me, that's why!" He raises his voice.

I'm not moved at all, because he ain't the only one in this bitch who can catch an attitude. "Look, Taz, I'm a grown-ass woman, and I do what the fuck I wanna do. Please don't ruin this by trying to run me like I'm a child or some shit, because this ain't that kinda party. I'm not like them bitches you used to deal with, so don't try to play me like I am."

"You damn right. You're not Osha, fo' sho, 'cause her ass woulda had enough common sense to know that what I said was what was supposed to happen," he responds frankly.

What the...? This nigga done clearly lost his mind. "What the fuck did you just say to me?" I walk over toward him and stand inches from his face. "If you ever in your muthafucking life compare me to that bitch again, I promise you ain't gon' never have to worry about me again. You can bet your life on that!"

"I wasn't saying it like that, Brandy. I just—" he starts to explain, but I block his dumb ass out and walk back over to get my clothes.

I grab a pair of jeans and a shirt and slam the bathroom door behind me. *How dare he compare me to that bitch? He's damn right I ain't nothing like her, because I'm a bitch who's all about my paper. I ain't the dumb ho who sits at home crying by the phone 'cause my nigga is out fucking some other bitch. I'm the type who'll be out fucking just like his ass is, without a worry in the world. He lucky I didn't bust him in his mouth for saying some slick shit like that to me! I can't believe he tried to play me like I'm some average bitch.*

I bend down and step into the black Roberto Cavalli stretch cotton jeans and pull them up, fastening them at my waist. I slip the beige, black, and cream animal-print tunic his ass forked out $900 for over my head, then remove my silk scarf. Using a wide-toothed comb, I unwrap my hair and allow it to fall. He took me to the shop two days ago and got a wash, wrap, and flat-iron. After putting a small part down the front of my head, I open the door. Standing in the corner of the room, I slip my feet into my Christian Louboutin peep-toe platform sandals.

"I'm out," I say over my shoulder as I pick up my Chloe bag and make my way out the door and close it behind me. As soon as I start my truck up, the low fuel light flickers on, letting me know I'm in desperate need of a gas station. The closest one I can think of is on 33rd in Lorain, and since I have a taste for Wendy's, I decide to head over there.

I pull up to the pump, grab my purse, and exit the car. Inside, I wait impatiently behind a guy whose playing the lottery. He's constantly calling off number after number to the clerk, who punches them into the machine in front of him. After about five minutes, it really begins to piss me off, because it seems as if he's playing every damn number in the world. When he does finally move out of the way, I slide my money into the slot, inform the clerk of what pump I'm on, and turn to walk out the door. After tossing my purse on the seat, I go around to pump my gas. As the fuel continues to drain from the nozzle, I look up at the black Infiniti G27 that's pulling up to the pump beside me. I have to do a double-take because it's looks identical to Xavier's, but I'm sure there are quite a few of them on the streets.

I laugh. *What are the chances that I'd run in to him here anyway? It's been months since I last saw him, and even then*

53

he stormed out because I flipped out about a dream. When the driver side door opens, I realize the chances are pretty damn good, because it's his ass, and he's looking mighty good, if I do say so myself. Playing it off, I roll my eyes, continuing to squeeze the lever since I've still got $20 left to pump.

From the corner of my eye, I see him smirk before closing the door behind him. He swipes his debit car at the pump, and while his back is to me, I take the opportunity to steal a glance at his outfit. He looks all laidback in a pair of Polo khaki shorts and a white t-shirt. The matching khaki Polo hat has a blue jockey on it, the same color as the one on the leg of his shorts, and his feet are clad in a fresh pair of Air Force 1s. As he picks up the nozzle to pump his gas, he looks over at me, and we lock eyes. Without even an acknowledgment, he turns around and commences to do what he came to do.

I snort in frustration. *This son-of-a-bitch has a lot of fucking nerve to avoid speaking to me. If he thinks I'm gonna break my neck to say something to him, he's got another thing coming. This ain't that type of party.*

The nozzle clicks, letting me know I'm done filling up. I glance at the pump to make sure the whole $50 was deposited into my tank before hanging it back in its place. I open my car door and take my seat. I start the ignition and pull my seatbelt across me before pulling off toward the street. There's a lot of traffic, so I have to wait for a safe chance to exit the gas station. While I wait, I take a quick look in my rearview mirror at Xavier; he's done with his gas and is waiting for his receipt. When the light changes, I hit the gas to head to Wendy's before I hit the freeway to go home.

It feels good to be back at my house after being gone for a week. When I'm finished smashing my food, I figure it's as good a time as any to do my weekly cleaning, and laundry is the first thing on my list. After I put a load in, I put clean sheets on my bed and vacuum all the carpets. Mopping the kitchen is my last task, and when I'm done, it's about time to put another load in. By the time I finish, I've got a slight headache. Inside my room, I unscrew the top off the Imitrex and sniff it up into both of my nostrils. It's only 3 o'clock in the afternoon, so I decide to lie down for a quick nap. After wrapping my hair, I climb into bed and place my head completely under the covers. The headache only worsens, so I massage my temples with my fingers until the pain subsides. Not long after that, I'm fast asleep.

***

"Get out," he says to me after he opens the trunk. I don't move a muscle. He soon grows tired of waiting on me, so he reaches in to grabs hold of my arm and forcefully pulls me out.

"Ouch!" I howl as I fall to the ground, landing right on my knees.

"Get up!" he orders.

I stand up slowly, knocking away the gravel that's embedded itself in my knees. When I look up, I see that we're standing in front of the house. I've been here the whole time! Pitch went into the house and left me outside in the trunk like a bag of dirty laundry. When he nudges me in the back with his hand, I begin to walk. My hands do a poor job of concealing my unclothed body as I walk up the stairs and into the front entryway. Standing in the foyer, he closes and locks the door behind us. I trip over my own feet when he powerfully pushes me toward the back of the house. The basement door is open right ahead of us, but beyond that, I see nothing but darkness.

I move as he guides me down the first step, but I've already made up my mind that I'm not going any further. He shoves me again, and I stumble before I reach my arms out and grab the wooden arm rail, holding on for dear life. My

*body jerks and shakes as he tries unsuccessfully to remove
my hands from around the rail, but I'm holding on with
everything in me. I have no intention of going down those
stairs. Without a doubt in my mind, I know Pitch is sitting
down there waiting for me, and I'm terrified of what he's
going to do when I finally get there. Even though I'm ready
to leave this Earth, I don't want to make my exit while being
tortured and abused, and I know that's what Pitch has in
mind.*

*"Let yo' fucking hands go, or I'm gonna break every one
of your fingers." The bass in his voice booms loudly in my
ear. When I turn to look up at him, I see a mask of irritation,
but the look in his eyes tells me he's serious.*

*"Well, do what you gotta do" I tell him smartly, but at
the same time, I'm scared of him actually doing it. I hang on
to the rail with all my might, tightening my fingers even
more.*

*He says nothing else and just walks past me and down
two of the stairs. He turns around and faces me before
bending over and reaching for my hands. I press my hands
together as tight as I can, but he still manages to get hold of
my left pinky finger. I watch in terror as he pulls my finger
back and twists it, breaking it. The sound of my finger
breaking will forever be etched in my mind. I yell so loudly
that I'm surprised the neighbors across the street didn't hear
me. As I stare at it, all bent and hanging from my hand, I
can't believe he actually broke it. It hurts so bad that my
breath temporarily catches in my chest, and I forget to
breathe. When he grabs hold of my ring finger, the fighter in
me lashes out. I let go of the rail, lift my right leg up, and
kick him right in the stomach.*

*He stumbles down at least six stairs before catching his
balance and running back toward me. I begin to kick my legs
wildly, trying to keep him away from me, because I know he's
going to hurt me bad. My right leg misses; he catches it in
midair and begins pulling on it. I grip the rail once again but*

can't hold it as tight because of the pain in my broken finger. He yanks one more time, and my hands instantly release. The back of my head bounces up and down as it hits each stair on the way down; it feels like it's going to explode. I try to sit up to protect my head, but when I do that, my back gets all banged up. Even though it's only ten steps, it seems like a thousand. By the time I land on the floor, I'm actually glad to be lying on a flat surface.

I shriek when he grabs a handful of my hair and begins to drag me over to the corner of the basement. It's extremely dark, and I start swinging my arms at his hands, hoping to somehow force him to let me go. I don't want to go over there because I'm scared of what's going to happen once I get there. He reaches down and punches me in the face, causing me to stop, but only for a minute. I began swinging my arms again but stop immediately when I hear Pitch speak.

"Stop doing all that stupid shit before I get up."

I move my head from side to side, but I don't see him anywhere.

"Aw, don't get scared now," he says.

I look behind me and see that he's slowly walking down the stairs. "I-I'm sorry, Daddy. I promise I won't do it again!" I cry out, as I can't bear to let him hurt me anymore.

"I know you won't—at least not after I'm done with you."

The corner of the room suddenly lights up, and I notice a medium-sized dog cage. It's lined with newspaper, and there are two plastic dog bowls inside it. Across from that is a small television with a generic-looking DVD player on top. The guy lets go of my hair, and my head falls to the floor with a thud. Pain shoots through the back of my head, and even though I've never been shot before, I believe that's as close as I'm going to get.

"Get in the cage," Pitch tells me as he walks over beside me.

"Huh?" I ask, certain that I heard him wrong.

"Bitch, I just told you to get yo' ass in that fucking cage!" he yells.

I get on all fours and crawl over toward it. I guess I'm not moving fast enough, because I receive a swift kick in my behind, and I drop flat on my stomach from the pain.

"Move yo' muthafucking ass, ho!"

I quicken my pace, but I'm still confused as to how I'm going to fit inside that tiny thing. It's meant for animals, for small dogs, and I don't think I can possibly squeeze in there. If I do manage, it's gonna be even more cramped than the trunk, and I won't be able to move. Still, I have no choice, so I open up the door and begin to climb in. When I'm all the way inside, I have to maneuver myself to be able to sit down. I get as comfortable as I can and turn around to look at Pitch. I flinch when he reaches into the cage and grabs hold of my broken pinky finger. Pain shoots from my hand and up my arm when he pops it back into place, but I'm too scared to cry. He then closes the gate and fastens a small lock on the outside, securing it. I watch him as he walks over to the TV and powers it and the DVD player on; a blue screen lights up the dark area.

On the video is Trixie, completely naked and tied to a bed. Blood is everywhere, and there are little gashes covering her legs and arms. Her chest is also injured, and I cringe when I notice that her nipple seems to be barely attached to her body. As the camera rotates, I see a few females off to the side. While most of them look horrified, one is smiling. Trixie's once-beautiful hair is standing up all over her head, as if a five-year-old hacked away at it with dull scissors. She cries and begs Pitch to let her go as she wiggles and tries to free herself from her confinement.

The camera stops spinning and lands right in front of her face. When she looks directly into it, I start to cry. It seems as if she's looking right at me. There are bruises all over her face, and both of her eyes are swollen. Her nose is crooked, as if it's been broken. When she opens her mouth to talk, I can see that quite a few of her teeth are missing, and it looks like some others might be broken off. Her hair is caked with blood, and she looks nothing like the Trixie I remember. Pitch walks over to her and hits her in the face with a closed fist, causing her head to jerk back violently. I turn away; I can't stand to see him hurt her.

"Lift your fucking head up and watch before yo' ass get strung up next," he threatens.

I pick up my head just in time to see Pitch pull out his penis and urinate all over her face. She tries unsuccessfully to move out the way of the stream of pee, but because she's tied up, she can't do much. A sadistic laugh comes from deep in his gut as he continues to humiliate her in front of everyone in the room. Once he's done, he shakes his penis, and the girl with the smile on her face comes over and stands directly in front of him. She's wearing a long, orange-colored wig that matches her bikini top, as well as white leather pants. She's a big-boned girl, but she has a real flat stomach; with those large hips sticking out, she resembles a horse. A bunch of makeup covers her face, but she's somewhat cute underneath. When she gets on her knees and opens her mouth, I almost throw up. What kind of person would want to suck urine off a man's penis?

"That's right, Kandi. Clean Daddy's dick off like a good girl," he tells her.

"You know I gotta take care of you, Daddy," she replies in a baby voice after she's done.

Pitch just laughs and begins to stroke her hair with his right hand.   "You must wanna be Daddy's bottom bitch, huh?"

"Yes, Daddy. I'd love that."

"In that case, you gotta prove yo'self to me."

"I will. I'll do whatever you want me to do," she replies eagerly.

He lifts her off her knees and whispers something in her ear. When he's done, she turns and walks away, only to return a moment later. In her hand she holds a handle with a razor blade attached to the end. She struts over to the bed and climbs on top of it, straddling Trixie's stomach. Using the razor, she slices a deep line across Trixie's forehead, causing her to scream out in pain and jerk around wildly. She follows that cut with three more, one down each side of her face and one across her chin. I cringe; I can almost feel her pain. Kandi uses her weight to stop Trixie from moving around so much before raising the blade again. The next cut goes from the corner of her forehead, down past her nose, past her cheek, and stops right above her jawline. She cuts her again the exact same way on the opposite side of her face, till she looks like she has a huge X inside of a bloody square on her face.

    Trixie continues to cry out in extreme pain as Kandi climbs off of her and walks back over to Pitch. She hands him the razor, and he pats her on the ass as she walks away. The other girls watch with nervous looks on their faces because they don't know what's going to come next. My face is drenched with fresh tears because I can't believe he'd do something like this to her. Yes, she took money from him, but it's not as serious as he's making it out to be, and he didn't have to treat her that way.

    "So, are you gonna tell me where she is now?" Pitch asks.

    Trixie doesn't reply at first and only stares at him as the blood runs down her face and into her eyes.

    "I'm not telling you shit!" she yells.

    Kandi returns with a bottle of alcohol in her hand. She twists off the top and holds it up for Trixie to see. Pitch gives her another nod, and she tosses the liquid all over Trixie's body.

    Trixie yells and begins to flip around the bed, like a fish out of water; a look of agony covers her cut-up face that used to be so beautiful. I know the alcohol has to burn like hell on those fresh cuts, but all Pitch and Kandi do is laugh. My vision becomes blurry from all the tears I'm crying. It hurts me so bad to see them doing that to Trixie, because she doesn't deserve this. I feel like it's all my fault, that she's suffering because of me. If she wouldn't have tried to help me get away, none of it would have ever happened. What was it all for anyway? Nothing, that's what, because I'm right back in the same place I started, only worse.

The video cut off with Trixie still jerking, and the screen suddenly goes black.

Pitch stands in front of the TV with a smirk on his face, then turns it and the DVD player off. Then he and the guy turn and made their way up the stairs. Once they get to the top, the lights go off, and I'm still in the cage, surrounded by darkness. I'd usually be scared, but since I've got so much on my mind, I welcome it.

***

My eyes pop open, and I roll over to look at the clock. It's 9:15, so it didn't turn out to be much of a nap. My headache is gone, but for some reason, I still feel drowsy. Minutes pass with me lying in the same spot, and even though I've slept the entire day away, I don't feel like getting out of bed. Turning my head to the side, I close my eyes. When I open them again, my eyes focus on the clock. This time says 10:10. *Damn! What the fuck just happened? I swear I thought I only closed my eyes for a second, but it's been almost an hour. I just know I need to get my ass up before I fuck around and go to sleep again. That wouldn't be good for me, because I'm sure I'm gonna have a headache when I do finally wake all the way up.*

My cell phone vibrates on the nightstand, but by the time I pick it up, it stops. The notification says I have four missed calls, and I see a familiar number on the call log: Xavier.

CHAPTER SIX

"What the fuck does he want?" I ask myself, still staring at the screen. That question gets an answer before I know it, because it starts to vibrate again. I take a deep breath and answer, not eliminating the annoyance from my tone. "Hello?"

"I know you ain't acting funny toward me," he says.

"Boy, what the hell you talking about?"

"I'm talking about the fact that this is the fifth time I've called you."

"Um…okay. What's your point?"

"My point is, why haven't you been answering my damn calls, woman?" he jokes.

"Can I help you with something, Xavier?" I say, unmoved by that ha-ha shit. *This nigga just seen me at the fucking gas station and didn't utter two words, and now he wants to call a bitch and spark up a conversation? Where they do that at?*

"Damn, it's like that?"

"Hell yeah, it's like that. Yo' ass ain't speak to me at the gas station, so what you want now?"

"You didn't speak to me either," he shoots back.

"I also didn't just call you five times either, did I?" I hear him chuckle.

"So…what's up, Xavier? What do you want?" I ask again.

"I'm just calling to check on you and see how you're

doing."

"Well, if I recall correctly, you told me—and I quote—it was fun while it lasted."

"Yeah, I said that, but only because I was pissed at you back then."

"What's changed?"

He doesn't say anything.

"Hello?"

"Yeah, I'm here."

"What's changed?" I repeat.

"I realized I'm in love with you," he states.

My words catch in my throat, and I can't come up with anything to say.

"Brandy, did you hear me? I said I'm in love with you."

"What are you—" I try to speak, but he cuts me off.

"Just hear me out, hear me out. Ever since I left your apartment, you've been on my mind. I tried to push you out, but you always somehow found your way back in. You're the first thing I think about when I wake up and my last thought before my eyes close," he says sincerely. "About two weeks ago, I met someone."

My heart drops. "Xavier—"

"Just listen, because I got more to say. I met this woman, and she's beautiful just like you, Brandy. She likes the same things I do, and she's open about what she wants in a man, so I figured I'd see where it goes. I spent the night at her house last night, and we had sex for the first time. Then I—"

"I don't want to hear this, Xavier!" I interrupt. I can feel myself getting sick at the thought of him touching another woman. Even though I haven't actually said it out loud before, I'm in love with him as well. I just haven't done anything about it because I'm in no mood to get my heart broken again.

"Please let me finish, baby. I gotta tell you everything," he pleads.

"Okay," I say, but inside I really don't want to hear any

more.

"We had sex, and all I could think about the whole time was you. I couldn't even perform because your face kept occupying my mind. I couldn't even cum because I wanted to be with you, not her. I guess she must have noticed the distant look in my eyes, because she stopped and asked me what was wrong. I couldn't tell her I was thinking about another woman, because I didn't want to hurt her feelings, so I told her it was nothing."

Fuck that bitch. Who cares about her feelings anyway?

"The only way I could finish up and get her off of me was to imagine making love to you. When I saw you at the gas station today, right after I left her house, I was stuck. It felt like it was fate for me to run into you, like something telling me we're meant to be. You've been heavy on my mind, baby, and then I just happen to run into you today, of all days. You gotta see what I see, Brandy."

"What are you trying to say, Xavier?" I ask, wanting to make sure I'm clear on what he's telling me.

"I'm sayin' I want to see where this can go between us. You're the woman I want to see when I go to bed at night, the woman I want lying on the pillow beside me when I wake up in the morning. I want you to be my woman. I want you to open up and tell me about your life. I want to be the shoulder you cry on when you're feeling down, the person who protects you from all the pain in this world. Most of all, I want you to allow me to do all those things and trust me with your heart."

"Xavier, I-I don't know." By now there are small tears rolling from my eyes and down my face. "It's hard for me to trust anyone. I've just been burned so many times."

"I understand that, but everyone is not the same. The only way you'll ever know is to give someone a chance…and I'm that person."

I sniffle quietly into the receiver. Roger had said similar things to me, and that hadn't landed me anywhere but devastated and heartbroken. "I-I-I just don't know what to say," I tell him truthfully. I have no clue what I'm going to do or what I'm going to tell this man who is expressing his love for me.

"All I'm asking is that you give me a chance—a chance to show you there are still good men out here. If you can honestly tell me you don't give a shit about me, I'll hang up this phone right now and leave you alone forever. You'll never have to worry about me bothering you ever again if you tell me right now that you don't want me."

"I'd be lying if I said I don't care about you, because I do. Thing is, I just don't want to get hurt."

"I'll tell you what. Whenever…if ever you feel like I'm gonna do you wrong, you can just cut me off. All I need is a chance, Brandy. I swear, you won't regret it."

"How about we start off slow and see where that takes us? I'd be comfortable with that."

"I'll take that," he says, seemingly content with my answer.

There's a long pause for a moment, and neither of us says anything. I'm not sure what's on his mind during that time, but mine is racing.

"I didn't get a chance to tell you since we haven't talked, but I bought a condo."

"Aw, shit! I'm happy for you. Where at?"

"Off Detroit Avenue, in an area called Battery Park."

"Oh, okay. Those new buildings they built not too long ago?" I ask, having seen them a few times before. "When can I come see the place?"

"What are you doing right now?"

"Nothing but lying in the bed." I glance over at the clock again; it's 11:00.

"Do you wanna come over now?"

"Sure. Give me about an hour and a half. I'll call you when I'm almost there," I say, tossing my covers aside.

"Okay. See you in a few."

After we disconnect the call, I climb out of bed and place my phone back on the nightstand. I don't make it through the threshold of the bathroom door before the phone vibrates again. I retrace my steps over to the bed and pick it up. The small mail icon on the screen tells me I have a voicemail. Since my line didn't beep while I was on the phone, I figure it must be a message he'd left before I answered. In the bathroom, I get myself together, then take a shower.

Forty-five minutes later, I'm standing in front of my closet, dressed in a lace La Perla bra and a matching thong. I look through my wardrobe and settle on a burnt orange Black Label cashmere ruffle cardigan. I decide to leave the top two buttons undone so my black bra is revealed, since it matches my Blue Label Pointelle leggings. I pull out my makeup bag and grab my M.A.C eye shadow. I brush a small amount of orange and chrome yellow above my lids and apply some mascara to my silk lashes. A coat of Surf, Baby Strange Potion lip gloss is spread evenly on my lips. After I finish giving my face a onceover, I stand in front of the mirror and unwrap my hair; instead of the part, I opt to comb my bangs down. My outfit is complete when I slide my feet into my new burnt orange, yellow, and black tricolor Python Patchwork Prada boots. After I fill my Bottega Veneta hobo, I grab my phone and head out the door.

By the time I get down the stairs to my vehicle, the clock reads 11:45. I realize I'm late, but I know he won't mind—just as long as I get there. I pick up my phone to call Xavier when I make it to 49th, and he gives me the address. After we hang up, I see that the voicemail icon is still at the top of the screen. Since it's working my nerves, I check the message, just so I can delete it.

"Hey, baby, it's Taz."

I roll my eyes but keep listening.

"I know you're probably looking at the phone, wondering what the hell I want, but I'm just calling to see what you're doing and to let you know I'm sorry about earlier. I didn't mean to compare you to her. It just came out like that. You're nothing like Osha, baby, and that's exactly why I fell so quick and hard for you. When am I gonna see you again? I miss you already, baby. Anyway, I won't go on and on about it. Just call me when you get a chance. Talk to you later. I-I love you."

I saved the message and hung up the phone, shaking my head. *It's crazy that I gotta dog a nigga for him to act like he got some damn sense. If I was all up his ass like Osha was, he'd be shitting on me just like he did her. Humph, as long as his money comes to me, I don't give a shit! I'd be a fucking fool to allow this nigga to play me like he did his babies'-mama. I mean, this nigga was fucking with me while he was with her—all in my face every chance he got, even in the house he shares with her. What kind of fool does he take me for?*

I pull up at Xavier's place and smile. It really looks nice from the outside. I climb out of the car, hit my alarm after the door closes, and strut right up to his door. My boot heels click with each step I make on the pavement. I push the doorbell once, and it chimes as it echoes throughout the house. A few seconds later, the door opens, and Xavier stands before me with a huge grin on his face. The aroma of food hits my nose, but before I get a chance to say anything about it or even step into the entrance, he picks me up off my feet and hugs me tight. *I guess he's happy to see me.* "Hello to you too." I giggle when he releases the hold he has on me.

"I'm sorry, Love. I'm just happy to see you."

"Love?" I ask, confused.

"I don't like all that baby-boo-bay or other cheesy shit people call their other half, so I'ma call you Love because that's what you are to me. You're the love of my life," he explains.

I don't say anything, but I do blush hard as hell.

"I wanted to tell you now, in case I didn't get the chance

for the rest of the night."

"What's that?" I ask.

"You look…beautiful."

I beam inside when he says it; he always knows just what to say. It almost scares me that he's such a perfect, total package. Not only can he fuck me until I'm damn near comatose, but he's also kind and gentle.

"Thank you."

"You are more than welcome." he pauses for a moment, while looking out of the door. "I see your driving a Camaro now.Is that a rental or did you trade your truck in?"

"My truck was totaled and I ended up with a Camaro as a rental. I liked it so much that I went ahead and purchased a new one." I tell him truthfully.

"Damn, were you in an accident or something?"

"Not exactly. I'll explain that later, because it's a long story."

He nods and we make our way up the stairs, where he gives me an official tour of his home. The living room is a nice size, with light hardwood floors and a fireplace. Four tall windows look out to the patio, which overlooks the rest of the apartments. The kitchen is small but open to the dining room. It has dark granite countertops and stainless steel appliances. A loft area sits at the top of the stairs and gives a clear view of the living room. While upstairs I see that one of the spare bedrooms has a queen-sized bed, nightstand, and dresser, while the other one has been turned into an office. The master is decked out in all black, with a huge armoire, dresser, two nightstands and a king-sized bed. I burst out laughing when he picks up a remote control and hits a button and a forty-two-inch plasma TV pops out at the foot of the bed. All in all, his house is nice; still, it could be better, with a woman's touch like mine. .

"You should let me decorate," I tell him when we head back downstairs.

"Damn. It's that bad?" he asks with a look of shock on

his face.

"No, I'm not saying that. It actually looks really nice. I just think you should hang a couple pictures and put a few knickknacks around the place, maybe even paint a few walls."

"Well, do with the place whatever you want. You're my woman now."

I don't say anything, because the sound of that puts a huge lump in my throat.

He senses my resistance and backs off a bit. "Just tell me how much you need, and I'll make it happen."

"Sounds like a plan." I smile, biting the corner of my lip, a habit I have when I start to get nervous.

"Do you want something to eat?"

"What do you have in mind?" I ask, having forgotten about the food I smelled when I first got here.

"Follow me."

We get up and walk over to the dining area, where the five-piece dining set is located. I take a seat after he pulls out my chair and watch him disappear into the kitchen. Moments later, he sits a chocolate chip martini in front of me and a rum and Coke in front of his chair. I bring the glass to my lips and take a sip as he brings out the food on small platters. For starters, we have bacon-wrapped persimmons wedges with little toothpicks stuck through them. Dinner consists of seared scallops and tenderloin steak with Manhattan sauce. We eat in silence, and I ponder how good the man is to me. He can cook his ass off, even better than I can, and I couldn't possibly make anything that tastes that good. *I'm beginning to think he's a keeper.*

"How was dinner?" he asks, as we both plop down on the couch.

"It was wonderful. I don't think I could eat another bite. Hell, I was already full, but when you brought out that chocolate éclair crepe cake, I had to have a piece." We both laugh as I rub my stomach. "By the way, thank you."

"You're more than welcome, Love. I'm just glad you liked everything."

There's an awkward silence, because neither of us can think of what to say next. I lean in and do what's natural to me, which is to kiss him. When he pulls away from me, I'm shocked and disappointed at the same time.

"I'm not turning you down, if that's what you're thinking," he says when he notices the look on my face.

"Well, what are you doing then?"

"I didn't call you over here for that. I just called you over here to sit and chill with me. I don't want you to feel or think that every time you're around me, we have to have sex."

I start to interrupt, but he stops me.

"I told you earlier that I love you, and I meant every word. Let's just spend the night getting to know each other. We have more than enough time to make love."

I can't say anything, because I've never heard anything like that from a man. Every guy I've fucked with has wanted pussy, even Roger. Sure, he expressed his undying love for me, but before the night was over, I was either sucking his dick or spread-eagle on the bed.

I tell Xavier I'm open to trying something new, though, so we just sit on the couch and talk. We continue to make small talk for a few hours, before taking our conversation upstairs. Once there we get undressed and take a nice, warm bubble bath together and talk some more. After we get out of the tub, we get in bed, naked, and just talk. I look him in the eyes as he tells me everything I want to know about him. He tells me all about his life and how he's worked hard for everything he has.

He also tells me he wants to get married and have children someday. I just sit there, listening to every word that comes out of his mouth. He explains to me that one of the main reasons he was so ready to leave Chicago was because there was nothing other than his family there. They were sad to see him go, but he had to do what was best for him. As we talks, he tells me that his breaking point was when his high school sweetheart broke his heart, about two years ago. "I thought we were happy," he says, "and there was no sign she was doing wrong. When I found out she was pregnant, I was scared but also happy." Once that happened, he proposed to her because he wanted his child to be raised by both parents. Everything was going well until the child was born.

They had just gotten home from the hospital when an unknown man came knocking at the door. "I opened it," says Xavier, "and the guy asked for my fiancée. He looked kind of rough, so I stood by my girl in case he might try anything. The look on her face when she saw him was one of sheer terror. Then the guy said, 'Why the fuck you ain't call and tell me my child's been born? When he said that, my heart dropped," Xavier says.

As much as she tried to deny it, the following day, they went to get a blood test done. It turned out that the unknown man was his fiancée's ex-boyfriend and was indeed the father of Xavier Jr. I notice that he's getting a little choked up when he gets to that part, because never once did she tell him there was even a remote possibility that he wasn't the child's father. After he finishes with that story, he explains to me that I'm not the only one that who's been hurt. He lets me know that he's also got trust issues, but he wants to put his trust in me. He tells me she hurt him to the core, and he promises that he'll never do anything like that to me or anyone else.

I know he's not lying to me, because by the look on his face, it hurts him to speak about it. My heart aches when I see him hurting like that, and I want to be the person who makes him happy again. I wipe the tear from the corner of his eye and tell him I'll never hurt him either. I tell him I'll try to trust him. It's then that I push all the doubt out of my mind and tell him my story; every horrifying detail.

CHAPTER SEVEN

The following morning, I wake up still enclosed in Xavier's arms. Truthfully, I like how it feels. I lie in the bed and think about all we learned about each other in just one night. We talked until the sun came out, something I've never done before. It feels good to have someone to talk to, someone to listen. I told him about my life and everything that's happened up to this point. I let him know about my mom, the woman who'd turned me out to tricking for cash. I told him about how my father deceived me and made me believe he was saving me from a horrible life, only to turn around and do the same thing my mother had done for years.

Xavier listened to me when I needed him to and was a shoulder to lean on when I cried, as I relived that all over again. I've never felt so loved in my entire life as I did when he put his strong arms around me. I finally know what it feels like to have someone who actually cares about me, someone who doesn't want anything in return. He could've tried to take advantage of me, but he didn't. I thought surely he'd push me away when I told him about all the men that I've actually had violate my body, but he didn't move or act like he wanted to. He just held on to me and let me get everything out of my system.

When I told him about being shot at and that I could have died, I had to calm him down; he got really angry about that. I didn't tell him the entire story, just that Angel was upset because I didn't want to deal with him anymore. I

72

couldn't tell him I stole the man's shit and put him in jail, because I know for a fact that Xavier wouldn't take that well. Throughout each story I shared, he listened and gave me a shoulder when I needed it. I don't know where this is going to lead, but for right now, I'm entirely onboard.

I roll out of his grasp and prepare to climb out of bed but stop when I see Xavier looking at me through a pair of sleepy eyes. I give him a quick smile and sit up, but before my feet have a chance to hit the floor, he has his arms around me, pulling me back down toward him.

"Stop, silly. I gotta pee," I tell him, giggling. When he loosens his grip, I go into the bathroom to handle my business. When I come back into the room, I find him sitting on the edge of the bed, rubbing his eyes with the back of his hand.

"Damn. It's almost 4 in the afternoon," he says after looking at the alarm clock.

"I know. It's like we slept the whole day away. What time did we go to bed last night?"

"I've got no clue. I just know it was early in the morning, because the sun was out."

Naked, I walk around the bed and pull out one of his drawers. I remove a t-shirt, pull it over my head, and let it fall down past my butt.

"I see you're getting comfortable," he jokes.

"Am I not supposed to?"

"You cool. You can do whatever you want in here. *Mi casa es su casa.*"

I burst out laughing; he's always being silly.

He pulls me close to him, and we lock lips, neither of us caring that neither of us has brushed our teeth. I guess this is this love thing after all, because anybody else would've got the shit knocked out of them for that. We part lips, and I climb over him and back into the bed, grabbing the remote in the process. I hit the button to make the TV come out of the foot of the bed. It's actually pretty cool, even though I didn't like it the first time I saw it. I scroll through the channels, and all I can find to watch is *Madea's Family Reunion*. I haven't seen it in a while, so I fluff my pillow and lean back to watch it. Xavier lies back down and does the same, pulling me closer to him, and we watch the movie in silence.

We must have dozed off, because when I open my eyes again, it's dark outside. Xavier has his arm around me, and he's knocked out. I don't move; just lying in his arms makes me feel refreshed. I've been lying in the man's bed all day, and he has yet to try to fuck me. Even though I want nothing more than to feel him deep inside of me, this is much better.

He moves a bit as he wakes up from his slumber, and I lean over kissing him softly on the lips. Slowly he opens his eyes and just gazes at me before breaking into a full-blown smile.

"What?" I ask.

"Nothing. I'm just happy you're here for real. I thought I was dreaming."

I blush once again. Something about the words he says makes them always perfect and always right on time. "No, it's not a dream, Xavier. I'm really here."

He smiles again before sliding out of bed and retreating into the bathroom. Moments later, I hear the shower running. I reach over and rummage through my purse, assuming this is as good a time as any to check my phone for missed calls. I turned it off last night while I was waiting for him to bring out dinner because I didn't want to be disturbed, and there ain't no telling who the hell would be calling. I figure it could be that butch bitch Meka, crybaby-ass Sade, thieving-ass McKenzie, or bug-a-boo-ass Taz. Either way, I wasn't trying to be bothered. As soon as my phone powers on, it begins to ring in my hand; it's Taz. I listen to see if the water is still on before I answer it. "Hello?" I say in my best sleepy voice.

"What are you doing?"

"Nothing. Just lying in bed. I don't feel well," I lie.

"Why was yo' phone off all day?" he asks.

Damn! Didn't this lousy-ass nigga just hear me say I don't feel well? "It was off because it died. Damn! I tell you I'm sick, Taz, and you want to give me the fucking third degree," I lash out, trying to remain as quiet as I can.

"I'm sorry, baby."

Bullshit. I swear I'm so tired of hearing him say the same shit every day! He's gotta be the sorriest muthafucka I've ever met.

"You want me to come over and take care of you?"

"No, I'll be okay. I just made me a bowl of soup and a glass of ginger ale, and I'm heading back to bed in a few."

"Oh, okay. Are you tryin' to keep me away from your house or something?"

"What?"

"It just dawned on me that I've never been to your place before. Why?"

"You've never asked. We've always done our creepin' at yours," I state matter-of-factly, knowing there ain't know way in hell he's ever coming to my house...period.

"I'm just playing." He gives a nervous chuckle because he knows what I said is true. "Anyway, I was just calling to let you know I'm leaving out tomorrow afternoon, and I'll be gone for a week. Me and this nigga Dan are gonna meet my people to work out some better prices for this shit."

"Okay. Well, when do you think you'll be back?"

"Probably next Friday. We're s'pose ta stay at dude's mansion for about ten days. He's having a balla party, and you know ya boy gotta be in attendance," he brags.

"What 'bout me?" I pout, acting as if I give a damn.

"I got ten of them things for you. You won't be broke while I'm gone."

My ears perk up at the mention of money. "I wasn't talking about money. I'm just gonna miss you, baby," I lie.

"I'll be back before you know it."

I hear a man, apparently this Dan, say something in

the background.

"Hey, baby, I gotta go. Call me in the morning so you can come pick that up before I leave, okay?"

"Sounds like a plan."

The shower water cuts off, and I know Xavier will be stepping out soon.

"Okay. I gotta go now though. I feel sick," I say, faking a gag.

"A'ight. See you in the morning," Taz says before we disconnect the call.

No sooner than I drop my phone back into my bag, Xavier emerges from the bathroom with a towel wrapped tightly around his waist. My eyes wander over the small beads of water that are all over his body; he looks good enough to eat.

"I have an idea," he tells me, walking over to his drawer.

"What is that?"

"Have you ever been to Myrtle beach?"

I shake my head while using my hands to brush the loose stands of hair back into my tangled ponytail.

"Well, in that case, let's go."

"When?" I ask, getting excited.

"We can leave tomorrow. We'll drive, if you're down."

"Hell yeah, I'm down!" I screech, jumping up and wrapping my arms around his neck.

This couldn't have worked out any better. Taz is gonna be out of town for a week, so he won't be breathing down my fucking neck. I hope them hoes keep his ass busy so I won't have to duck and dodge his calls every day. That would be wonderful.

About thirty minutes later, I finally climb out of bed and take a shower myself. I decide to stay the night, and we order Chinese food. For the remainder of the evening, we sit in front of the TV watching movies.

The following morning, I wake up and brush my tangled hair into a much neater ponytail; I'm glad I have a good perm. After I'm done, I get dressed, preparing for the busy day ahead. Not only do I have to meet Taz, but I also have to go home and pack for our trip. I kiss Xavier on the lips and tell him he better be ready when I get back, then walk out the door at around 11:00 a.m.

In my car, I use my phone and call Taz to see where he wants to meet. He answers and tells me he's still getting ready and that I should just come to his house, unless I want to wait till later. I don't have time to wait, so I let him know I'll be there in a second, because I've got shit to do. It takes me less than ten minutes to get to my destination because Taz's house is not far from where Xavier lives. This could be both good and bad, and I'm not quite sure how it's going to turn out.

I don't bother to knock because the door is slightly ajar. I walk in and head to the back of the apartment; I hear movement in his room. There are clothes everywhere, and it looks as if everything he owns is lying on top of his bed.

"Hey, baby," he greets.

"Hey." I push a few items aside before taking a seat on the messy bed. "Need some help?" I offer.

"Hell yeah. I don't have a clue what I'm wearing."

I spend the next hour helping him pack for his trip. I make sure he has everything he needs, from swimming trunks to casual wear. When I'm done, we pack everything in his black canvas monogram Louis Vuitton roll-away suitcase and matching carryon. As he zips them both up, I grab the toiletry bag that completes the set and head into the bathroom. Inside, I open up the cabinets and remove the personal items he needs: toothbrush, paste, deodorant, shower gel, and cologne. When I hand it to him, he hands me a stack of money, wrapped tightly with a rubber band.

"Thanks for the help," he tells me sincerely.

"No problem. You know I gotta look out for my baby." I smile. "I've gotta go though, honey. You have fun and be safe." I grab the sides of his shirt and pull him in for a hug.

"I will," he tells me after I kiss him gently on the lips.

"You also betta let them hoes know you have a woman at home…and that the bitch is crazy!" I can still hear him laughing as I make my way out of his apartment and into the elevator. As soon as I hit the ground floor, I jump into my car and hit the freeway, as I've still gotta pack my own shit.

It doesn't take long to get everything I need out of my closet and onto my bed; while I was driving, I visualized all the clothes I'll be taking with me. I carefully fold and place all my garments in my suitcases. I figure we'll be at the beach most of the time, so I make sure to pack a few pairs of flip-flops, shorts, and tanks. I throw in a few night-on-the-town outfits, and sexy swimsuits are a must. I walk around the house and check to make sure everything is where it's supposed to be and that I haven't forgotten anything. After lugging both suitcases into the hallway, I push the button on the elevator so I can go down to the garage. Using the remote control, I pop my trunk and place both bags inside, then shut it. Once I'm in the car, I pick up my cell, scroll through the call logs, and hit send.

"Hey, sexy," his baritone voice speaks through the receiver, instantly wetting my panties.

"Hey, honey. What you doin'?"

"Finishing up my packing. I just got off the phone with the rental car place. I'm just waiting on you to get her so we can go pick it up."

"Okay. I'm on my way."

By the time I make it to Xavier's, I'm even more excited about spending the entire week with my man. It sounds funny coming from me, because nobody could've ever told me I'd say some shit like that and mean it. *My man? Damn! I got a man…and I love it!*

I enter the house and see that he's finished packing; there are a Marc Jacobs carryon and backpack sitting by the door. I call out his name, and he comes down the stairs dressed in a pair of dark blue Levi's, a gray and purple LRG hoodie, and a pair of gray, purple, and blue Jordans; he looks cute.

"I forgot to grab my cell phone charger. You ready to go?" he asks.

"Sure am."

"Okay. Well, I was thinking we should go pick up the car and come back here and load it up then, since we gotta bring my car back."

"Sounds good."

It takes us about two hours to get back to his place from the airport. As soon as he opens the door to his apartment, I dart past him, headed for the bathroom. He laughs when I almost bust my ass while running in my black, five-inch Giuseppe Zanotti platform pumps. I don't even care, because I have to pee. I close the door behind me and plop my ass down on the seat with little time to spare. "I don't know why I didn't go when we were at the airport." I sigh as I relieve my bursting-at-the-seams bladder. When I'm done, I wipe myself, stand up, and flush the toilet. I pull up my mocha Brunello Cucinelli stretch cargo pants, fasten them, and wash my hands. "Don't be laughing at me," I say when I round the corner from the bathroom.

"I'm sorry, Love. It's just that you almost took a spill." He chuckles.

I give him a fake pouty face and turn my back to him.

He gives in and walks over and places his arms around my shoulder, pulling me closer. A soft kiss on the forehead brings a bright smile to my face. "You're so damn spoiled," he says.

"And you know this man!" I turn around and give him my best Chris Tucker impersonation.

"You so silly."

We both laugh.

"You ready to go?" he asks as he picks up both his bags off the floor.

"As ready as I'll ever be," I say, and we walk out the

door.

Once everything is packed securely inside the trunk of
the red Chevy Tahoe, we put the alarms on our vehicles and
drive off, headed to our destination.

With all the stops for food, gas, and bathroom breaks, it
takes us about fourteen hours. I keep reminding Xavier that
I've never been on the road this long before; I've always
traveled long distances by plane. He seems worried that I
don't like our little road trip, but I quickly explain that I
actually love it! Riding in the car with him all those long
hours gives me a chance to get to know him even better. We
swap stories about what we like to do and the places we want
to see, and it's so fun. The craziest part about the whole trip
is the fact that I don't doze off once. Our conversations are so
good that they keep me wide awake.

We pull up at the townhome Xavier has rented for our
week's stay, Kingston Plantation. It's about 10 a.m. when we
arrive. On our way to the townhome, we pass the pool area,
with lounge chairs scattered all around; there's plenty of
adequate seating if we ever decide to leave our room long
enough to swim. The townhomes all look the same, light on
the outside. From where we stand, it looks to be pretty nice. I
use the key to open the door, while Xavier gets all the bags
out and brings them in. I'm way too curious to wait till he's
finished, so I give myself a tour to check everything out.

The living room is painted a mustard color with
burgundy and gold decorations. The colors match perfectly
with each other, even with the beige leather furniture.
There's a bedroom downstairs, done in a nautical theme; it
matches the small attached bathroom. Directly beside it, is a
six-seat dining room table and a spiral staircase leading to the
upstairs area. I walk to the top of the stairs and see a loft. It's
something like Xavier's and offers a perfect view of the
living room. The master bedroom is spruced up with royal
blue and gold; the silk drapes match the bedspreads. The
master bath has a hot tub, and I plan on using that bad boy

before this vacation is over. Everything is nice inside, and I know we're going to enjoy the place. The only thing I don't like is the green carpet that runs throughout the entire house. *Who the hell thought of some shit like that? It makes me feel like I'm walking on a golf course or something!* On my way out the master, I run right into Xavier, who scares the shit out of me. I hold my hand on top of my chest, breathing hard.

"That's what yo' ass gets for not waiting for me before you looked at everything." He laughs.

"I was only trying to check it out and make sure you're going to like it," I lie, causing him to laugh again. I give him a small tour, and he agrees with me about the funky carpet.

Since we're both beat from the long drive, we lie in the bed and fall asleep, still fully dressed in our clothes.

***

"Wake up, sleepyhead," he says.

I slowly open my eyes. When they finally focus, I see Xavier standing over me with flowers in his hand.

"They're beautiful!" I exclaim. I pull myself into a sitting position before taking the bouquet out of his hand. "What are they?"

"Rainbow roses."

The name fits them perfectly, because they actually looked like real rainbows, and the frosted lavender vase really makes them pop. For a moment, I just sit there admiring twenty-four of the prettiest roses I've ever seen. "Thank you so much, baby!" I pull him close and wrap my arms tightly around his neck.

"You're more than welcome, Love. Now get up and get dressed. We're about to go to dinner."

I climb out of bed and place my flowers on the nightstand beside me. "How should I dress?" I ask, walking toward the bathroom.

"It doesn't matter. Everything looks good on you."

My lips form a bright smile. *I swear, I love this man.*

An hour and half later, I'm showered, dressed, and ready to go. I don't really have much time to spend on my hair, so I just pull it back into a bun. It's nice out, so I decided to dress light. Even though I've have no clue where we're going, I figure I can't possibly go wrong with my strapless embroidered ABS dress. It's simple yet classy. I add my brand new pair of silver mirrored Jimmy Choo sandals and the matching mini-bag. When my makeup is finished, I step out of the bathroom and into the master, where Xavier is waiting.

"You look beautiful."

"Thank you." I smile, striking a pose.

We head down the stairs and out the door, into the night. The restaurant is only a short distance away, so we decide to walk. He grabs hold of my hand, and we start to make our way toward out destination. A slight breeze blows, but it feels good against my skin. I'm wearing a John Hardy sterling silver necklace that hangs low and sits just above my belly button; the pendant glimmers every time one of the many lights hit it. The sky is a lovely shade of blue, and there are so many stars up there that it looks like it can't possibly be real—like we're walking in a dream. It feels good to be away from all the madness at home. *Truthfully, I could stay in this moment forever.*

"I'm happy you decided to come here with me," he says as we stroll down the street.

"Me too."

Xavier wasn't lying when he said the restaurant is only down the street, because it only takes us about three minutes to get here. I can tell right away that Omaha Steakhouse is my kind of place. The outside is bright yellow, and there are people eating on a deck, sitting on patio furniture. As soon as we enter, the host asks us where we'd like to sit; since it's such a wonderful night, I tell him the patio will be fine. After we're seated, the waiter comes over to take our drink and appetizer orders. Xavier asks for a bottle of Clos du Val Cabernet Sauvignon and a platter of scampi with Bruschetta as our starter, and the waiter scurries away to retrieve it for us.

Dinner is wonderful. I enjoy my baked stuffed shrimp, mashed potatoes, and Omaha chopped salad, and Xavier devours his twelve-ounce filet mignon, shrimp bisque, and a Caesar salad. It's so cute when he cuts off a few pieces of his steak and feeds it to me. I do the same thing, and by the time we finish our appetizers and entrées, we're practically stuffed. Still, we find room for dessert: crème brulee. I've never had it before, but Xavier promises me I'll like it. Turns out he's right, because I'm hooked after the very first spoonful; it's so delicious that I finish mine even before he finishes his. Just like that, I have a new favorite dessert!

Xavier pays the tab, and we get up to leave. As we walk past the bar, a few of the guys sitting at the bar start saying shit, even though they can clearly see that I'm with my man. I guess they figure since they outnumber Xavier, they can do whatever the fuck they want, but they're dead wrong.

"Damn! Shorty got a fat ass!" I hear one of them say. "I'd bend that big ol' thang over and wear it out!"

They all share a laugh.

I turn around and notice that the heckler is some fat, roly-poly-looking muthafucka with a bald head. "I wouldn't even let yo' fat ass get near me, you ugly bastard," I snap. *His fat ass got a lot of damn nerve, especially when his ass is way bigger than mine.*

"Bitch, you better watch yo' mouth," he yells.

That's Xavier's cue, because before I know it, Xavier's all over him, right up in his face. "What'd you just say?" He steps over to him with his hands hanging calmly by his side. Even though he looks relaxed, the fire in his eyes is unmistakable.

Everyone within ear shot freezes, waiting to see what's about to happen.

"Aw, man, it ain't nothing," the fat pig squeals, bitching up. Just like I thought, he was all talk until he realized that Xavier isn't some punk who'll let that shit slide.

"I think it is something. Not only were you being rude to my woman, but you just disrespected her by calling her a bitch."

"My fault, dude. I was just…caught up. Won't happen again," he apologizes.

"I'm not the one you need to be apologizing to."

The porker looks at me and smiles all crookedly. "Sorry 'bout that, ma'am. I didn't mean no harm. It won't happen again."

I don't say anything and just turn my back and walk out of the restaurant with a smile on my face. *My man just stuck up for me and didn't have to throw a punch to do it. I think I could get used to this.*

When we get back to the townhouse, we take a bath together. When we're finished, Xavier washes my hair and even sits beside me while I braid it up. In bed, we start our night off right by making love. I lie on my back with my legs rested on his shoulders, a position we've done before, but it doesn't feel the same. This time is feels much different. It's so much better, as if it's exactly what's supposed to happen. We don't rush through it; we simply take our time enjoying the other person.

As we climax together, tears begin to run slowly down the sides of my face. Never in my life have I cried during sex, at least not due to happiness. This time, I can't help myself. It's kind of embarrassing, but I relax when I see the smile on Xavier's face. When he places gentle kisses all over my face, everything feels perfect. There's no place in the world I'd rather be right now. *God, I love this man!*

CHAPTER EIGHT

We both wake up early, ready to get our day started. We've only got six days left in Myrtle Beach, and I know they'll fly by. Today, our plans are to go to Family Kingdom, an amusement park. The park is about thirty minutes away, and we want to get there early so we can really enjoy the full day. I know there will be long lines for most of the rides, but I want to ride as many as I can before it closes.

Xavier and I take a shower together, which proves to be hard because we can't keep our hands off each other. I suck him off, just to get him through the day, and then we both dry off and proceed to get ready.

The first step for me after my shower is to do my hair. I braided it up last night, because I want to wear a curly look today. I didn't have time to stop at Zema's before we came here, but it wouldn't have mattered anyway because I knew it'd end up getting wet. As I take down each of my French braids, I'm happy to see it came out pretty good. Looking in the mirror, I notice that it'd look really cute hanging down, but since we're going to an amusement park, I don't want it to be flying everywhere. Instead, I opt for a high ponytail, thinking maybe I'll wear it down later. Teasing the exposed hair hanging from the ponytail, I give it a real curly, poufy look before spraying a small amount of oil sheen throughout.

As I go through my outfits, I take into consideration that we'll be walking all day. I don't choose heels, because that'd

85

be like signing a death certificate for my toes and feet. Instead, I settle on a pair of black and gold Gucci thong sandals that buckle around my ankle. I don't even want to deal with flip-flops, because I'll be damned if I'm going to lose one of my shoes on a ride; that would be so embarrassing. I wiggle my way into a pair of dark denim Rock & Republic shorts, before looping my gold belt that matches the flecks of gold in my black Gucci halter top. When I'm finally dressed, I make my way into the bathroom to do my makeup.

Before I even unzip my cosmetics bag, Xavier runs in grabs my hand, stopping me. "Don't. Don't put any makeup on."

"Why not? You don't like it?" *Here it goes. Now his true colors are coming out. He doesn't want me wearing makeup? What's next, no revealing clothes?*

"It's not that I don't like your makeup. It's just that...well, you don't need it. You're gorgeous enough without it, Brandy," he tells me sincerely, placing his hands on my shoulders. He turns me around and forces me to look at myself in the mirror. "Don't you see it? You're absolutely beautiful, girl. You don't need that shit."

Truth is, I know I'm beautiful. I've always known that. For some crazy reason, though, I believe makeup gives me more of a grown, dressed-up look. When I was younger, I used to see the older girls strutting up the street in their makeup. I wanted to be just like them, but I knew there wasn't a chance in hell that I would. When I got to Pitch's house and Trixie showed me how to apply makeup and how to dress up, I was in heaven. It was exciting to be able to dress like the women I'd always wanted to be like. Now I'm the girl everyone stops and stares at. I'm the chick all the guys wish they could come home to at night. *I guess he's right though. Even though I like to wear makeup, I'll see how it feels to go without it.*

"Thanks. I'm not gonna wear it today, but I'll see how I

feel later."

"Good. It's a first step...and I'm sure you'll see exactly what I mean."

I put my hand is his, and we walk down the stairs and out the door.

There's not much traffic, so it takes us a little under a half-hour to get to the park. After driving around for five minutes looking for a parking spot, we finally find one when a minivan pulls out. We back in, climb out of the truck, and walk to the front gate. I'm glad I thought to pull my hair back, because I would have been miserable as hell in that hot sun if I'd have left it down. At the gate, Xavier pays for our wristbands, and we hurry into the park, trying to decide what we'll do first. My excited ass pulls Xavier over to a ride called The Hurricane; it looks like it will be fun. It turns out to be a really fast-spinning ride that has my stomach feeling queasy as hell by the time we get off. I guess that's a lesson learned. "I'll be damned if I'm getting on any more spinning rides," I say. "I don't like those things at all."

We stayed until the park closed at 10 p.m., and even then, I didn't want to leave. I had such fun that I can't help smiling all the way back to the townhouse. We rode both go-kart tracks, the Figure 8 and the oval. I beat Xavier's ass both times, though he swore up and down that I cheated. Of course I rubbed it in, letting him know every chance I got how much he sucked at it. The two scariest rides in the entire park are The Swamp Fox, a rollercoaster, and The Slingshot, with seats that go high as hell up into the air up a pole in the middle, then plummet down after hanging riders in the air for a minute. I thought for sure I was a goner on that one! It was all new to me since I've never been to an amusement park before; the closest thing I'd ever gotten to a rollercoaster was watching the commercials on TV. Actually riding one, I was screaming till I was damn near hoarse.

It wasn't just the scary, dropping, looping, fast rides that were fun. We also rode antique-looking track cars; Xavier sat in the back while I drove. He kept brushing up against my neck, making me think there was something crawling on me, and I almost crashed twice. The bumper boats were fun, until Xavier started squirting water all in my head. I screamed bloody murder; I didn't want my hair to get wet, knowing my shit would turn into an afro within minutes. I tried my best to spray his ass right in the mouth, because he thought it was so funny to see me panic, but it didn't work out the way I planned. Since my hair was already damp, I agreed to go on the log ride with him. We sat in a long, hollowed-out log, kind of like a canoe, and went up and down hills, getting splashed all over the place. It was a lot more fun than I expected it would be.

The last ride we got on was the best ride of them all, the Ferris wheel. It went up pretty high, and I have to admit I was nervous as hell at first; I thought we would tip over, causing us to fall to our deaths. Xavier told me everything would be okay and that he'd protect me. I was still leery, but when he asked me if I trust him, I had to think about it for a moment. Thing is, I do trust him, so I cuddled in my man's arm as the wheel went 'round and 'round. The stars shone brightly in the sky, and when Xavier leaned in to kiss me, it was magical. I joked and told him he must have put some voodoo or something on me, because I was hooked on him. He laughed and teased right back, saying I must have done the same thing. "I'm all the way in with you, Love," he said.

By the time we pull up back to the townhouse, I'm still pumped from our trip to the park. Instead of going in the house like we planned, Xavier grabs a blanket, and we walk over to the nearby beach. There are a few couples sitting around, just like we plan on doing. I bend down to help Xavier lay the cover down, and we both kick off our shoes and have a seat. He places his arms around my waist and pulls me closer, between his legs. I close my eyes and listen to the wave's crash in the distance. *This place is wonderful. I wouldn't mind seeing this every day. That'd be so refreshing!*

With my eyes still closed, I calculate figures in my head, speculating how much a condo might cost down here. *I'd really consider moving here.* As soon as the thought enters my mind, the comfort of Xavier tightening his grip on me brings draws me back to reality. *It just won't work. He just moved from Chicago to Ohio, so I know there ain't no way in hell he'll be ready to relocate to South Carolina, especially after he just bought a house.*

"What's on your mind?" he asks, noticing the tension in my body or the questioning look on my face.

"Nothing much. Just thinking about a few things."

"Like what? Fill me in."

"Like I said, it's nothing."

He reaches for my chin and turns my face slightly so he can look me in the eye. "Brandy, you can talk to me about anything. I told you I love you, and I mean that from the bottom of my heart. That means your problems are now my problems. I would say vice versa, but before I let my problems become yours, I'll try my best to solve them. I don't ever want to be a burden to you."

My eyes begin to gloss over, till I think I might cry.

"I want to be the person who gives you everything you need, and even though I'm not the richest man in the world, I've got enough to make you happy. Tell me what's on your mind."

I take a deep breath and let him know how I feel. "Well, I-I was just thinking about how nice it would be to live here, how nice it'd be to come here all the time, that's all," I say, trying to give him just enough so he'll back off, but he's too smart for that.

"Okay. So what's the problem?"

I don't say anything.

"That still doesn't explain the pain I just saw in your face. If we're gonna do this—this you-and-me thing—you need to trust me as much as I trust you."

I take another deep breath and lay all my cards on the

table. "The problem is that I want to move here, but I can't because I don't want to…to leave you." The tears pooling in my eyes begin to fall down my face. My shoulders start to tremble while I try to hold them back.

"Who says you'd have to?" he asks.

"Wh-what?" I ask, confused. *Is he saying what I think he's saying?*

"Hear me out before you go all crazy on me." He cracks a smile. "Let's go home and see how you feel in, say, six months. If you still feel this way, I'll make the moves to make it happen."

"Oh my God. Are you serious, Xavier?"

"As a heart attack, Love."

"I-I can't believe it!

"We just need to make sure it's what you really wanna do and that you aren't just feeling a vacation high. It's the end of August now, so if you still want to move here by February, I'll make the necessary arrangements. We can make the move by the summer of 2011—that is, if you want to move with me and not on your own."

I can't believe my ears. "Of course I'd move in with you," I squeal, "but let me get this straight. You'd up and move, give up your new house and everything, just to be with me?" I ask.

"No, *we* will up and move to be together. Don't you understand how much I love you, girl?" He pulls me into a tight hug from the back, and I nuzzle my head into his chest.

Now that I have my mind set on moving here, I know I've got to get on my grind as far as my money goes. I have enough right now, but the greed in me won't allow me to let Taz off the hook; I want his paper too. I realize I'm just gonna have to move quicker when it comes to him; if Xavier and I are going to me moving to Myrtle Beach in less than a year, I need to get my hands on as much money as possible. I'm gonna suck his muthafucking ass dry, and he won't even see it coming. *I can already see it: a whole new life. No more crazy bitches trying to fight me, no stalking ex-lovers, and no niggas shooting at me. Just me and my man. Here in South Carolina, I can start fresh and be whoever I wanna be. I can leave everything from my past behind. I'll see a psychiatrist first thing, somebody who can help me work through my problems. I'll tell them everything I've been through, and they'll tell me how to make my life easier. Once I'm free from all the bullshit, I'll finally be able to live a normal and happy life—a life with a man who really loves me.*

I break from my daydream when I feel Xavier staring at me. He has a slight smile on his face and doesn't break eye contact, even when I catch him in the act. "What?" I ask.

"Nothing. I just can't stop thinking about how beautiful you are."

I melt on the inside because my man always knows how to make me feel good. "Aw. Thank you baby."

"I'm serious, Brandy. I don't think you understand how glad I am to have you in my life. When I left Chicago, I didn't think I'd ever meet anyone who could make me feel the way you do. Shit, truthfully, I didn't figure I'd find anyone at all. My only mission was to come here and open up my restaurant, and everything else was pushed to the back burner. When I saw you at the gas station that day, it felt like something drew me to you. I wasn't even going to talk to you again, but something inside me forced me to. Looking back, I know we're destined to be together. I truly believe that."

Great. He's getting me all teary-eyed again. I try to keep the tears from coming out of my eyes, but there's nothing I can do about it. "I'm glad I met you too, Xavier. I've told you what I've been through, and never in a million years would I have thought I'd be where I am today. For the first time in years, I'm truly happy with my life. I'm not faking anything just to get something in return. I'm just…happy." The tears pour down my face rapidly, and I don't try to stop them anymore. I want him to know this isn't a game; it's how I really feel—no bullshit, no lies, and just me and him. I'm actually in love, and for once in my life, I'm not scared to accept or admit it.

We sit at the beach for a few more hours, just talking. It amazes me that we still have so much to talk about, as I've never had anyone in my life like him before. Everything with Xavier has been new and different. Even with Roger, it was more about me talking and him listening. He never really gave me too much information about himself, and looking back, I understand why. He was living a secret life that he didn't want me to know anything about. Xavier doesn't mind pouring out his life story to me or listening to me pour out mine. We've talked about everything under the sun and still haven't reached the end of our long conversations. My heart skips a beat when he mentions marrying me someday. He says he wants to spend the rest of his life with me. He knows I can't have any children, and he's fine with that. "There's always adoption," he says.

If I wasn't all the way onboard before, after he said that, I am now. I lie in his arms with my eyes closed, daydreaming about a small but beautiful wedding. I can see myself walking slowly toward him, my groom-to-be, while he stands at the altar with a huge smile on his face. I'm sure he won't be able to believe how gorgeous I'll look in the wedding dress I'll hide from him until that glorious day. I picture the two of us shedding tears of joy as we exchange vows, before we say our final "I do" that makes us husband and wife.

My thoughts go from my wedding to being a mother, taking our baby to the park for play dates. I smile when I think about him coming home from a long day at work, walking over, and kissing me on the cheek before picking up our little bundle of joy and babbling baby talk and kissing the little one on the head. *We'll sit at the dinner table, surrounded by a delicious home-cooked meal I've prepared. I'll ask him about his day at work, and he'll ask me what the baby and I have done all day. Finally, I'll have my happily-ever-after—something I never thought I'd have.* I've always seen my future quite differently, always assumed I'd have to keep trying to get over on someone just to provide for myself. Now, I'm much more comfortable with Xavier than I've been all these years, fucking for money.

We finally decide to head back to the house as the sun begins to rise. I slide my feet into my shoes before leaning over to help him to fold up the sand-covered blanket. It seems as if the townhouse is much farther away than it was last night, but I'm sure it's only because we're exhausted after staying up all night. When we make it back, we drop the blanket in the middle of the floor and head up the steps. We don't bother with showers, and I assume Xavier is even more tired than I am, because by the time I finish using the bathroom, he's already in bed, snoring lightly. I watch him for a minute, then undress and climb under the covers beside my man. The second my head hits the pillow, I'm out like a light.

***

Since we got in so late, I assumed we'd sleep in, but Xavier apparently didn't have the same idea, because he's up way before I'm ready to be. I don't even know what time it is when I felt him tap me lightly on the arm, but I'm sure it's no later than 10 in the morning, because it sure feels like I just closed my eyes. Still lying in the bed, I try to play dead and don't even acknowledge the fact that he's nudging me.

Being the silly person he is, he uses his finger to gently force one of my eyelids open.

I can't fake it anymore and burst out laughing. "That was kiddie as hell, and you should be ashamed of yourself for even doing some shit like that!" I scream, still laughing.

"I knew yo' ass wasn't asleep." He laughs along with me. "I saw your eyeballs moving under your lids."

"So what? I'm still sleepy, bay," I whine, after my laugh is over. "We just went to sleep a little while ago."

"Girl, get yo' ass up!" He chuckles.

"I don't want to!"

"Brandy, it's 3 o'clock in the afternoon. You've been asleep for eight hours."

"Stop lying!" I yell without even attempting to glance at the clock.

"I'm serious."

"Well, then I'm about to sleep eight more, because I'm not getting out of this bed," I let him know before pulling the covers up and over my head. I instantly feel a cold draft when he snatches it back off of me, exposing my naked body. My eyes shoot open and reach down to grab it back, but he grips my legs and pulls them to the edge of the bed.

"Get yo' ass up!"

I try to slap his hands away, but he's relentless.

He picks me up and carries me into the bathroom. My ass is in the air, and my breasts are bouncing on the back of his shoulder. He continues to hold me, not letting me down. With me still over his shoulder, he reaches in the shower and turns the water on. I stretch my arm until my hand is by his butt and pinch his ass with my pointer finger and my thumb. In turn, he pops me on my ass with an open hand, making a loud smacking noise. I feel him move just enough to slide down his boxers before putting us both under the spray of the shower water. I scream and start to wiggle because the water is cold as hell, but he continues to hold me close to the nozzle.

"Ah! What are you doing? The water's so cold, Xavier!" I yell, but he does nothing to adjust it.

"I'm waking your ass up! Are you gonna wake up now?"

"Yes! I'm awake! I'm awake!" I shout.

Using his free hand, he grabs the knob and turns it to the hot side. The temperature starts to warm up, and I'm glad; I've already got goose bumps all over my ass.

"You play too damn much." I playfully hit him in the chest after he puts me down.

He doesn't say anything. He just places his arm around the small of my back and pulls me closer to him. His full lips connect with mine, and our tongues begin to slow-dance. I moan when he reaches back to grip my ass cheeks, and I feel his dick poke me in the stomach. It's hard as a rock, and I cream between my legs just thinking about him entering me. I break our kiss and turn around, spreading my ass cheeks so he can do just that. My eyes close involuntarily when he begins to rub his dick up and down the slit of my opening. I start to push back into him; I can't wait. Using his hand, he stops me, letting me know he's in control. He slowly slides the head in but pulls out quickly.

"Don't do that, baby," I whine, hoping he'll stop teasing me and give me what I want.

"Shh," he says to me in return.

Once again, he only puts the head inside before pulling it back out. When he goes to do it a third time, I reach back and grab his hips, keeping him inside me. I tighten my pussy muscles and squeeze the head of his member as tight as I can. He sighs before smacking me on the ass with a little force and extends his arms just enough to grip both of my shoulders. I sigh when he begins to pump in and out of my juicy tunnel. Removing my hands from his hips, I place my right hand flat on the shower tile, while fingering my clit with the left. It feels like my body is floating; that's how good it feels every time he drives in and out. Our bodies connect to an ideal rhythm as we move in sync with each other. As he thrusts in, I push my ass back so we meet perfectly in the middle.

"Ooh, fuck!" I pant. "Aw shit, baby! Get this pussy!" I cry out.

I bend over more and grab hold of my ankles. Before long, I feel a familiar tingle. I'm in the perfect position to get my spot hit. Repeatedly he continues to poke it, bringing me closer and closer to the orgasm I've been dying for since the last time we were at my place. The tingle starts deep in my body and continues to rapidly work its way outward. When it reaches my toes, I almost lose my balance with the anticipation, because I know I'm almost there. Quickening the pace of my fingers, I can feel it's coming soon. I want to make sure it's as good, if not better, than it was before. Xavier begins to grunt, gripping shoulders tighter and tighter; I know he's about to cum to. Using my hands as leverage, I push myself off the wall and throw my ass back with everything in me. The water is raining down on us, and I don't even care that my hair is soaking wet. The hot water running down the crack of my ass only heightens my enjoyment.

Xavier reaches out and grabs hold of both of my breast and applies just enough pressure to cause my nipple pleasure, with a small mixture of pain. He begins to pump faster and faster, and I continue to rub my clit with my fingers at a very quick pace. Just then my eyes roll in the back of my head, and my breath briefly gets caught in my chest. *I-I can't breathe!* Usually a person would panic when suffocating, but I totally welcome it because I know it's only temporary. My muscles tense up, and my whole body begins to get so hot it almost burns. No sooner than I hear him grunt, my body starts to convulse. With every thrust he gives me, I spew more and more of my fluids out. My knees buckle, and I slowly start to fall to the ground. Had it not been for Xavier placing his arms up under my armpits, I would've busted my ass.

"Damn, baby. You okay?" he asks, placing me gently on the floor of the shower.

The water is pouring down on my hair, but I don't care because my body is still tingling.

"Hey, are you okay?" he asks again.

"I don't know what it is about yo' ass that makes me cum like that. This shit is crazy!" I say, shaking my head back and forth. I sit for a little while longer while the heaving in my chest subsides.

"You know what it is?"

I reach up and grab hold of his extended hand and pull myself into a standing position. "No. What?" I tilt my neck upward so I can stare directly into his eyes while I wait on his reply.

"Don't play crazy and act like you don't know good dick when you come across it."

"Naw, I don't know about *good* dick." I turn my back to him and allow the cooling water to drizzle onto my face. "That's what you call *great* dick!" I laugh.

We both wash up quickly, because the water quickly goes from cool to chilled in a matter of minutes.

It's 4 o'clock by the time we make it back to the bedroom. I take a seat on the edge of the bed and rub lotion all over my body, from the neck down. Xavier throws on a pair of *Diesel* briefs and some basketball shorts. He leaves the room and heads downstairs. I walk over to the dresser and pull out one of Xavier's t-shirts, then pull it over my head. I don't bother to put on underwear because there's no need; I know they'll more than likely be coming off soon anyway.

"What do you want to do today?" Xavier asks as soon as my feet hit the bottom of the stairs. He's in the kitchen, sitting at the island, going through the planning book we got when we arrived.

"I'm not sure, but I really just wanna chill," I say, still exhausted from that nut he just brought out of me.

"How about we grab something to eat and catch a movie? I've been waiting to see *Lottery Ticket* for a minute, and its showing at the Cinemark, not too far from here. I believe it's in the mall, so we can even do a little shopping if you like.

"Well, after that, you ain't gotta twist my arm! I'm down!"

We both laugh.

"What do you want to eat?" I ask, taking a seat on the couch. I fold my legs and place them up under me, pulling

97

his shirt down over them to stop the chill from the air conditioning.

"How do you feel about a seafood buffet?"

"A buffet? You must want to have a fat girlfriend," I joke.

"On second thought…maybe we should go somewhere else."

I poke out my bottom lip and act like I'm mad.

"I'm just kidding, baby. You know I love you either way."

"It's a good thing you changed that shit up!"

We decide to catch the last movie, which starts at 9:50. Since it's only 4:30, we have a little more than five hours to kill.

I run upstairs and stop in the bathroom to figure out what to do with my hair. Since my hair is still damp, I decide on a wet bun. I know it will look cute wet, but it'll also dry into a neat style. Using the comb and brush, I smooth it back to the nape of my neck and secure it with a scrunchie. I bend and twist the exposed ends and clip them in place with bobby pins before spraying it with a light mist of oil sheen and tying it up with my silk headscarf.

I guess we both decide to dress simple, because a t-shirt and jeans are what we both wear. Xavier throws on a pair of Ralph Lauren jeans, a polo shirt, and a pair of Jordans. I on the other hand opt for some 7 jeans, a Gucci tank and a pair of matching high top sneakers. Once we're both dressed, we head out the door.

CHAPTER NINE

The sunrays hit my eyes and awake me from my deep sleep. I lift up and turn around, trying to position myself comfortably so I can squeeze a little more sleep out of my body, but it's not working. I realize it's no use and that I might as well get my ass up and out of bed. Xavier isn't in bed beside me, so I assume he's already downstairs, watching television. I slowly climb out of bed, make it up nice and neat, then head to the bathroom. I exhale as I sit on the toilet and relieve my bladder of all the fluids that had a chance to sit there overnight. When I'm done, I walk over to the sink, wash my hands, brush my teeth, and wash my face. No sooner than I put my toothbrush back into its holder, my cell phone rings.

At first, I consider ignoring it, but thinking it might be Taz, I decide I oughtta pick it up; I don't want to piss him off and make my plans all that much more difficult to pull off. I reach into my bag, pull out the phone, and sigh. "Osha? What the fuck does she want?" I say to myself. *I haven't talked to her since we went to dinner, and that was two weeks ago. I hope she's not calling to cry on my shoulder, because if she is, I'm gonna hurt her feelings. I'm really not in the mood for her whiny shit today because I'm too busy having fun with my man.* "Hello?" I say into the phone after I hit the talk button.

"How the fuck you think it's cool to fuck around with Taz, Brandy? What type of bullshit you on?" she yells in my ear, catching me totally off guard.

Before I reply to her, I tiptoe over to the door and out into the hallway to make sure Xavier's still out there. When I see that the coast is clear, I walk back into the room and inside the bathroom, closing the door behind me. "Girl, what in the world are you talking about?" I ask, playing dumb, wanting to find out just how much the bitch knows.

"Don't try to play me, Brandy. I already know the truth." I take a seat on the edge of the tub and cross my legs.

"You apparently don't know as much as you think, 'cause I've got no clue what you're talking about."

"So you gon' tell me I'm crazy, Brandy?" she asks.

"Either that, or you getting your information from a liar," I say matter-of-factly.

"Okay. Well, open the picture I just sent."

I glance down at my phone and see the text notification. I touch the top of the screen and slide it down with my finger, revealing that I've got a picture message from Osha. When it finally downloads, my hand flies up to my mouth; I'm shocked to see a picture of me and Taz holding hands, taken the day we went to the mall together. *How the fuck did she get a picture like this? Has this bitch been spying on me or something?* I don't even know what to say, but since I've already been caught in a lie, so I don't say anything at all.

"So what? Now you ain't got nothin' to say?" she asks after a few too many seconds pass.

"Not really," I say truthfully, because I really ain't got shit to say.

"That's fucked up, Brandy. I thought you were my friend. You been in my house and shit. This is really fucked up, and you know it!"

I still don't say anything and just listen to her vent.

"I should've listened to Zema when she told me to watch yo' grimy ass!"

"Girl, fuck you and Zema's bum ass!" I say, breaking my silence. *This bitch ain't about to talk to me any ol' kinda way.* "Yeah, I'm fucking Taz. Now what?" I raise my voice, just loud enough to get my point across but keeping it low enough so Xavier doesn't hear.

"Have you fucked him in my house?" she calmly asks— a little too calmly for my taste.

"Naw, but he damn sure tried," I tell her honestly. "Look, don't get all pissed at me because yo' man came on to me. It ain't like y'all together no more, so I don't know what the problem is."

"Bitch, the problem is that you've been in my house, around my kids and my family, while you fucking my man."

"You mean your *ex*-man," I correct her with a chuckle.

She doesn't find the shit amusing at all and begins yelling and screaming loudly in my ear. "I don't give a damn if we're broken up. He's still my baby-daddy, bitch! You violated our friendship in the worst way, and you better trust and believe that yo' triflin' ass is gonna pay. I'm going to beat the fuck outta you when I see you, and it ain't gone be nothing you can do about it but take the ass-whooping like the ho you are! You ain't shit, Brandy. I swear, you ain't shit!"

I roll my eyes and glance down at my French manicure. This conversation is really boring me.

"I can see why these bitches be coming for your neck, because you shady as fuck! You can add me to the list, because *whenever* I see yo' ugly ass, I'm gonna hurt you bad!"

I laugh out loud when she calls me "ugly." *She's reaching now.* "Girl, bye! Yo' ass wish I was ugly. Matter fact, you wish you could look this good. You can't fuck with me on my worst day boo-boo, so don't even play yo'self out like that. You're an average bitch, while I'm top notch. You'll *never* be on my level." I laugh again, just to piss her off.

"Top notch? Get the fuck outta here, bitch. You far from top notch. You're just quick to climb on a dick, that's all.

Bitch, you wore out. Don't nobody want you for real. You're only good for a quick fuck, and once these niggas get done with you, they toss your ass out like yesterday's trash," she says, then laughs like it's her turn.

This bitch really thinks she's getting to me. What she don't know is that I don't let that little shit bother me. Hoes like her wish they could be me, if only for one day. "Well, I must not be yesterday's trash to Taz, because since he's been fucking with me, he hasn't been by to see you or the kids, has he?" I shoot back.

Clearly, my words pissed her off, because she starts screaming again. All I catch are bits and pieces of what she's hollering before I hang up on her. *I'm not about to sit on the phone and let the girl yell all types of negative shit about me. Fuck her and that bitch Zema. Neither of them hoes can fuck with me. I can't wait to go to her shop when I get back, and I bet her ass ain't gon' say shit. If she does, it's gonna be a sad day at Tresses, because the clients will have to witness their hairdresser getting her ass beat. I promise you that! I actually want her to say something out of pocket so I can knock the fuck outta her for even running her mouth about me in the first place. That bitch don't even know me! She's lucky her man is too broke, because she'd be calling my ass talking shit too. Both those hoes need to concentrate less on me and worry more about keeping their men happy. Apparently, what they doing ain't working.*

I really need to get my number changed. Shit! If it ain't one thing, it's a-muthafucking-nother. I'm tired of people blowing up my phone, talking all reckless. Roger just won't let go, and even though he hasn't called in a while, I know that doesn't mean he won't. Sade calls every blue moon, but I hang up whenever I hear her voice. Her dumb-ass cousin hasn't called for a while, but it's all just too much. McKenzie just stopped calling, only because she got shipped over to the county, where her calls aren't free anymore. I heard she got eighteen months behind that shit, something about it not being her first time caught stealing. Now Osha's playing tough too. I shake my head, place my phone back inside my bag, and head downstairs to see what Xavier's up to.

"Hello, sleepyhead," he tells me from the couch while he watches basketball highlights on ESPN.

"Hey, baby." I curl up beside him, totally dismissing the conversation with Osha. I don't like basketball, but I don't mind watching, just to spend time with him.

We have two more days in Myrtle Beach, so we decide to spend a day just chilling. We've done so much these past few days. Two days ago, we went to this place called Express Water Sports, where we got on this huge inflatable banana and allowed a jet ski to pull us around the water. I had such a blast doing that! We also did a little jet skiing of our own. I was afraid to ride by myself, so I got on the back of Xavier's because I didn't want to fall off. That was a lot of fun also. The same place had scuba diving, but Xavier did that by himself because when they were helping me get suited up, I swore I saw a shark swim past. Of course they tried to calm me down, telling me I was just seeing things, but I didn't give a fuck what they said. There was no way I was getting in that damn water!

Yesterday, we went fishing and dolphin watching. I actually enjoyed fishing, even though I didn't think I would. Neither one of us caught anything, but we had fun trying. Dolphin watching was the coolest because we got on a small speedboat and watched as the dolphins hopped out of the water; a few of them did tricks. It was amazing to see them so up close, and I wasn't even scared like I thought I'd be. I even reached over the edge of the boat and touched a dolphin's head. Its skin was soft and smooth but also had a wet and rubbery feeling to it. They have extremely small teeth, and when they open their mouths, it looks as if they're smiling. Dolphins are really friendly creatures, and even though they're weird-looking, they're kind of cute at the same time.

Xavier took me to the House of Blues afterwards, where Hootie and the Blowfish were playing. I've never heard them or any of their music before, but they did a great job. I really liked "Let Her Cry," even though it wasn't exactly about me. I also liked "Only Wanna Be with You," "Time," and "Hold My Hand," which almost made me cry. I've never been to a performance like that, and I look forward to going to more places with Xavier. I don't know how many times I'm going to realize this, but he's nothing like anybody I've ever messed with. Xavier's just…different. He likes to go to plays and nice restaurants. It's not just the normal with him; he likes to think outside the box. I like that in him because he'll force me to do the same, and anything other than what I've been doing would be a good change in my book.

We sit in front of the TV for a few more hours before ordering food from a place called Wok Express, a Chinese/American restaurant that delivers. We order pepper steak, a crab stick, and shrimp fried rice for me, while Xavier wants that nasty-looking egg foo young, shrimp on a stick, and beef fried rice. There's a little while before our food is to be delivered, so to waste time, I sit on the floor as he applies grease to my scalp. I was sure he'd tell me to do it myself, so to say it shocked the hell out of me when he told me to grab the comb and the grease is an understatement. I sit on the floor between his legs and after showing him exactly what to do, he jumps right in and does it perfectly. Once the food is delivered, we sit in front of the TV and eat in silence as we watch reruns of *The Jamie Foxx Show*.

***

We wake up bright and early, facing a busy day ahead of us. It's our last day here in Myrtle Beach, and I'm going to be so sad when we leave tomorrow. Other than the bullshit-ass call from Osha, everything else has been relaxing and drama free. I'm definitely not in a rush to go back to my regular life, where there's always some nonsense going on. I'd much rather stay here and spend time with my baby, but of course I know that's not even an option. We both have things to settle, and neither of us can do them from here. It's cool, though, because it won't be long before we're back, and I won't ever have to deal with the people from my past again. If everything goes according to plan, by this time next year, we'll be living in Myrtle Beach.

Our first stop of the day is breakfast; I'm looking forward to it because I woke up hungry. I'm already packed up for our return trip tomorrow, and I've only left out the few pieces I plan on wearing today and tomorrow when we pull out. Xavier is in the room ironing his clothes, while I'm in the bathroom flat-ironing my hair. I'm tired of putting it in a bun, and the curly look is getting old, so I decide to wear it straight. Since we're not going to be getting wet or doing anything strenuous, I don't see how it could possibly get messed up. Once I'm done with my bangs, I unplug the flat-iron and get my washcloth. The oil I use can get a little messy, so there's always some on my neck or sometimes on my forehead.

When I walk back into the bedroom, I see that Xavier is almost dressed. He doesn't have on shoes or socks yet, but he's already wearing his black Sean John jean shorts with a red, black, and white t-shirt. He takes a seat on the bed, facing the door. As I walk by, he moves his head in the direction I'm walking and just stares at me. I don't even let it bother me, nor do I ask him what he's looking at; I just go about my business and get dressed. I continue my stride over to the other side of the bed and stand there before dropping my robe and exposing my nude body. Picking up my leopard fishnet and lace thong from my pile of clothes, I turn around and bend over, purposely putting my ass all up in his face.

"Keep playing, you gon' fuck around and be the reason we end up spending our last day in bed," he warns in a serious tone.

"Dang! I'm not doing nothing but getting dressed." I giggle. I pull my underwear up until the middle of the thong disappears in the crack of my ass.

"Yeah, okay. Get dressed then." He smirks before turning his body completely around, until he's facing me.

I continue to take my time getting dressed because I know he's looking. I decide not to wear a bra, because my cream crochet dress wouldn't look right with one. I pick it up and step into it before sliding it up my body. Once my head is through the hole, I adjust the bra part so my breasts won't pop out. I bend down and slip my feet into the Stuart Weitzman crochet espadrilles Xavier bought for me the other day and secure them around my ankle. They look really good against my manicured toes, and when I look in the mirror, I see that Myrtle Beach has been good to me. My normally dark skin looks as if it's been kissed by the sun. I didn't think dark-skinned chicks could get a tan, but I guess anything is possible. Sliding a pair of Stella McCartney glasses over my eyes, I walk over to the door of the bedroom, letting him know I'm ready to go. My tan Chloe bag is swung over my shoulder before we walk down we stairs and out the door.

We stop at a place called Croissants Bistro & Bakery, which isn't far from the townhomes. As soon as we enter, we're greeted by a young-looking white girl with blonde hair. She's dressed in a black, button-down, long-sleeved shirt and black khakis. Her black, slip-proof shoes look as if they've seen better days, but everything else is neat and well put together. She asks us if there are only two of us, then waltzes off to a private table in the corner of the restaurant. No sooner than we take a seat, our waiter comes over and asks us what we would like to drink. He's dressed just like the white girl, but his shoes look as if he's never worn them before; I silently hope today isn't his first day on the job, because I can't stand when someone gets my order wrong or takes all day. *If he does that, he'll fuck around and not get a tip. I don't care if it ain't my money!*

106

Moments later, he arrives with an orange juice for me and a glass of apple juice for Xavier. We both put our orders in, and he disappears once again. I take a look around while I'm waiting. From the looks of things, it seems the place serves pretty good food.

"So...you ready to go home tomorrow?" Xavier asks.

I don't answer him right away, because I know he knows damn well that I ain't ready to leave yet. Shit, if I had it my way, I'd never go back. "No, I don't want to go back." I tell him seriously.

"I know, Love. Did you at least have fun?"

"Yeah, a blast. I'm really glad you brought me here baby. I've really enjoyed my time here with you. I know it's gonna be different when we get back home."

"Why? I don't understand what you're talking about," he asks, looking at me with confusion on his face.

"For the past week, we've slept together every night. It's going to be weird to go home and lie in my bed alone."

"You don't have to be alone, Brandy. We can still sleep together every night. I love spending time with you, and you're more than welcome to stay at my house for as long as you want. I'd love to see your beautiful face every morning."

I tilt my head to the side and smile at him warmly. "I'd love to wake up with you also, but I don't want to ruin what we have by being too clingy. You know what I'm saying?" I don't give him a chance to reply. "I don't want you to get tired of me because I'm in your face all day every day" I sigh.

He picks up the glass and takes a swig of his juice.

"I just don't want what we have to change," I tell him truthfully.

"Listen to me." He places the glass back on the table. Before he continues what he's saying, he looks me deep into my eyes. "As long as you continue to be the person you are, nothing will ever change. I want you to quit second-guessing yourself. I don't know how many times I have to tell you I love you before you'll understand and believe me. I'm not going anywhere, Brandy. That's something you never have to worry about."

After we finish eating, we head to Broadway at the Beach and stop inside the Build-a-Bear Workshop. Even though it's a kids' place, I want us to make a stuffed animal for each other. As soon as we walk through the door, I see a bunch of stuffed animals and small clothing line the walls. I look at all the children inside the store; the excitement on their faces is priceless. I smile because I feel the exact same way they do. In fact, I feel like a kid all over again. Instead of being used and abused, I feel like I'm supposed to feel: loved. I watch the children interact with their moms and dads, and a small amount of envy takes over. I'm a bit jealous of them because they actually have a chance to act their age, to be kids. They don't have to go through the shit I had to endure. Still, I'm happy for them. I don't think any child—naw, fuck that…any person—should have to go through the shit I've had to deal with.

Xavier touches my hand and jolts me back to reality. We walk around the store hand and hand, looking over everything they have. After a few minutes, we're right back where we started. We decide to go our separate ways so we can make our animals in private. I walk to the back of the store and pick up the teddy bear I've had my eye on since we walked in, a fluffy brown one with a dark brown nose. I decide to get a business suit for him, because it reminds me of Xavier, who's all about his business. The suit is pinstriped and blue, with an Oxford shirt and a red silk tie. I top it off with a pair of black loafers, giving the bear the appearance of a furry little CEO. I laugh out loud when I picture the final project.

On my way to the bear-stuffing machine, I see Xavier still piecing his together, with his back turned to me. I ask the worker for help, and she suggests a sound box and explains that I can record a message to put inside the bear. I record my message, then place the sound box inside and put the bear on a stuffing machine. I carefully step on the tiny pedal. Once my bear is stuffed and stitched up, I grab him and his outfit and go over to the dressing station. It takes me a few minutes to completely dress my bear before I walk over to the counter and pay, a total of $45—money well spent, as far as I'm concerned. I know Xavier will like the bear and love my little message. The clerk hands my receipt to me and places the bear in a box, that's decorated like a house on the outside.

I stand by the front door as I wait for Xavier to finish his bear. It takes him a few minutes to show up, but when he does, he has a box and a bag in his hand. I can't wait to see what he's made for me, so I reach for the bag and try to peek inside. He pulls it back teasingly, before handing it back to me. Even though I'm excited to see it, I first want him to see what I made for him. We walk over to a nearby bench and take a seat. I hand him my box, and he smiles when he opens it.

"Squeeze his paw," I say.

"Okay." He lifts the bear's arm up and squeezes the left paw lightly.

"Xavier, I love you with all my heart. You are my breath of fresh air in the storm I call my life." Even though the message is only ten seconds, it's exactly enough time for me to tell him exactly how I feel.

"See? Now you can hear how much I love you, even when I'm not around."

He smiles, tells me he loves it, then kisses me gently on my lips. When he asks me where I got the suit idea from, I explain to him that it's how I view him: a man about his business.

When it's my turn to check out my bear, I open the box and see a pink Hello Kitty bear dressed in a white and pink robe and pink, fuzzy house shoes. Upon opening the robe, I see that the bear is wearing a frilly white and pink baby tee and a pair of pink and white ruffle panties. I laugh out loud.

Not only is the bear cute as hell, but it's also dressed sexy in some shit I'd actually wear. I gently place the bear back inside the box and put my hand in the bag to see what else there is. I pull out a pink, silky Hello Kitty bed, with a Hello Kitty head for the pillow. There's a pink blanket on top of the bed, decorated with Hello Kitty faces. I put the beautiful little thing back in the bag and stand up. I pull Xavier up and throw my arms around his shoulders, then kiss him repeatedly all over his face; he put a lot of thought into my bear, and I love it.

After putting both our gifts inside the truck, we head over to Ripley's Aquarium to check out the ocean life. It's very crowded inside, with a lot of families walking around. There are even a few schools and daycares in attendance. Everyone is taking pictures and videotaping the animals. I even pull out my phone and snap a few shots myself. The exhibits consist of sharks, turtles, snappers, sawfish, and stingrays, and it's a really cool place. We only stay for a couple of hours, though, because we still have to make it home in time to get dressed for our plans later tonight.

It takes us about a half-hour to make it back to the townhouse, around 5 o'clock. We have reservations on the casino cruise at 7:00, and the cruise lasts till 1 a.m. Since the GPS tells us it will take at least thirty-five minutes to get there, we have to rush to get ready. I wrap my hair up while Xavier is in the shower so I don't mess it up while I'm getting ready. I plug in the iron so I can run it over his black Armani slacks and checkered black, gray, and white Armani button-up. I pick up the black Prada loafers from the closet and place them at the foot of the bed; all he has to do when he gets out of the shower is put everything on.

A few minutes later, Xavier emerges from the bathroom with a towel wrapped around his waist. Even though I know we have things to do, it's hard not to pounce on his sexy ass! He looks so good standing in front of me with droplets of water resting on his chest. He looks down at the bed, smiles, and thanks me before sitting down to put his carefully laid-out things on. I take that as my cue to move my ass and jump in the shower myself. It doesn't take me long at all, and in no time, I'm wrapped in my robe and back in the bedroom, rubbing lotion all over my body. Xavier isn't there, so I assume he went downstairs; that's fine, because his ass can really be a distraction! Since it's our last night here, I want to make sure we don't miss that cruise, and if I mess with Xavier, I know we will.

I walk slowly down the stairs to give Xavier the full effect of just how sexy I feel. The black, sleeveless RED Valentino Bow Dress feels wonderful against my skin. It's form fitting but not so tight that it's uncomfortable. By the time I make it to the bottom of the steps, he's already walking over to me with a smile on his face. We meet in the middle, by the kitchen area, where he grabs hold of my hand and lifts it above my head before twirling me around in a circle. The heels of my red Valentino patent-leather peep-toe pumps click lightly on the floor with every step. When I'm standing face to face with him again, I let go of his hand and strike a pose.

"You look beautiful," he says.

"You're looking mighty spiffy ya damn self," I kid before giving him a bright smile.

"Shall we go?" he asks.

I don't answer. I just tuck my red leather red Valentino clutch up under my arm and nod my head in the direction of the door.

CHAPTER TEN

The alarm sounds loudly in my ear, and even though I know I have to get up, I don't want to. We have to leave today to head back to Ohio, and I really want to stay here. I lightly tap a snoring Xavier on the arm before slowly climbing out of the bed. He begins to stretch as I walk past him and into the bathroom to start getting ready. Once my teeth are brushed and my face is washed, I come out and pick up my Juicy Couture jogging outfit off the top of the dresser and slip it on. I look up when I see Xavier come out of the bathroom, still stretching and yawning.

"Are you ready to go?" he asks.

"No, but I don't have a choice," I say, shrugging my shoulders.

"Well, you know what we have to do. Like I said, if this is really what you want, we'll be back soon."

"I know, and I completely understand. It just seems like that's so far away." I wiggle my foot into my white Air Max, before tying the laces.

He looks at me with a serious face before speaking. "Patience is the key to life, Brandy. Anything worth having doesn't come at the drop of a dime. You have to wait on it. You'll be fine, and we'll be back before you know it."

I don't reply and just begin working on the next shoe. Even though I know what he's saying is true, that doesn't change the fact that I don't want to wait. I know we have to go back to Ohio, because we've both got loose ends there

112

that need to be tied up, but in my mind, that stuff won't take almost a year to do. Truthfully, I could get the things I have to get done in about two to three months. All I have to do is bleed Taz dry and put my condo up for sale. At first, I considered keeping it, but then I realized there'd be no reason to. If I have it my way, I will never visit Ohio again, so it's pointless not to sell it. Even if I rented it out, I'd have to keep ties with the tenant, and I don't want to fool with that.

I offer Xavier a weak smile and stand up, preparing to go downstairs. As I pass him, he grabs hold of my arm and pulls me close, into a tight embrace. He brings his lips really close to my ear and whispers that he loves me, then lets me go. I don't say anything; I'm too upset, in a way. I know I shouldn't be angry with him, but I can't help it. It's his idea to make me stay in Ohio for another year, not mine. Like I said, if it were up to me, we'd be back here by Christmas. I exhale and hit the corner on my way down the stairs, preparing to leave the place I've grown to love.

***

We don't do much talking during the twelve-hour ride back home. I guess we're both lost in our thoughts; I know I am. For most of the ride, I simply sit back with my head resting on the reclined seat, thinking about my future. My mind races for the entire ride; for the first time, I am truly excited about a change. In the future, I don't want to have to get over on anyone. I just have to finish that up with Taz. My plan is to get as much money from his ass as possible, before cutting him off and moving to South Carolina. *As soon as I do that, I don't plan on keeping in touch with anyone associated with my past, other than Xavier.* About an hour from home, my head actually starts to hurt because I'm thinking so hard. *I'm so ready to move on, to try and get past the bitterness about all I've been through.*

A little after 10 o'clock, we park in front of Xavier's

house. I'm more than ready to get out of the truck since we haven't stopped once for four hours. I step out and stretch my legs, which were starting to feel a bit cramped. I walk around to the back of the truck to meet Xavier as he pops the latch on the trunk. One by one, he begins to remove our bags. The only noises I hear are cars passing by in the distance; neither of us utters a word. I lift up my trunk and allow him to place my bags inside it, then close it and turn to face him.

"Are you okay?" he asks.

"Yeah. Why?" I place my hands on the back of my car and lean back.

"Because you've been quiet since we left. I figured you had a lot on your mind, so I didn't want to bother you, but before I let you leave, I need to know you're all right. I need to know that we're okay."

"I'm fine," I try to assure him, smiling.

He exhales. "Okay. Well, I guess I'll talk to you tomorrow, unless you want to come in and stay here."

I can see a glimmer in his eyes, and I know he really wants me to stay, but I can't. "Naw, I'm gonna head home. I haven't been there in a week, and I need to check on my house."

The disappointment shows on his face, but he smiles to let me know he understands.

I reach out and give him a warm hug, followed by a gentle kiss, then hop into the front seat of my car. I stick the key in the ignition and roar the engine to life as I reach over and secure my seatbelt across my body. I see him waving at me as I pull off to head home.

The ride to my house is a quick one, and I'm shocked when I pull into the garage and realize I didn't even have my radio home. I never—and I mean never ride without music playing, but I guess that goes to show that my plans with Xavier are really weighing heavy on my mind. I hop out, get my bags out of the trunk, and lug them onto the elevator, where I push the button for my floor.

It's pitch black inside my house, so dark I have to feel the wall in order to find the light switch. Once I click the lights on, I drag my luggage inside and sit it by the door. I'm not in the mood to unpack just yet, so I decide I'll let it stay there until tomorrow. I catch the blinking of my answering machine out the corner of my eye. When I press the button to listen to the message, Taz's voice booms through the speaker, disrupting the quietness of my house.

"Naw, nigga, you betta strap up with that ho. You fuck around and have a baby out in this bitch and don't even know about it!" He laughs loudly at his own joke. "Oh, hey, baby! I'm just calling because I haven't talked to you almost a week, and I wanted to make sure you're okay. I'll be home the day after tomorrow, and I'm hoping I can see you when I get back. A'ight…well, I'm about to get off yo' machine, 'cause you know I don't fuck wit' 'em. Oh yeah…why the hell yo' ass ain't at home?"

Beep.

I can't do nothing but shake my head. *This nigga has a lot of nerve.* I know he couldn't have been too worried about me, because he didn't even call my cell. *His ass must really think he slick, calling the house phone. He knows I'm more than likely not home anyway. Funny that he's trying to cover his ass just 'cause he thinks I care. This message only proves I got this nigga right where I want him. Truthfully, I don't give a flying fuck what he does or who he does it with. He could be suckin' and fuckin' every bitch in the city for all I care. Hell, I got a man! What Taz doesn't know is that his days are numbered, because once I'm done juicing his ass, he'll be just a distant memory, like all the rest. The message was sent the day before yesterday, so more than likely, he'll be back home sometime tomorrow.*

My arms involuntarily extend over my head, and I yawn loudly; this, in turn, causes my eyes to water. I'm sleepy as hell, and my body is tired and drained. I go back and forth with myself, because I don't even feel like taking a shower.

Apparently, my body wins, because I start to peel off my clothes on my way to my room; in no time, I'm up under the covers, lying back into my pillows. Before my head fully hits it, I'm out.

***

The following morning, I awaken to my cell phone blaring in my ear. I roll over and snatch it off the nightstand and glare at the screen, only to see that it's Taz. I decide not to answer, because I'm really not ready to wake up, so I press ignore. I don't even bother to put it back where it was, because I just don't even have the energy. Instead, I drop it beside my pillow and close my eyes again. I doze back off in no time, but my eyes shoot back open when the phone begins to ring for a second time. "Ugh! What the fuck does he want?" I turn my head slightly and peek at the clock on the wall. "He's calling at 9 o'clock in the damn morning?" Once again, I hit ignore. When it rings again, I totally lose my cool and answer it, even before the first ring is finished. "What?"

"Damn. Hello to you too," he says sarcastically.

"What do you want, Taz?"

"What the hell is wrong with you?"

"Why are you calling my phone like a damn lunatic?"

He doesn't respond.

"Hello?"

"Yeah?"

"What the fuck?"

"Stop all that fucking yelling, man! I'm just calling to let yo' ass know I'm back in town, but now you got some damn attitude! Fuck it!"

Now I'm pissed off, because not only did he wake me up out of my peaceful sleep, but he also has the audacity to talk shit to. He's got me all fucked up! I sit up in bed and tear into his ass. "First of all, yo' ass need to calm the fuck down, because last time I checked, you called my phone *numerous times* at 9 o'clock in the damn morning, waking me up outta my sleep. Second, you can hang this bitch up, because I ain't the muthafuckin' one today. I'm not in the mood for your shit, Taz." I start to think this is the perfect opportunity to put his ass right where I want him. "You've been gone all fucking week and only called me once. Are you fucking serious? I've waited by this phone since the day after you left, and you couldn't call me to say shit. You couldn't even answer the phone when I called you. I must have called your ass about a hundred times, so don't call here talking shit, or you'll end up talking to the fucking dial tone!"

"Damn, baby, I'm sorry. I was just busy as hell, and then my phone didn't really have any service out there. Soon as I saw that I had a few bars, I called you."

I chuckle to myself, because it's the sorriest excuse I've ever heard in my life! Of course I haven't called his ass once, but he doesn't know that, because his phone was more than likely powered off at times. He could've come up with something better, but he didn't even bother. "Is that right?" I ask him skeptically. "You must think I'm a damn fool, Taz, because that don't make no damn sense."

He exhales loudly in my ear. "Well, I'm sorry you don't believe me, 'cause that is what happened. Come on, baby! You know I'd—"

I cut him off. "Taz, you know I don't like being lied to, so you better come with something better than that, or it's gone be some shit for real."

"I promise you, baby, that's what happened," he continues to lie.

"Yeah okay. Has Osha called you yet?"

"Yeah, but I ain't answer. She called me, like, thirty times."

This nigga is so fucking dumb! How in the hell would he know she called him if he didn't have no signal? I don't even bust his ass, because I know it'd be pointless, plus I've got something else up my sleeve. I go on to tell him about her calling me and threatening me, how she played on my phone the whole night and just wouldn't leave me alone. I exaggerate and embellish the story, too, just to really piss him off. I tell him she said she's been playing him all along and that the kids are some other nigga's, not even his—that he's been a dummy to take care of them. I tell him Osha said their real baby-daddy was sent to jail, so she just wanted to find a nigga with money. I pretend like she told me about the tape she made with that dude and say she sent it to herself. I even tell him the kids belong to that dude, and that he was on the tape because he just got out of jail.

Taz is mad as fuck when I mention that part, and I hear him breathing all heavy. "I'ma kill that ho!" he roars loudly in my ear.

"What are you gonna do about her disrespecting me, Taz? I'm your woman now, and I don't appreciate her calling me up and telling me she has more power than me. I'm the HBIC in this muthafucka, and you betta let her ass know," I say, filling his head up. "Them fucking kids ain't yours. That bitch has been playing you for years. That nigga probably lying all up in the shit you bought, playing Daddy to the kids you *thought* were yours." I'm relentless, and I'm not gonna let up for shit.

"Naw, you got me fucked up! That bitch getting the fuck out of my shit, and she's about to go right muthafuckin' now! Lemme call you back a little later, baby." Before I even get a chance to respond, he hangs up in my ear; usually I'd flip out on him for that, but since I know he's going to fuck her whole world up, I let it slide.

It's 2 o'clock before Taz finally calls me back. I'm sitting on the couch watching TV, anxious as hell to answer; I really want to know what he did to her. He tells me he went over there, but nobody was home. He says he then called Dan, and they packed up all the stuff that belongs to her and the kids and tossed it on the front lawn. "Then I called a locksmith and had him change the locks," he says, "so the bitch can't get back inside."

I almost die laughing when I think about how salty Osha's going to be when she gets home and sees all her shit outside. *I can just picture her walking past everything with a look of amazement on her face, damn near running to the front door, only to have her key not work. That's what that ho get for fucking with me. She and everybody else needs ta learn I ain't that type of bitch.*

After we wrap up that part of our conversation, I switch gears a bit and begin talking about my favorite subject: money. I lie and tell him Taz I spent the ten racks he gave me and was broke while he was gone, one of the reasons I'd been trying to call him. I tell him I was out shopping and saw this bag I desperately wanted, but I couldn't purchase it because I didn't have enough money.

"Damn, baby. My fault. If I'da known you was gonna go shopping, I woulda left you more. I just figured that would be enough to get you through the week. Where's the bag? I'll go get it for you."

"That's the point, Taz. You can't! It was a limited edition Gucci, and they only made a few of them," I say, lying my ass off.

"I'm sorry, baby. Next time I'll make sure to leave you more money," he responds, thinking that's going to be the end of it.

"I don't want to have to go through that," I whine. "Why can't I have more control over your money?"

"What? Girl, you tripping," he says, attempting to brush me off.

"How you figure that? I am your woman, right?" I ask.

"Yeah, but—"

"But what? I'm sure Osha had more control over your money than I do, didn't she?" I grill.

"Naw. Um…she really didn't," he stammers.

"You're a fucking liar! Did you forget I was her friend? Nigga, please don't lie to me again."

"Come on, Brandy! Why you trippin'?"

"I'm not. It just seems to me that you don't trust me."

"It's not that I don't trust you."

"Then what is it? You can't tell me you do, because if you did, we wouldn't even be having this conversation. You came after me and wanted to do this, but now you're gonna sit here and play the fuck outta crazy? How the fuck are we supposed to work toward something when you don't even trust a bitch?" I inquire.

He doesn't answer me right away.

"Tell me, Taz!"

"Calm the fuck down, girl! I didn't say I don't trust you, a'ight?"

"Well what is it then?"

Again, he doesn't reply.

"Right! Just like I thought, yo' ass bullshitting, and you think I'm dumb. What you don't know is that I can make your money grow for you for real. Don't sleep on me, Taz."

"Grow, huh? Is that right?" He chuckles, which only irritates the hell out of me.

"Yeah, grow. I mean, it ain't like you ain't doing shit with it anyway. I don't see why you tripping so hard. All you do is throw it away on bullshit and nonsense."

"Don't tell me how to spend my fucking money, Brandy! I'm a grown-ass man, and I can do what the fuck I want with it," he snaps in my ear.

I realize I've made him pretty angry, but I don't let that deter me. I just continue trying to prove my point. "I'm not saying it ain't your money. All I'm saying is that I can make your shit legit, invest it and make it seem like you own a business or something. That way, when the police come knocking, you'll have proper paperwork to show them."

"Naw, I'm good. How about you don't count my money and just stick to counting yours? I got my end covered. I know how to control my funds, so just stay in your lane, sweetheart," He says in a very serious tone.

I know I musta heard him wrong, because I'm damn sure this son-of-a-bitch didn't just say what I think he said. "Stay in my lane?" I plant my feet firmly on the floor as I stand up from the couch. I'm not sure why I feel the need to, since we're only on the phone, but somehow, it makes me think I'll be able to hear him more clearly.

"That's what I said," the nigga has the balls to say.

"Sure, I'll stay in my lane, but you best do me a favor."

"What's that?"

"Let me ride in this bitch, dolo!" I yell before hanging up the phone. *Who the hell does this nigga think he fucking with? I ain't that wack-ass bitch Osha, and I ain't about to bow down to the lame. He can kiss the crack of my ass after I take a shit for all I care. That's just how little I give a fuck about this nigga.*

My phone begins to ring again, and of course it's him, but I choose not to answer. *He's gonna learn how to talk to me and respect me. I know he'll be calling me in a few days, begging me to talk to him. It never fails.*

***

It's been a week, and I have yet to take *any* of Taz's calls; believe me, he's made many. I just don't feel the need to talk to him at this moment, because I'm still pissed and don't want to be bothered. He has a lesson to learn anyway, and the best way to teach someone a lesson is to completely ignore their ass. It's always worked for me. I still can't believe how he spoke to me the last time we were on the phone. *Stay in my lane? For real, nigga? For real, he ain't even in my lane, so what the fuck that mean? I got his bitch ass though, and when I put my plan into effect, he ain't even gonna have a clue what hit him.*

I just got off the phone with Xavier, who just had to rush back to Chicago because of a family emergency; his mama's been hospitalized, and the doctors don't know what's wrong

121

with her. He said his brother called and told him their father found her passed out in the bathroom and called 911. After a few days and numerous tests, the so-called experts still don't know what's going on. I told him I'd pray for her and to keep me posted on what's going on. It broke my heart to hear the cracking in his voice as he explained how worried he is. I could tell he was fighting hard not to cry. I wish I'd been there to console him and let him know I'm here for him whenever he needs me. We told each other, "I love you," and, "I miss you," before hanging up.

I climb out of bed, and no sooner than I begin to walk away, my cell rings. Before I even get close enough to pick it up, I already know it's Taz calling; he's been calling at the same time every day. I snatch it up, ready to hear what he has to say. "Hello," I say, as dry as possible.

"Why haven't you been answering or returning any of my calls?" he has the audacity to ask.

I pull the phone away from my ear and stare at it in disbelief. *This dude has to be slow or something, because if he doesn't know why I've been ignoring his ass, I don't know what to tell him. Robbing his dumb ass blind is gonna be a lot easier than I thought.* "What do you want, Taz?"

"Damn! So it's like that? You ain't got time for your nigga no more?"

"Last time I checked, *my* nigga would trust me. *My* nigga wouldn't try to control every fucking thing in our relationship, and *my* nigga wouldn't have told me to stay in my lane."

"You still on that shit?" He chuckles in an attempt to humor me.

I, on the other hand, don't find the shit the least bit funny. "Hell yeah, I'm still on it. You hurt my feelings, Taz, and I don't know if I can forgive you for that shit," I say, pretending to tear up.

"Come on, Brandy. Don't be like that. I wasn't even

trying to hurt your feelings. You know I love the fuck outta you."

I don't say anything.

"You do know that, right?"

"I thought I did, but now I'm not so sure. You made me feel like a jump-off or some shit, the way you played me. You claim you want me to be your woman, yet you played me like a chicken-head as soon as you got a chance. Sad part is, I was trying to help you out for real. I was trying to make your shit seem legit and make sure that if the cops come knocking, you'll be okay. You say you want to be with me, but you won't let me plan for our future. I ain't with that shit, and before I allow someone to make me feel less than what I am, I'll be by myself."

"Be by yourself? Are you serious?"

"As a heart attack. I don't need this, Taz. I have enough going on in my life; I don't need your shit too. I don't need your baby-mama calling and playing on my phone every day, threatening to kill me on sight. I don't need you claiming you trust me when you really don't. I can do bad by myself...for real," I say, going in for the kill. "I'm a good woman, and I'm sure there's a good-ass man out there who'd be willing to give me everything I need without me having to beg and plead for it. I think we should go our separate ways, because this here ain't gonna work. It'll give you a chance to find that female who will allow you to talk to her any kind of way and feed her money only when you feel like it. I'm not going to be that bitch, so I'll just let you go." I sniffle. "Goodbye, Taz."

I hang up the phone, but in no time, it begins to ring again. I don't answer and just continue to let it ring out. As soon as it stops, it begins to ring again and again and again. He won't give up, but there's really no reason why he should. He knows I'm one of the best he can get. Not only am I one of the prettiest, but I'm also the flyest bitches in Ohio. Even if he doesn't say it, I know he knows he hit the jackpot when he upgraded to my fly ass; Osha could never compare. Yeah, I'm flipping out about money, but he knows I got paper; I can do without his money. Hell, I don't want to, but I can always find someone else to suck dry. "Hello," I answer.

"Brandy, what the hell is your problem?" he yells in my ear.

"Look, if you're calling to be all loud and shit, you can hang up the damn phone now. I'm not in the mood for all this today, Taz."

"A'ight, look…I'm sorry about flipping on you, but you came out of left field, and I didn't know how to respond. I know you don't believe me when I tell you, but I do love you. You're right. I do have some trust issues when it comes to my money, but—"

"I understand all that, but I haven't asked you for shit, Taz! You are the one who wants me to depend on you. You've always just given me money, so please don't act like I've been leeching off you since the beginning. I got my own house and ride, and I had all my own shit long before I met you. I'm not some hood-rat bitch you saved from the projects. You know me."*Well at least he knows my representative.*

"I know, and you're right. What are your plans as far as investing?"

I rub my hands together greedily, knowing I've got his ass right where I want him. "Well, I was thinking we could open a business account at a local bank and say you're co-owner of a club or something. I know a few people who'll vouch for it, and it would seem like you're a silent partner and are just financing the club. All the money that goes into that bank account will seem like the owner is paying you back slowly, with interest. Most of your money would be pushed through there, so if anything happens, your ass will be covered. We can do the same thing with a restaurant, and before long, all your money will seem legit. Then you won't have any problems paying for stuff businessmen pay for," I say, giving him the rundown. Everything I'm feeding him is bullshit, but he won't have a clue until it's too late.

"Hmm. Well, it seems like you've got everything figured out."

"Yeah, like I told you, I've been thinking about our future," I lie, as I've only been thinking about my own future. "While you were gone, I started thinking of ways we can begin to live legit. I don't want to wonder if you're going to call me late at night and tell me you're caught up in some shit, Taz. That would kill me. I love you, and I want to make this work—for both of us."

"Damn, baby. I didn't know you felt like that." He sounds shocked.

"Well, I do. I want to be your wife one day, as well as the mother of your children. I just can't do that until I know I don't have to be looking over my shoulder every second of the day. I want to feel comfortable with our lives together. I want to grow old with you, Taz." I continue to feed him the bullshit, which he's eating up. I can tell he's feeling everything I'm saying, because he keeps saying, "Damn, baby," all sentimental and shit.

***

Over the next two weeks, I find out that Taz still hasn't let Osha come back. She and the kids have been staying with her cousin in some projects, Joy Park Homes in Akron. From the pictures I've seen on the Internet, Joy Park ain't nothing like what she's used to, so I know she's salty. She lost everything she had because she wanted to befriend me. I laugh every time I think about it, because this bitch really thought she had a new best friend, and that couldn't have been any further from the truth. When she called him after she realized her key didn't work, Taz went over there and took all her stuff out of the Escalade. I bet the look on her face was priceless when he handed her the keys to that old-ass Trailblazer he allowed her to keep. It's been in the garage for years, and it isn't even going to run long anyway. Word on the street is that she's pissed and coming after my neck whenever she sees me. But I ain't worried about that ho or anyone else.

   As far as my plan goes, I've got the faux paperwork drawn up and am starting to put it into motion. I even got a fake ID. The first name is the same as mine, but since Taz doesn't know my last name. I changed it and made it something totally different. It's funny that a man can claim to love you without even knowing your fucking last name. What kind of shit is that? I used the fake ID and opened two separate bank accounts. Not only did I open the one I told Taz about, but I also opened another one for myself. The only one he knows about is the first one, which is for the fake business; it has Terrence Young, Taz's government name, on it. The other one I'll use to clean out the first bank account. It's also under the fake name, so when I withdraw every dime, the money will never be traced back to me. My plan is going well, and there ain't shit anybody can do about it.

CHAPTER ELEVEN

*A*bout two weeks goes by, and I have yet to be released from my new home, the cage. My legs are cramped, and my back is hurting something terrible. I really just want to die, but for some reason, Pitch wants to keep me alive. What that reason is I don't know; I just want it all to be over. I'm tired of suffering, and I just want to be free. The plastic bowls in front of me were recently filled with dog food and toilet water, but now they're empty. In this cooped-up space I'm forced to call home, dog food is all I'm allowed to eat. I guess this is Pitch's way of breaking me down, and it's working.

I'd been locked up for almost four days before I actually gave in and started to eat. I tried to hold out as long as I could, but my stomach literally started to touch my back, and I realized I didn't have a choice. I almost threw up after I took the first bite, but I held it in because I knew if I did, not only would it hurt, but it was all I had to eat. I knew if I didn't eat it, there was nothing else coming. Now I just hold my breath and swallow huge mouthfuls, trying not to gag. Sometimes it works because it's gone much faster, and I don't taste it so much.

Now the toilet water is a different story altogether. I'm not absolutely sure, but I swear on everything that I love that there's urine in it. It smells just like pee and always a light tint of yellow. I know Pitch would do some grimy shit like that just because he can. He wants to make me suffer, though

I'm not sure why. I don't know what I've done to him to make him hate me as much as he does. I know I'll never have the answer to that question, and if I continue to think about it, I would only give myself a headache or drive myself crazy. The only thing I know for sure is that he'll do anything and everything in his power to make my life miserable; pissing in my water would take it over the top. That alone makes me sick to my stomach, but I have to do what I have to do.

My nose starts to turn up out of the blue, and my guess is because this cage reeks. The smell of urine, feces, and my own body odor is enough to cause me to gag repeatedly. The stench invades my nose every second of the day, and I'm ashamed to say I'm getting used to it. Since I haven't been able to leave the cage for any reason, it was where I'm forced to do my business. The space is so cramped that I can't do much of anything else. The back of the cage was full of pee and shit, and it's starting to pile up day by day. My behind is covered with doo-doo; it's not like I can wipe myself or even attempt to. I can barely move my arms as it is, and Pitch has left me in here to die! I know that, so I constantly ask God to take me away from my misery. I want to die quickly—not a slow, suffering death. I believe I deserve better than that.

The dark basement illuminates when the door at the top of the stairs opens. I see a pair of feet sporting black gators; they slowly descend the stairs. I know without a doubt that it's Pitch. He stops briefly at the bottom of the stairs and just stares at me. My heart starts to beat rapidly in my chest, so loud that I'm sure he can hear it, even from the other side of the room. I'm scared to death, because I never know what to expect from him. I'm not sure if he's here to talk shit or to torture me more in some way. Either way, I don't want to go there with him.

"Today is your lucky day," he says in that deep voice of his, then chuckles. "You're finally going to get out of that cage for a while."

My face holds no emotion, because I know he's up to something. He walks over to the cage and slips the key in the lock. When it clicks, he pulls the small door open before stepping back a few paces. Taking that as my cue to move my ass, I begin to crawl out slowly. It hurts like hell to move, and with every motion, I feel like I'm going to die. Once my body is all the way out of the cage, I stay on all fours and just look at the concrete floor. I know it's not safe to assume he wants me to stand up, and I don't know what he'll do to me if I try. Pitch reaches down and grabs the back of my matted hair and yanks me into an upright position. Every bone in my body feels as if it's snapping into small pieces. It doesn't help at all that I instantly hear a bunch of cracking sounds. I can also feel and hear my hair follicles breaking from the force of his hands, but I don't make a sound, in spite of the pain.

"You smell like shit!" he jokes, then laughs at his own sick humor.

Still using my hair to guide me, he jerks and pushes me over to the corner of the basement. There's a water spigot there, something like a shower, except without any walls or any sort of enclosure. It's really just a small drain on the floor and a spout that hangs from the upper part of the wall. If I had to guess, I would have said that it was supposed to have been a shower, but no one chose to upgrade it. My thoughts are interrupted when Pitch violently shoves me toward it, which causes me to trip. Using my arms, I try to brace myself, but since I haven't moved them in such a long time, they don't work as well as they should. I crash, head first, into the wall with a loud thump, *causing my body to immediately to bounce back from the impact.*

"Get the fuck in there!" he yells as he pushes my dizzy body back over toward the wall.

I attempt to shake my head, but no matter what I do, my vision won't stop spinning. I begin to get lightheaded and reach out and steady myself on the wall for a minute with my eyes closed. This only lasts for about a minute before I feel a cold stream of water splash against my naked body. My eyes instantly shoot open, and my breath gets caught in my throat. I jump back and shriek, trying to get away from the freezing water. I attempt to back up a bit more, but Pitch pushes me back so hard I almost fall against the wall again. My breathing is heavy, and my naked body trembles as the cold water discharges from the rusty spout. A bar of soap falls to the floor after he tosses it toward me, but I don't pick it up.

"Pick up that fuckin' soap and wash yo' funky ass. Get that nappy-ass hair too...and you betta do it right," he warns.

I bend down and pick up the soap and slowly begin to rub it all over my body, building up a lather. He stands behind me as I bathe in cold water, as if I'm some kind of animal and not his child at all. Terrified of his punishments, I do exactly what I'm told. I wash my body and my hair as best as I can. After a while, the water doesn't feel as cold, and I begin to get used to it. Even though I don't like that I'm being forced to wash up, the soap and water actually feel somewhat good, somewhat refreshing against my filthy skin. I wash away layers of dirt, and I finally smell a little bit better. When Pitch sees that I'm finished, he tosses a towel at me and instructs me to dry off with it. When I'm done, I wrap it around my body and wait for his next command, as if I'm his obedient little puppy. I can't do anything until he gives me an order.

He leads me up the stairs and into the full bathroom off the dining area. Inside is a black, short skirt with a matching top, black fishnet stockings, and bright red heels. There is makeup neatly set up around the vanity, as well as a comb and a brush.

"You have an hour to get yourself together, so hurry yo' ass up." He starts to close the door, but stops. "Don't try no slick shit, because I will kill yo' ass this time. You hear me, bitch?"

"Yes," I reply.

"Yes what?"

"Yes, Daddy."

He looks at me one last time, then closes the door and locks it behind him.

Finally, I can exhale. I hurriedly do everything Trixie taught me. My hair is still wet, so I pull it into a tight ponytail, then tie a thick bun in the back. Next, I apply makeup. I first dab my eyes lightly with a tissue, as they've started to water lightly. I miss Trixie so much, and I still can't believe Pitch did her the way he did. I really thought he loved her, but I guess once she crossed him, all that went down the drain. As soon as I'm done with my hair and makeup, I pick up the skirt and shirt and begin to get dressed. Everything fits me perfectly. Not sure what else to do, I sit on the toilet and wait for him to come and get me. I already know he's going to take me out to the stroll. I'm not ready for it, but truthfully, I don't have much of a choice. Plus, anything's better than being locked away in a cage, day in and day out.

About ten minutes later, I hear the door being unlocked. Pitch opens the door and smiles when he sees that I'm already dressed. He instructs me to stand and spin around so he can get a full view of how I look. I did as I was told, slowly turning around in a circle, then stopped. He grins again, showing off his one gold tooth, and tells me he's proud of me for following directions. He also mentions that if I keep doing what I'm supposed to do, life will be much easier for me. I don't say anything; I only nod to let him know I understand what it is that he's telling me. We walk through the dining area and out the front door, then head over to the car. As we get closer, I see that the guy from the store is driving, and there's someone else in the back seat. Upon closer inspection, I can see it's the girl with the orange wig, the one who'd tortured Trixie in the video.

Pitch climbs in the front seat, and I got in directly behind him. The girl from the video is sitting beside me, wearing a stone face and looking as if she's got an attitude. Her eyes are focused straight ahead, and she doesn't so much as acknowledge the fact that I'm sitting just inches from her. I don't give too much of a damn though. If she only knew what I want to do to her, that funny-looking bitch would really be mad. I don't appreciate the way she treated Trixie in the video, and if I were to get some time alone with her, I'm sure she'd see just how I felt about it. This time, she's wearing a short black bob, and instead of a bikini top and leather pants, she's wearing an expensive-looking summer dress that comes down to her knees. I can only assume she's now his bottom bitch. As we head to our destination, I sit silently beside her, wishing her dead.

In no time, we're in downtown Cleveland, on a street called Superior. We slowly pull up and park in front of a dark brick building with a bunch of activity going on outside of it. Every building looks abandoned, except for the huge glass one that sits on the end of the street. That building looks pretty new, and the fresh shine on the windows lets me know somebody's taking good care of it. I wonder why it's next to the shit hole, North Point, according to the sign.

There are a bunch of half-dressed women standing around or walking in the front, and I know they're prostitutes. One in particular catches my eye; she's tall and has a very nice shape. Her long legs are covered with a pair of silver tights, and on her feet are black, open-toed shoe boots decorated with rhinestones. Her shirt is black and plain, but she's sporting a large silver belt around her waist, blending everything else together. I'll never forget her walk as long as I live; she was taking every step with confidence and power. I don't really get a chance to zoom in on her face, because she's too far away for me to see, but when Pitch calls her over to the car, I finally see who it is.

I gasp and jump back in my seat when Trixie comes into clear view. Our eyes connect for a mere second before she starts talking to Pitch; after that, she refuses to look my way

132

again. She looks nothing like the beautiful woman I remember. Instead, her face is covered with small keloids that must have come from the cuts all over her face. It's hard to look at her, a beautiful goddess destroyed. I cannot believe what they've done to her! I'm happy she's alive, and I want to hug her, but I know I can't—not only would Pitch knock the shit out of me, but I'm not even sure she'd accept the hug. I glance over at the chick beside me, the one who cut her up like that, and it takes everything in me not to punch the hell out of her; the heffa just sits there, smiling and cheesing like something's funny. Pitch wraps up their conversation, and Trixie struts away, not even bothering to look back.

I know he didn't really want to talk to her; he just wanted me to see the consequences for disobeying him, up close and personal. He doesn't have to tell me twice; I'm already a believer. A few seconds pass before I'm ordered to get out of the car. I follow closely behind Pitch and his new chick as we make our way into the building. At the front desk, Pitch laughs and jokes with the attendant before the man hands him a key. In no time, we're headed for a raggedy-looking elevator. I stand behind Pitch and his bottom bitch as he presses the button for the third floor. I have to hold my breath on the ride, because the elevator reeks of urine and stale body odor. We get off the elevator when the doors open, pass a few doors, and stop in front of one so Pitch can unlock the door with the key. Inside is a full-sized bed, nightstand, small table, and a old-fashioned TV with a shabby antenna attached to it.

"This is where you're gonna make my money," Pitch said, breaking the silence.

I hear him, but I choose not to reply. Instead, I nod my head to show that I understand what it is that he's saying.

"I don't trust you to be outside alone yet, because yo' connivin' ass just might try to get away again, so your customers will come here instead. When someone knocks on the door, let them in and do exactly what they want. They'll

be paying good money for your ass. You hear me?"

"Yes, Daddy," I answer meekly.

"I'm gonna leave John downstairs, and he'll collect the money. None of it will ever touch your hands—not until you show me I can trust you. I got a couple guys coming up in a few, so do whatever they ask and don't bitch about it." He turns to walk away, then stops. "Don't play with me, Brandy. If you fuck this up, I'ma do you worse than I did Trixie," he threatens before he and his sidekick walk out the door. .

When I feel the coast is clear, I finally break down and start to cry. I try to sit down on the edge of the bed but end up sliding off and landing on the floor. It doesn't make sense to try to get up, because the floor is exactly where I need to be. I'm scared, because I don't know the first thing about selling my body this way. I did it for my mother, when I was younger, but that was different. Those guys were people I knew. Now, I know I'll be stuck with total strangers, men I've never met, and none of them care that I'm only fourteen. So many thoughts run through my mind that I start to get a headache. I don't know what I'm going to do. I know I can't run, because if Pitch catches me—which I know he will— he'd damn near torture me to death. All I can do is go with the flow and do whatever the men want. There's not a damn thing I can do about it. .

My thoughts are interrupted by a knock on the door. I slowly walk over and peer through the peephole, squinting. My eyes buck and damn near pop out of my head when I see three dudes standing outside. I don't know how in the hell Pitch expects me to do more than one dude on my first try. I close my eyes and take a deep breath before I open the door. As they begin to walk in, I stand up against the wall to allow them to enter. Each stops to give me the onceover before continuing all the way into the room. I stand still, holding the door, in utter shock and disbelief that Pitch is really trying to do me dirty. He doesn't even give a damn that all these niggas at once will cause me pain.

"Hurry the fuck up," one says.

His command breaks my train of thought, and I begin to close the door. Something is stuck and prevents me from shutting it completely. When I look down trying to figure out the cause, all I see is Pitch's purple gator. I look up, and our eyes connect; a cold chill runs through my body, causing me to let go of the knob and allow him to enter.

"I changed my mind. I'm gon' sit in here and make sure you do what the fuck you s'posed to do," he says, then strolls past with that bitch hanging on his arm. He takes a seat in the chair beside the window, and she rests on his lap.

I turn to close and lock the door, but it's hard because my hands are shaking. A few thoughts cross my mind as I attempt to pump myself up before I turn around to face everyone. I put on my game face; I know if I don't, I'll surely cry in front of them. The fact that Pitch is standing in the room makes it all much harder, because I know I won't be able to ask them to stop if they're hurting me. I know my daddy will make sure I do everything I'm supposed to, and that alone scares me half to death. Once I'm composed enough, I turn around and prepare to do what I have to do. I figure if I just take my mind to another place, like I used to do when I was with my mom, everything will be fine. It worked when Harold was assaulting my body, so I'm sure it will work now.

I walk slowly to the bed and begin removing my clothes. All three of the guys are already naked, waiting for me to get started. The one closest to me, who doesn't look like he's much older than I am, is jacking off. He's medium height, light-skinned, and has a baby face. The second guy looks to be much older, with bits of gray speckling his beard. The third one appears to be Jamaican, because he's wearing long-ass dreadlocks that come just past his shoulders.

I place my hands on the bed and begin to climb across slowly, but Baby Face grabs my arm and leads me over toward him instead. I glance over at Pitch, who merely nods

*his head. Baby Face sits me down on the edge of the bed and
sticks his penis directly in my face. I already know what he
wants me to do, so I open my mouth and welcome him, all the
while feeling degraded as hell. After a few strokes, he
removes his penis from my mouth and tells me to get on all
fours. I have no choice, so I do as I'm told.*

*As I'm about to prepare to climb on the bed, Gray Beard
gets on first and lies on his back, then directs me to straddle
him. When I'm in their desired position, Baby Face once
again inserts his penis in my mouth. Next, he grabs my
ponytail and begins to pump my face forcefully. He's being
way too rough and is going so fast that I can't breathe, as if
he's trying to put the thing all the way down my damn throat.
I know I'm supposed to take it, according to Pitch, but the
dude is trying to kill me! I gag and try unsuccessfully to push
him back just a little bit, but he won't budge. Instead, he
moans and continues to thrust in and out of my mouth. As I
struggle to breathe, Gray Beard places one of his hands on
my butt while sliding his condom covered penis up and down
my slit with the other. As hard as he tries, I'm not getting
wet, but that doesn't stop him at all. I grunt when he enters
me, but no one can hear it because I still can't breathe.*

*I still haven't had a chance to recover from that assault
when I feel someone grip my hips; I know it has to be Dread
Head. Pain shoots through my body like fire when he
penetrates my rectum, showing no mercy. I open my mouth to
scream but can't because Baby Face still has control of my
jaws. All I can hear is the gurgling sound of my spit inside
my throat as I'm forced to take the unbearable pain. Tears
start to run rapidly down my face, but I can only let them fall
as Dread Head grabs hold of both my arms. He pulls me
roughly toward him and rams himself forcefully inside my
butt hole. It feels as if I'm going to shit myself, and the pain
is excruciating, to say the least. With red, tear-filled eyes, I
look over at Pitch. I'm not at all shocked by what I see. The
bastard has the audacity to wear a smirk on his face, as if*

he's thoroughly enjoying seeing me go through all this pain.

I force my eyes closed and attempt to let my mind go blank, but the three guys thrusting themselves in and out of each of my holes make that impossible. My vagina and rectum are on fire, and my mouth begins to get dry and cracked in the corners. It's still hard for me to breathe, but I have to hang in there. It surprises me that I haven't passed out, but I'm sure that would be way too good for me. With my luck, I'll have just enough oxygen to stay awake for the total assault. All I can hear is a series of grunts and groans, and all I can feel is pain and terror. With every stroke they administer, a piece of me dies.

I glance over at Pitch again and see that the girl is on her knees between his legs, sucking him off. His eyes are open and fixed on me, and on his face is a look of enjoyment. Even though nothing about him should amaze me, I still can't believe seeing his daughter treated this way would turn him on. I'm his flesh and blood, yet seeing me violated makes him feel like having his dick sucked. I seethe on the inside as she bobs her head up and down, and I silently pray that her jaws will lock up so she bites that crusty muthafucka he calls a dick off and leave him bleeding to death. I'm so caught up in my daydream of his demise that I don't even flinch when Dread Head smacks me hard on my butt. My body begins to go numb to everything they are doing, and the pain begins to subside. I sigh when I feel my mind finally begin to go free, and before I know it, I pass out.

***

I wake up to cold water being thrown on me by Pitch. I feel as if I've run a marathon. My coochie and butt are on fire, and only a hot bath helps at all.

After that, the same sort of thing happens to me every day. Pitch locks me in the room and sends various men up to come in and out as they please. My body is continuously used and abused, and there's not shit I can do about it.

About two months later, he loosens his grip on me and allows me to stand out in front with the rest of the women who work for him. Truthfully, I believe standing outside is more degrading than being in the room, in my opinion anyway. In the room, guys would knock on the door, already knowing what they wanted. Outside, I have to try to sell myself to them, and I don't like that.

My first day outside is terrible, because I don't really know what to do. New Year's is right around the corner, and there are so many johns outside, but I can't seem to get one of them. I stand out in the cold for hours, not really moving because I don't exactly know what to do. I'm freezing and the little skirt and cheap jacket do nothing to keep me warm; since I'm not moving, I'm even colder.

When I see Trixie, I damn near run over to get to her, but she continues to walk away. I call her name constantly, but she doesn't so much as acknowledge me. My feelings are hurt, and I began to cry as I sit all alone in the corner.

"Baby Doll, you're gonna have to get it together," I hear from behind me.

I smile instantly, knowing it's Trixie.

"Don't turn around. Just listen to me, okay?"

"Okay."

"You're going to have to start moving around and making money. If you don't have any money by the time Pitch comes back, he'll punish you. I'm going to need you to get off your ass and make it happen, Baby Doll. Do you understand?" she asks.

"Yes. Trixie, I miss you," I tell her, with tears rolling down my face. I want to turn around and hug her so bad, but I know I can't.

"I miss you too, Baby Doll. Don't think I don't."

"Then why won't you say anything to me when I call you?"

"Pitch told me to stay away from you. He threatened to

kill you if I don't. But don't you worry. I'm always here for you. That's why I'm out here right now, to keep an eye on you. If it wasn't for you, I woulda killed myself long ago. Look at what that muthafucka did to my face!" She must notice that she's raising her voice, because she pauses for a moment before going back into her whisper. "I love you, Baby Doll, and I hope you know that. I'd die for you in a heartbeat." She sniffles and starts to cry. "I want you to get away from this life. Take the first chance you get and don't look back. You need to make some money out here, though, because that's the only way you'll be able to get away from him. Pitch will kill your spirit if you allow him to, so keep the faith. It'll get better. I've gotta go, but I'll be watching you, Baby Doll." Just as quick as she walked up, she's gone.

"I love you too, Trixie," I say, but she doesn't hear me because she's already across the street, walking up to another john..

I took Trixie's advice and now do what I'm told. I've always been a quick learner, so I watch the other girls and try to mimic what they're doing. I talk the same way, dress like them, and act like them. It doesn't take me long to get it down, and in no time, I'm making the same amount of money as the old pros. Of course of few of them are upset about that, because I'm the young girl—the rookie—taking all of their clientele. I don't sweat it though. If it were my choice, I wouldn't be out here at all. I'd just be doing things kids my age are supposed to do, like going to school.

My birthday comes and goes without so much as a "Happy birthday" from my dad. I don't know why I'm disappointed; I shouldn't have expected Pitch to say anything. He's not exactly a loving father. Instead, my daddy is the man who put me out on the ho stroll at the age of fourteen, as if it was the right thing to do. Trixie never forgets, though, and she sings "Happy Birthday" to me; that makes my day. At least I know someone in this world gives a damn about me.

Cachet

The following month, I'm able to add someone else to that very short list: Roger.

CHAPTER TWELVE

I wake up with a bad migraine. It hurts so bad when I first open my eyes that all I can do is close them quickly. I reach into my nightstand and grab the small tube of Imitrex, quickly twist off the top, slide it into my nostrils, and inhale. I drop it back inside the drawer, then just lie there, unable to move. My eyes feel like they're going to pop out of my head at any given moment, and I silently pray the pain will go away quickly. I don't know how much time passes, but it seems like an eternity before it finally starts to clear up. *I need to let my doc know I need something stronger, because the Imitrex isn't working as well as it used to be. Maybe I'm starting to become immune to it.*

After getting myself together for the day, I decide to head to the mall to pick up something nice for Xavier. When I talked to him last night, he told me his mother is feeling a lot better, and he just got back to town. He then told me he's going to stay in the house all day. I know he's still feeling worried, and I want to cheer him up. It's a chilly October day, actually Halloween, so I decide to be cute but warm. My black and cream checkered, long-sleeved DKNY crepe dress stops just above the middle of my thighs. I pair it with black wool tights and some black knee-high Christian Louboutin boots. After removing my scarf, I comb my hair out and allow it to fall gracefully across my shoulders and down my back. My final touch is a black Eugenia Kim floppy hat with the cream feather on the right side and my Gucci clutch. The only makeup I put on is a little M.A.C. lip gloss, and then I grab my keys and leave out the house.

It takes me a little less than two hours to find everything I need at the mall. I even find something for myself; I simply have to buy the wool Gucci coat that seemed to be calling my name from the rack. After I pay for everything, I pull up to the doors, and a nice gentleman brings my bags out and places them inside my trunk. I smile, hit my horn twice to show him my appreciation, and pull off, leaving him waving by the doors. A warm, tingling feels invades my body, because I know Xavier is going to love the things I bought for him; they are going to look so nice in his new townhome. Little by little, his house will look more like a home, and the kitchen appliances I purchased are just the beginning. He'll now have everything he could ever want or need in a kitchen, and I pieced everything together well, if I do say so myself.

As I prepare to make a right onto Cedar Road, I do a double-take when I see Xavier's Infiniti fly by me, heading toward the opposite way. He's supposed to be at home all day, so when I see four heads in the car, I'm confused. I make up my mind that I not going to wonder long; and as soon as the road is clear I pull out and go in the direction he just went. I'm a few cars behind him as he sits at a red light, and he can't see my vehicle. When I see him put his right blinker on and began to ease into the lane to make his turn, I do the same. Following that turn, he makes a left and pulls into the parking lot of The Cheesecake Factory. I wait a while before pulling in and parking a few spaces away.

I was accurate about there being four people inside the car, confirmed when they climb out one by one. There's a nice-looking older gentleman in the back seat who looks like he could be about fifty. He's dressed in a pair of cream slacks, a dress shirt, and a dark blue blazer. A well-dressed woman steps out right after him, dressed in a purple wool bar jacket over the matching dress, sheer stockings, and black pumps. From where I'm sitting, she looks like she could be the wife of the gentlemen, because when she steps out, he places his hand on the lower part of her back. Xavier is next to climb out, clad in black dress pants, a white button-up, and an Armani leather jacket, which looks very good on him. I chastise myself; because right now I can't focus on how sexy he is, because the person who gets out last is a woman.

Instantly she puts me in the mind of the model Eva Marcille. She even has the same skin tone. I squint so I can get a closer look just to make sure it's not her. Regardless, she's a beautiful woman, and I instantly envy her good looks. I'm not saying she's prettier then I am, but there is something about her that looks innocent. Not only is her skin blemish free, but it looks as if she's never had a rough patch in her entire life. She's dressed simply but cute in a pair of dark denim skinny jeans and a white wife-beater under a tan pea coat that matches perfectly well with her tan ankle boots. I have the exact same $2,500 Chameleon duffle Fendi bag, so I figure the bitch either has money or Xavier is breaking her off something proper.

I damn near lose it when I see him drape his arm lovingly around her shoulders and guide her to the front door. My blood begins to boil. I want to hop up out and run up on them and beat him and that bitch's ass! I sit there for a minute, then climb out of my car and make my way inside. The hostess greets me and asks if there's only one in my party. I want to say that my other half is probably eating appetizers with his bitch at this moment, so I'm forced to be by myself, but instead I just nod politely and say, "Yes."

She leads me to my table, which just happens to be a few seats away from theirs. Even though Xavier's back is to me, I still pull my hat down over my face, just in case he just happens to turn around.

When the waiter comes, I brush him off quickly by ordering a glass of water and a slice of chocolate cheesecake. I don't even have an appetite, so I know I'm not going to touch either, but I have to make it seem like I'm there for a reason besides stalking my man.

From my seat, I watch them intently as they talk and laugh; all the while, I'm mad as hell. The older couple is sitting on one side of the table, and Xavier and his bitch are on the other. Every time they share a laugh, she places her hand lovingly on his back. They seem so comfortable with each other that it makes me sick. I can't help myself; I need to know who these people are and what the hell he's doing with them, so I decide to take my chances and call his phone to see if he answers. I scroll to his number on my phone and make the call, all the while watching him closely from under the brim of my hat.

Seconds later, he touches his pocket before reaching in and pulling his phone out. There was not any ringing, so I figure he must have it on vibrate. He glances down at the screen, and then excuses himself from the table.

"Hey, Love," he says into the phone, a little too chipper for my taste.

I bite down on the inside of my jaw in an attempt to stay calm. What I really want to do is flip out on his ass, but I keep my cool.

"Hey. What are you doing?" His background is quiet, and there's a hell of an echo, so I figure he's in the restroom.

"Nothing. Just sitting here watching a little bit of TV," he lies. "What you getting into?"

"I ain't doing shit myself. How about I come over with something to eat so we can watch TV together?"

"That sounds like a perfect idea." He pauses. "Damn! I forgot I have to run out for a little while. Maybe later tonight?"

"Yeah, that's fine. I'll see you later then."

"A'ight. I love you," he says.

"Yeah…me too." I hang up the phone with my heart feeling heavy. He just lied to me, and when we first got together, he promised that was something he'd never do. I suppose that promise was a lie too.

I continue to sit at my table as I watch him walk up and take a seat back beside ol' girl. The waiter brought their food while he was in the bathroom, but I guess they wanted to wait until he was back, because once he's seated, they all dig in. Halfway into their meal, Xavier reaches in his jacket pocket and pulls out a small velvet box. I narrow my eyes and try as hard as I can to see what's inside it, but I can't make it out from where I'm sitting. The older gentleman stands up quickly and begins to shake Xavier's hand proudly.

The woman I assume to be the man's wife hops up and walks around the table to give him a big, heartfelt hug. I'm confused as hell and have no clue what's going on until I peep the girl sliding a ring on her finger. Instantly, she begins to jump up and down with excitement, then wraps her arms around his neck tightly. The whole restaurant gets quiet as onlookers try to figure out what all the commotion is about. Moments later, they all stand and begin to applaud. At that moment, I realize I can't just sit here and watch this shit any longer. I push my chair back; drop a twenty on the table, and dash out of the restaurant, not bothering to look back.

Every piece of food inside my stomach comes up in the parking lot. I brace myself against my vehicle and choke and gag until I can't do it anymore. My head is pounding, and I feel like shit. I reach in my bag and grab a piece of tissue to wipe the spit off my mouth, then take a seat on the curb. I'm parked near the grass, so the trees shield me from the beaming sun, and the breeze helps me feel a little better. I close my eyes and see the image of her with the ring on her finger, hugging him. I realize that I can't continue to sit outside this restaurant, because I don't know what I'll do when they decide come out.

It takes a minute before I'm calm enough to climb into the driver seat. I start the engine and begin to drive home. During the entire ride, I'm in a zone, and it's a wonder I get home at all. Pulling into the parking garage, I grab my bag and walk aimlessly toward the elevator.

As I stand directly outside my apartment, it all hits me again, and I break down, collapsing to the floor. I begin to cry hysterically. I can't help it, and I can't stop, even though I want to. *How could he do something like this to me? He said he loves me, and this is how he proves it?* My insides ache, and my soul hurts. It feels as if I can't breathe. I inhale deeply, but it's still not enough air, and I feel as though I might be dying. I'm sure I'm dying of a broken heart. Still on the floor, I reach up and stick my key in the lock and push the door open. I don't even bother standing up; instead, I just crawl inside, nudging the door closed behind me. I kick my boots off while lying on the floor, face up. I clutch my chest with my hands and attempt to ease the pain I'm feeling, but it doesn't work. I don't think anything will.

My hands are still on my chest, and I can feel my heart beating, but it feels like something is missing. A piece of me died when I saw him with her, and I can't even explain how I felt when she slid that ring on her finger. He proposed to another bitch, after he told me I'm supposed to be his wife. I feel myself getting queasy again, so I jump up and run to the hall bathroom, causing my hat to fly off somewhere between there and the living room. I make it in just enough time to put my head in the bowl and throw up. It feels like I'm throwing up my insides, because I can't possibly have any food left in there. I lift my head out of the bowl for a second, just long enough to unzip my dress so I can slide it over my shoulders and over my legs with the tights. Clad in nothing but a pair of panties and a bra, I just sit here in case anything else wants to come out. Tears roll down my face, and I don't even try to wipe them away. I don't see the point, as there will be plenty more anyway.

My mind drifts back to when I was younger. *Was my mother right when she said I'll never be shit to anyone? Was her life like that? Is that why she turned to drugs? It would make perfect sense, because I feel like getting away right now. I don't want to be inside my body anymore. I just want to go far away. I'd like to go somewhere so I don't have to deal with this pain I'm feeling anymore. Anything would be better than where I'm at right now, because I feel like dying. I can't kill myself, because I'm too damn chicken. I don't want to feel the pain, but I'm also afraid of dying. The cold toilet bowl feels good against my hot skin, and I figure I can sit here all day. I just want to go to sleep, but I know I can't, because I have too much on my mind.*

It's crazy, but as much as I hate Xavier, I find myself wishing he was here to hold me and tell me that everything's going to be okay. I know it sounds ridiculous, but I really don't give a damn; this is how I feel. My body craves his touch in the worst way right now. I want him to squeeze me tight and tell me it's all a big misunderstanding and that I'm the one he loves. I want him to tell me he's sorry he hurt me and to promise that he'll never do it again. I'd scream and cry and tell him it's over, but he wouldn't leave; he'd make me listen to him. He'd beg and plead and tell me he can't live without me. Then he'd explain to ol' girl that I'm the love of his life and that we have plans already that she is no part of. I'd spend hours crying on his chest while he stokes my hair lightly with his fingers, and we'd end the night making love like it's our last time. *Yeah, that sounds good, but I know it won't happen because that's not how my life goes. Nothing good ever happens to me, and it's about time I learn to accept it.*

Forcing myself to stand up, I flush the toilet and reach in the cabinet to pull out a terrycloth washcloth. My head is spinning, and all I can do is shake it to try to clear the images of him and her together. Of course it doesn't work, because that horrible nightmare is burned into my brain, forever etched in my memory. Turning on the knob, I drop the washcloth inside the sink and watch as it soaks up the cold water. I reach in the bowl, grab it, and wring it out, then close my eyes. The coolness of the material feels wonderful as I dab it lightly around my face. My eyes open, and I just stare at myself in the mirror. Once I get a good look at my bloodshot, puffy, swollen eyes, I go from sad to mad in seconds.

"What the fuck is wrong with me?" I yell at the top of my lungs. "Am I not lovable? What's so damn wrong with me that nobody will truly love me?" I ask myself. I'm still crying, but not because I'm sad; these tears are all my salty anger coming to the surface.

Years ago, I sat in a bathroom and cried over someone who claimed to love me. At that moment, I vowed to myself that I'd never let myself get in such a predicament again. Now, here I am, lying on the floor, crying my eyes out over yet another nigga who claimed unconditional love, only to lie to me in the end. *What the hell is wrong with me? Mama was right. I must be weak. These muthafuckas think they can just make empty-ass promises that they've got no intention of keeping. I'm gonna have to make an example out of Xavier's ass and show him I'm not the bitch to fuck with.*

I gather my things off the bathroom floor and drop them in the hamper. Back inside the living room, I reach into my purse and pull out my phone, before texting Xavier: "What time do u want me 2 come?"

Xavier: "About 8. Cool wit u?"

Me: "Fine. C U then."

I laugh out loud after I press the last button. *This nigga don't know what he's getting himself into. He done fucked with the wrong bitch!*

CHAPTER THIRTEEN

"Hello!" I yell.

"What's wrong, baby?" Taz asks.

"I'm on my way to your apartment. I need you," I sob into the receiver.

"What's going on?"

"Please just be there, Taz. Please."

"I'll be there in a minute, baby. I'll see you there." He disconnects the call.

It takes me fifteen minutes to make it to his apartment, and by the time I pull up, he's standing outside his car, waiting for me. I climb out of my car and walk over to him slowly before falling into his arms and crying like a baby. He keeps asking me what's wrong, but I don't say anything and just squeeze him tight, like I'm holding on for dear life. The blood running from my nose smears all over his white t-shirt, but he doesn't mind.

Dan is sitting in the passenger side of the car. When he sees how upset I am, he tells Taz to call him a little later, and then pulls off, leaving us standing there.

I try to talk, but nothing comes out but blubbers because I'm crying so hard.

Taz picks me up and carries me into the building and onto the elevator, all the while gently kissing me on the forehead and telling me everything's going to be okay. Once we're inside his apartment, he places me on the couch and walks off toward the bathroom. He emerges a little while later with a warm washcloth in his hand, which he tenderly uses to wipe the almost-dried blood away, all the while looking at me intently.

I don't say anything and only stare at him with tear-filled eyes.

When he's done, he takes a seat beside me and holds me close to him. No words are spoken, but I know it's his way of letting me know that he's here for me, whenever I'm ready to talk.

I never knew Taz had such a caring side, but I lay my head on his shoulder and close my eyes, as the tears continue to fall.

"He...he raped me," I whisper after a long silence.

"What!?" Taz jumps up in a rage, almost knocking me down. "Who? What muthafucka raped you?" he demands.

I sit up and gradually begin to tell him what allegedly happened to me before I called him.

"There's this guy named Xavier. We were really cool, like best friends...until I told him you and I are together. After that, he started acting funny toward me, like he didn't really want to be bothered. He ignored my calls, so I eventually accepted it and stopped calling him." I paused to swallow the mouth full of saliva. "Today, he called me out of the blue and asked me if I'd help him decorate his new place, a townhouse he just bought. He offered to pay me if I'd be his interior decorator. I didn't see anything wrong with it. Like I said, we were like best friends."

Seeing the tears rolling down my face, Taz gets up and brings me a box of Kleenex.

I pull out a few sheets and dab both of my eyes, then continue. "He gave me the address, and I met him over there a few hours ago. Everything was going fine. He showed me the entire house before we sat down to discuss the budget. He offered me a glass of wine, but I declined because I didn't feel like drinking. That was when he...when everything changed." I stopped for effect. "He began to yell and called me a stuck-up bitch, then accused me of thinking I'm too good for him since I'm with you. I told him that's not true." I weep, shaking my head, and fiddle with my hands the whole time. "I just...I—"

"Take your time, baby," Taz says, holding it together for my sake, even though he's clearly upset.

"I got tired of being disrespected, so I got up to leave. When I stood, he walked right over and slapped me in the face with the back of his hand. I fell to the floor and hit my head on a chair on the way down. That's how I hurt my eye. He didn't care, though, because he stood over me and smacked me in the face again, busting my nose. When he straddled me and began to try to try to take off my pants, I lost it and started to kick my legs. I tried to...to get him off of me, but...God, Taz, he was so heavy!" I said, wailing. "He just...he raped me over and over again, and there wasn't anything I could do about it. I tried to fight him off, but he was too strong, and fighting only made him angrier. He kept slapping me and choking me, until I thought I was going to die. I can't believe he did this!"

Taz sat back down and pulled me close again, letting me cry on his shoulder. "It's going to be okay, baby. I'm gonna handle this shit for you. I promise."

"Shouldn't we call the police?" I ask, knowing damn well he'll not want to involve the authorities.

"Don't worry about the police. You let me get that bitch-ass nigga. Just give me his address, and I'll handle the rest."

I pretend to hesitate at first but finally give him all the information he needs to track down Xavier and dispense a little street justice on his ass for doing me wrong.

Taz carries me upstairs into his bedroom and places me on the bed. He then walks into the bathroom and begins to run me a bath. As soon as the tub is full, he carefully removes my clothes and carries me into the bathroom, then sits me in the warm, sudsy water. It feels so good, and I lay my head back and close my eyes. I don't open them until I felt a soapy washcloth trail down my arm. I lift my body up and allow him to wash my back, then stand up and let him get my legs. When it's time to wash my private parts, I flinch, because it's pretty sore down there.

"I'm sorry," he says before rinsing me off with the sprayer from the top of the faucet. He then dries me off and wraps me up in a big, soft towel and carries me back into the bedroom, where he places me gently on the edge of the bed. He walks away, only to return moments later. I accept the t-shirt and pull it over my head. When I climb under the covers, he removes his clothes and does the same. He wraps his arms around me and pulls me as close as he possibly can and squeezes me tight. His warm body feels good against my skin, and I actually feel safe. It doesn't take long before I'm sleeping, snoring lightly.

***

When I wake up, it takes me a second to remember where I am. I look around and realize I'm in the bed alone; Taz is gone. I call his name, but receive no reply. I figure he must've stepped out. I climb out of bed and head into the bathroom to pee. I grimace when the urine finally begins to come out because it burns like hell. Cutting it off with my muscles, I try to push as little out as possible so that it won't hurt so bad, but it doesn't work. I exhale when I'm finally done, wipe myself gently, and wash my hands. Standing in front of the mirror, I just look at myself for a minute. Even though my face is bruised and my nose is sore, I still smile. I can't help it; I know Xavier's going to get what's coming to his dumb ass, and that makes me very, very happy.

Yes, I stretched the truth when I told Taz what happened, but there was no way I was going to give him all the real facts. I couldn't tell my so-called man that I caught my real man cheating, nor could I tell him I went over to Xavier's house, fucked him silly, and did all this damage to

152

my own face. I ain't no fool! The look on Xavier's face was priceless when I told him I wanted to have rough sex. His ass couldn't even keep up, so I had to take over. He was amazed when I kept yelling, "Harder! Harder!" Yeah, that shit hurt like a muthafucka, but I'm a woman on a mission. *I wonder what Taz is gonna do to him. I bet he'll kick his ass real bad, but I don't even care.* As far as I'm concerned, Xavier did this all to his own dumb ass for doing me wrong.

I rush back into the stall when I feel myself begin to get sick. I crouch down in front of the bowl, barely making it as vomit spews from my mouth. No sooner than it stops, it starts back up; this continues for a few minutes. Tears pour out of my eyes, and my stomach is killing me, but no matter what I do, I just can't stop it. *What the fuck is wrong with me?* My head is spinning, and I feel dizzy. For a moment, I wonder if I'm coming down with a stomach virus or something. If I am, I can only hope it passes fast, because I don't know how much longer I can take this. At the sink, I wash my face and brush my teeth before going back to bed. The nauseous feeling is still here, but at least I'm not throwing up anymore. It takes me a while to get comfortable in the bed, but when I do, I peacefully drift into Dream Land once again.

***

Hours later, I awake to Taz coming up the stairs and into the bedroom. The clock reads 3:24 a.m. I sit up and turn on the bedside lamp, only to see him standing in front of me with blood all over his white shirt.

Panic takes over because I think he's hurt, and I walk over to him quickly. "What happened to you?" I ask, lifting his shirt and trying to inspect the damage.

"Nothing. It ain't my blood," he says, pushing my hands away.

I look at him, confused.

"It's ya boy's blood, Brandy."

I don't say anything. Instead, I just sit on the bed, wondering what the hell happened. "Do you wanna talk about it?" I ask, praying he will.

"Yeah, after I get out of the shower."

I watch him as he strips down to his plaid Dolce & Gabbana boxers. He says nothing, as he balls his bloody clothes up in the corner and walks into the bathroom. The whole time the shower water is running, so is my mind. I can't help thinking about all types of scenarios and shit that could've happened. I'm all over the place, and I'm damn near about to go insane, because everything I'm coming up with sounds crazy. My head begins to hurt as I silently curse him for taking such a long shower. I want to know what happened, and I want to know now! When I hear the water stop, I exhale and wait patiently for him to come back into the room. Minutes later, he enters with only a towel around his waist. *I swear, if I wasn't so sore and thirsty to know what happened, I'd be ready to fuck.*

I take a seat on the edge of the bed. Xavier tells me that he and Dan went over to Xavier's house, knocked on his door, and he answered as if he didn't have a care in the world. Dan asked him if his name was Xavier, and when he replied that it was, they attacked him. They dragged him up the stairs and into the living room, where they beat and stomped him until he was unconscious. Then they trashed the house to make the whole thing seem like a burglary. Finally, they put a single bullet in his head.

At Taz's mention that Xavier is dead, I get lightheaded. I didn't expect them to kill him. A single tear rolls down my face, but I quickly wipe it away before Taz is able to see it. Even though I feel like shit, I don't want him to know. In his mind, he just did me a favor and handled a problem for me; in reality, though, he just killed a man for absolutely nothing. Xavier is dead, and it's all because of me.

"It's over, baby. He'll never hurt you again," he whispers in my ear. "No one will."

All I can do is nod my head, because there's nothing left for me to say.

"What if you get caught?" I jump up from the bed and race into the bathroom to grab one of the small garbage bags from the cabinet. I shake it open, bend over the bloody pile of clothes on the floor, and begin stuffing everything inside of it. "We gotta get rid of this shit."

"Don't worry, baby. I took care of everything," he says, rubbing my back in a circular motion, trying to calm me down. "Dan's dumb ass wanted to keep the gun, because he said it's his favorite, but other than that, we cool. They'll never trace back to us." He shrugs.

"I still want you to dump these clothes in the morning, Taz."

He nods his head to let me know he will.

I swear, Niggas are so fucking dumb. They give away way too much information about shit. Not only did he tell me he killed a man, but he even told me what gun was used. I know exactly what gun he's talking about, because every I've seen Dan, he's had it on his hip. I don't say anything, but I store all this information in the back of my mind for a later date; I never know when it might come in handy. I sit on the bed, zoned out, because it's a lot to process. Even though I never wish death on anyone, I figure it is what it is. He fucked with me and was dealt with; it's as simple as that. I kinda feel bad about it, but I'd be lying if I say I'm going to lose a bunch of sleep; truthfully, Xavier did this to himself. I'm the victim here, and if I have to make an example out of every person I run into, that's exactly what I'll do!

***

I stay at Taz's place for about a week, but he still bitches about me wanting to go home. I swear I thought this nigga would chain me to the bed, because every time I want to leave, it was a problem. I still have a few outfits over there, so it really isn't anything for me to get dressed and get ready to step out. It's the beginning of November, and it's cold as hell outside. I'm glad Taz brought my Gucci coat in with him, because I totally forgot about it. I sent him out to get the stuff I purchased for Xavier's kitchen and told him I bought it all for him. He had the biggest smile on his face when he opened all the bags. I helped him put everything away, and it looks just as good in his house—if not better—than it would have in Xavier's.

Not really feeling like dressing up, I throw on a pair of Citizens of Humanity wide-leg jeans and a plain white t-shirt. I have an appointment at the shop in less than an hour, and I can't wait until Zema works her magic on this head, because it really needs some TLC. I've been pulling it back in a ponytail for the past week, and my locks are kinking up. I slide my feet into my plaid UGGs, then lace and tie them up. Taz is gone, so I don't have to hear his mouth as I walk out the door. Looking at the clock, I realize he just might be on his way home, so I grab my coat and make my way to the elevator.

The chilly air hits me as soon as I step out the door, and I temporarily rethink going out. I push those thoughts to the back of my mind and march to my vehicle. The belt on my coat is pulled as tight as it could get it, but it still does nothing to stop the wind from chilling my body. It takes a while before the heat actually comes on, because I haven't driven it for a while, but once it does, it feels great! I finally remove my coat and slide the seatbelt across my waist. I have a little less than a half-hour before my appointment, so I put my car in gear and pull out, ready to head to Tresses.

I pull in front of the shop with minutes to spare, but I don't waste any time because it looks like the place is packed. I'll be damned if I have to wait, so I put my coat back on and hurry my ass inside. I walk up to the front desk and let the girl know I'm here for my appointment and take a seat in the waiting area. The bald-headed-ass chick in the seat beside me has a small baby in her arms. The kid can't be any older than six months, and it's not wearing anything but a sleeper. I don't see a car seat or a diaper bag, so I'm hoping like hell the bitch has a snowsuit in her purse or something; if not, she needs her ass beat. A smell assaults my nose and causes it to instantly turn up. It smells like shit, and I know it's coming from the baby. It upsets me that the bitch just sits there like she doesn't smell it, and I know damn well she has to.

Trying my best to ignore the stench, I have a look around. I can tell from all the bitches walking around that it's the first week of the month. I've never seen the place packed before, but then again, I've never been here at the beginning of the month. A few minutes later, Zema shows up, ready to take me in the back. I speak, but she barely acknowledges me; she only rolls her eyes and keeps her back to me. I assume she's spoken with her bestie, Osha, and now she's got an attitude, but I really don't give a damn. As long as she does my shit right, she ain't gotta say two words to me. I follow behind her and envision myself drop-kicking her right in the back. I laugh to myself, causing her to turn around to face me. I give her a look that says, *"Try me, bitch,"* and her scared ass turns back around quickly.

I remove my coat and hang it next to her work station, then take a seat in the chair. She drapes the cape around my body, secures it around my neck, and begins at the base of my scalp. It takes her about fifteen minutes to apply the relaxer to my new growth and smooth it out. Our next destination is the shampoo bowl, where she leans me back, sets the water temperature, and begins to wash my hair thoroughly, removing all traces of relaxer from my hair. The scalp massage relaxes my body and allows my mind to go free. When I'm back in the chair, she pins my hair up and begins to cut my ends evenly. A little wrapping lotion and a molded wrap later, she moves me over to the dryer, where she leaves me alone with my thoughts.

My mind is heavy, because I'm trying to figure out what to do next. Just a month ago, I had it all figured out, and now I'm so lost I don't know what to do. I still want to go to South Carolina, but I don't know if I can be happy there. *Are thoughts of the fun Xavier and I had going to haunt me daily? How do I go from knowing exactly what I'm doing to not knowing a damn thing? That's what I wanna know, and the sooner I find the answers, the better off I'll be.* Just thinking about Myrtle Beach brings a slight smile to my face. I had so much fun there, but as quickly as those happy memories come, they're gone again; I remember all the lies Xavier told me while we were there, all the false hope I was sold, and how I felt when I found out I'd been deceived. I know I said it before, but I will never again allow anyone to get that close to me. I'm over love and all the pain associated with it.

An hour later, Zema comes over and removes the dryer hood from my head. She pokes my hair with her fingers, trying to make sure it's dry. She then turns the dryer off and sends me over to the chair. I sit down and wait patiently as she goes into her office and does whatever it is that she needs to do. Five minutes later, she's back and starts running the comb in a circular motion around my head. Little by little, my hair begins to fall and take the shape of a wrap. Most people would be done at this point, but I don't care how straight the wrap makes my hair; I still want some heat to it. She rubs serum between her hands and applies it evenly throughout my hair to protect it from the hot temperature. Her last and final step is to flat-iron each piece of my hair to give me a bone-straight look. After she finishes the last piece, she spins the chair around so I can face the mirror and have a look at her handiwork.

As always, I'm impressed. I reach into my bag and pull out her fee, then place it in her hand. She looks down at it, huffs, and shoves it into her cape pocket. I guess she feels some kind of way because I didn't give her ass a tip this time. *Oh fuckin' well! If she'd have acted like she had some damn sense, I might have, but she didn't, so fuck her!* I stand up to get a better look at my hair but turn around when I hear commotion near the front door.

"Where that ho at?"

I figure there are probably some hood-rats up there beefing in the front, so I turn back around and finish checking out my do.

"What was all that shit you was talking on the phone?" asks a voice directly behind me.

I spin around quickly, wearing a smirk on my face. "Why hello to you too."

Standing in front of me is Osha, with her little sister Asha off to the side, both of them dressed in t-shirts, jeans, and Timberlands, with their hair pulled back in ponytails. Clearly, they're ready for ass-whooping. I can't do anything but laugh at the thought. By now everybody in the shop has gathered around to see what's about to go down, from the bitches in the waiting room to the ones with bags on their heads who were sitting under the dryer. I know each of them secretly hopes I'll get my ass handed to me since I waltz into the shop like I'm the shit all the time, but I can't help that I'm a bad bitch and every one of these hoes wishes she could be me.

"Don't try to be funny now, bitch. Say all that smart shit you was talking on the phone," Osha challenges.

I keep my voice calm because I want the bitch to know she doesn't faze me at all.

"Which part you talking about? The part when I called you a fucking bum, or the part about your baby-daddy being in love with me and fucking me silly every night?"

Ooh-ing and ah-ing erupts through the shop, and everyone looks shocked.

Osha reaches back and clocks me right in the face. It stuns me for a minute, and I can't believe the bitch actually had the audacity to hit me, especially with a weak-ass jab like that. It pisses me off, so I ball my fist up and hit her with a

159

solid shot to the eye. Her head jerks back, and she stumbles, but she doesn't fall. We trade blows back and forth, and while she gets a few licks in, they're weak as hell. I swear, the bitch can't fight worth a damn! She told me before that she never got in fights when she was younger, and now I can see that she wasn't lying.

Since there's no way in hell that she can win this fight, she rushes me and goes for my hair. I jump out of the way, and she crashes into the vanity, knocking most of Zema's shit to the floor. The thunderous sound of all the supplies and rollers and bottles falling to the floor causes everyone to jump, including me. Since Osha's back is to me, I use that to my advantage. I reach out and wrap my hand around her ponytail. She yells when I sling her little bony ass across the floor with all my might. Her body resembles a kid sliding down a hill, the way she helplessly glides across the floor. When she finally stops, she just lies there for a while, not moving. Seconds later, she tries to get up. I run over and kick her roughly in the stomach, causing her to fall back to the floor in pain.

"You ain't talking shit no more, are you?" I deliver another kick to her midsection.

Somebody jumps on my back and begins to pull the shit out of my hair.

"Ah!" I scream as I feel my hair being pulled from the roots.

"Get the fuck off my sister, bitch!" Asha yells, still grabbing my hair and holding on for dear life.

Ain't this about a bitch? I'm tripping because I didn't even notice her ass come near me. Those hoes got one up on me because Asha shocked the hell out of me. I begin spinning around in a circle, trying to shake her off, but her little ass is holding on with a death grip. She's not hitting me at all, just riding my fucking back like a cowgirl, using my hair as reins. Seeing no other way to get her off me, I back up and ram myself up against another one of the work stations

160

repeatedly. I finally feel her grip loosen, but that doesn't stop me from slamming her up against it once more just because. This causes the back of her head to collide with the mirror, shattering it and sending pieces of glass flying everywhere.

Asha leaps off of the table and squares up with me, as if she's really ready to get it in. I can see the fear in her eyes, and I know she's terrified of the ass-whooping I'm about to deliver. I glance to my right and catch a glimpse of Zema; she has a grin on her face, as if she's enjoying this shit. I make a mental note to whoop her ass at a later date, because I know she's the one who called the hoes up here in the first place. Asha takes the first swing, a weak-ass haymaker that I easily block. I block another attempt to hit me; I'm tired of playing with this little ho, so I hit her with a three-piece combo that puts her on her ass. She slips and slides on the broken glass, trying to get up, but she gives up soon after and just lies there.

I get a little too cocky, just sitting there and watching her struggle to get up, because I totally forgot all about Osha. She quickly makes her presence known by hitting me in the back of the head with a wire magazine rack she must've picked up from one of the work stations. I stumble forward and reach for the back of my head. Bright red blood spills between my fingers and onto the floor. I turn to face her, and all I see is red.

I'm gonna kill this ho, 'cause she done fucked up now. Rushing toward her, I hit her like a football player. We slide across the floor with me on top of her. Osha is too little, and she can't do anything to stop me as I climb on top of her and pin her down with my legs. Taking her hair in my hands, I lift her head and slam it into the floor over and over again. I want her head to bleed just like mine.

She screams and begs for someone to help her, but nobody moves. I continue to pound her head into the floor until I start to feel my fingers being soaked. When this happens, I ball up my fist and strike her constantly in her face. She turns her head from side to side in an attempt to stop my hits, but I keep on tagging her ass. Every hit lands on its intended target, and I rain blows down all over her face. Her nose is busted, and blood is leaking from her mouth.

"You fucking bitch! I told you not to fuck with me! I'll fucking kill you! Do you hear me?"

Osha's eye's are almost swollen shut, and blood continues spilling out of her nose and mouth.

I don't stop; truthfully, I don't give a fuck if the bitch bleeds to death. Someone screams, but I try not to hear anything going on around me, because I'm on a mission. Suddenly, a dull, throbbing pain starts in my side. I instinctively stop hitting Osha and grab the spot where I feel the pain. I close my eyes when I feel something sticking out of my side. I don't want to open my eyes and look; because I'm sure I've been stabbed. Finally, I force myself to look down in horror and see the handle of what looks to be a big-ass kitchen knife sticking out of my body. The pain hits me like a ton of bricks; it's excruciating! It burns, and I can't scream because it's so severe. When I look up, my eyes meet Asha's, and she looks terrified. Still, I'm sure she can't feel as afraid as I am right now.

I panic and pull the knife out, which causes blood to spew out of my open wound, down my body, and all over the floor. Everyone begins to freak out, and I can hear people on their phones, speaking to the 911 operators. Rolling off Osha, I clutch my side and land on the floor. The pain is bad, but it's burning more than anything. I'm getting dizzy, and it's hard for me to focus. I'm lying in the middle of the floor, bleeding profusely, yet no one even attempts to try to help. Seconds pass, and my body begins to start shaking. I can't stop, and I'm getting cold. Still holding the spot with my hands, I try to stop the blood from coming out. It doesn't help because I can still feel it seeping slowly through my fingers.

"I'm going to jail! Oh my God, I'm going to jail!" I hear Asha scream.

My vision blurs, but from the corner of my eye, I can see Osha slowly picking herself off the floor. She staggers over toward me, lifts her leg, and delivers a powerful kick to my head.

"I told you not to fuck with me, bitch! I hope you die right here on this floor like the dog you are." She then hocks up a bunch of phlegm and spits it directly into my face.

I can't do anything but watch helplessly as she stumbles over to a hysterical Asha and embraces her. In the distance, I hear sirens; it sounds like they will be here in a matter of minutes. This causes Osha to walk Asha to the door as quickly as possible, so that they won't be there when the police arrive; not a soul tries to prevent them from leaving. My body begins to weaken, and I feel myself losing consciousness.

This is it. This is how I'm gonna die. All those years of begging and pleading to be put out of my misery and this is how I'm going to leave this Earth? I've survived being beaten, mistreated, and abused, but I'm gonna lose my life to a scary bitch with a knife? I don't know whether to laugh or cry. I fix my gaze on the knife on the floor, its blade still covered with my blood; that's the last thing I see before before I surrender to a feeling of sleepiness.

CHAPTER FOURTEEN

*I*t's been a few months since I've been away from
Pitch, and I'm shocked that he hasn't found me yet.
*Maybe I've managed to stay off his radar, or maybe he just
gave up. Either way, I'm tired of looking over my shoulder
every second of the day. Sometimes I sit in my classroom and
get a chill just thinking about what he'll do if he ever catches
up to me. It scares me half to death, because I know the kind
of man he is, and I know he'll kill me if he gets a hold of me
again. What I don't understand is why he can't just let me go
and allow me to be free. What have I done to deserve the
pain he's caused me in the short amount of time that he's
been in my life? I don't think I'll ever get the answer to that
question.*

*All I want is a normal life. Is that too much to ask for? I
guess it is, considering that I can't seem to find happiness
anywhere. Then again, Roger does make me happy—happier
than I've ever been in my entire life. Not only does he
provide for me financially, but he also spends as much time
as he can with me, even though he's a busy man. I try not to
complain because I know what he does, and I also know if he
could, he'd spend every hour of his day with me. It gets
boring here sometimes, though, because I never have
anything to do.*

*Take today, for instance. It's Friday, and Roger's out of
town, handling business. I can't seem to sit still. I wanna go
out, but I don't have anywhere to go because I don't have*

any friends. There is this chick I know from Life Skills, Zema, but she seems too clingy for my taste. She just wants to sit up under me, and that shit is boring. To makes matters worse, all she wants to talk about is the shop her daddy is supposedly opening for her once she gets her diploma and finishes the cosmetology classes she's in. I don't believe a thing she says, but I'm not going to be the one to crush her poor little dreams, so I just grin and bear it; even though I just really want to tell her to shut the fuck up. It's sad how hard she tries to be my friend, even though I barely even speak to her when I enter the classroom.

As the day moves on, I realize there's nothing for me to do but to sit in the house and think. Trixie has been on my mind heavy lately and I can't shake the feeling that something has happened to her. I might be just overreacting, but I think he's done something to her because of my absence; I just can't prove it. I had a dream the other night about her, and it felt so real. It seemed like I could have reached out and touched her. In the dream, I was lying in my bed, and she walked through the door dressed in a white gown. Her face was clear of all the cuts and bruises from Pitch, and she looked as beautiful as she did the first day I met her. She glided over toward me and just stood there. I tried to sit up in the bed, but something prevented me from doing so, as if something was holding me down.

"Everything is going to be all right, Baby Doll. I've made sure of it."

I tried to open my mouth and ask her what she meant, but I was unable to.

She must have read my mind, because she said, "I know I played my part in what Pitch did to you, and I also know I can never apologize enough. I've traded my life for yours, and I did it so you can have a chance at a better one. You are the daughter I was never able to have, and I will always love you, Baby Doll."

Golden tears slid down her face and pooled at the floor

around her feet. I continued to lie in the bed, crying, because there was nothing else I could do. I wanted to get up and hug her and tell her it's all right; to let her know that I forgave her a long time ago and that I'll always love her; to thank her for always being there when I needed her, even when Pitch forbade her. She bent down and kissed me lightly on the forehead, and, just like that, she was gone. Since that night, that dream has been heavy on my mind because I don't understand what she was trying to tell me. I know it was more than a dream; it seemed to real to not mean anything at all.

I have an idea, so I jump off the couch and quickly race into my bedroom. I grab some black leggings and a black wife-beater, jump into them both, then slide my feet into a pair of charcoal UGGs. After tying the belt of the Burberry leather trench coat, I placed the matching hat on my ponytailed head. Lastly I slide my Jackie-O glasses over my eyes, grab my car keys, and leave, with my bag in hand. It takes me twenty minutes or so to get my destination, and once I get there, I realize that it still looks exactly the same. There are about fifteen girls out, but I can't tell by the look of them that it's only thirty degrees outside. I pull up in front of the building, and one of the girls instantly walks over to me as if I'm a trick.

"What you want?" asks the young chick, who can't be older than seventeen.

"I'm looking for Trixie," I say to her, hoping like hell she doesn't remember who I am.

"Who?" she asks, causing me to repeat myself. "Oh, Trixie. What you looking for her for? She's dead," she blurts out nonchalantly.

"What!?" I yell.

Like she's scared, she backs away from my car.

I don't want her to get away, so I ask her to get in.

She doesn't budge at first, until I flash her the wad of cash in my hand. After one glimpse of it, she climbs into my *car, and I toss the money in her lap, then drive off. There must be $1,000 in that knot, and I tell her she can have all of it if she'll just tell me what I want to know about Trixie. The greedy look in her eyes tells me she's down, even before she begins to start talking. It takes her all of five minutes to tell me what happened not too long ago.*

Supposedly, Pitch started beating Trixie up because one of his hoes young ran away, and she wouldn't tell him where the girl was. One day, Trixie got tired of being his punching bag, so she walked into his bedroom at his house and put a bullet in his head. The next to get it was his new ho, the video chick who was asleep beside him. Finally, she turned the gun on herself and ended her life.

I'm in total shock and can't do anything but sit there, stunned. She goes on to tell me that since Pitch has been gone, all the hoes have been reporting to John, the new man in charge. I'm about to ask her who the hell John is, but then I remember that he's the dark-skinned guy from the store, Pitch's driver, who broke my finger that day. After the girl's done telling me everything she knows, she asks me if I'm related to Trixie, because no one else has come around asking about her. I don't say anything and only pull up to the same spot I picked her up from. I unlock the door and signal for her to get out. She thanks me for my business and steps out of my warm car and into the cold weather, leaving me alone again. No sooner than I pull away, the tears start to spill out of my eyes and under my glasses; my heart is hurt. I finally know what that dream meant. Trixie traded her life for mine, and now that I know I'm finally free from Pitch, I have to make sure she didn't die for nothing.

***

A beeping sound wakes me from my sleep. I open my eyes, but my vision is blurry, and it takes me a minute to focus. Panicking, I try to sit up, but a sharp pain shoots through my body and causes me to lie back down. It's like déjà vu, because this same thing happened only a few months ago. I can tell I'm in Metro again, because the hospital room looks exactly as it did the last time I was here. That time, it was for being shot, but now I'm here, courtesy of Asha and her stupid knife. My mind goes back to the pain I felt lying on the floor, thinking I was going to die.

A middle-aged woman in Mickey Mouse scrubs walks in. Her hair is pulled back in a tight ponytail, and she greets me cheerfully. "Good morning!" she says with a bright smile on her face.

I don't say anything.

"Your poor boyfriend is gonna be so happy. He's been here day in and day out, checking on you."

I still don't say anything and just watch her.

She walks around my bed and begins jotting down information on the clipboard in her hand. Next, she takes my vitals and looks at my bandages, then heads out of the room.

"Excuse me!" I call out to her before she can hit the corner.

"Yes?"

"How long have I been in here?"

She flips a few pieces of paper on the clipboard and reviews the information on the chart. "You've been with us for a week, darlin'"

"Really? A whole week? Well, uh…do you know if I'm gonna be okay?"

"Yes, you're gonna be fine. How about I go get your doctor so he can explain everything to you?"

"Thank you."

A few minutes later, a white, older man enters my room. He's dressed neatly in a white dress shirt, a black and white striped tie, black slacks and black leather loafers. The lab jacket he's wearing looks to be brand new and his salt-and-pepper hair is mostly combed to the back, with just a small amount to the side. He gives me a warm smile, but I can tell by the dark bags under his eyes that he's tired.

"How are you today, Ms. Wilson?"

"I'm fine. Just wondering when I'll be able to go home."

"A few more days. You lost quite a bit of blood, requiring a transfusion."

"What!?" I screamed, sitting up and causing myself a great deal of pain. *A fuckin' blood transfusion? I'ma kill those hoes!*

"Don't worry. Everything is going to be fine. You'll have a small scar on your side from the wound, but everything else will heal properly."

I begin to relax, but his next words cause me to almost hyperventilate.

"I'm sorry, but we couldn't save the baby," he says with sadness in his eyes.

"What did you say? I was...pregnant?" I ask, unable to believe it.

"Yes. Two and a half months, to be exact."

He continues to talk, but I can't hear shit else. He eventually gets the picture and excuses himself, because when I finally come back to reality, I'm the only person in the room. *How could I have been pregnant? I thought I couldn't have any children after that crooked-ass doctor gave me that illegal abortion when I was a kid.* I lift my hands to wipe my tears away, and when I bring them down, they involuntarily land on my stomach. My mind begins to race as I attempt to make sense of it all. *That explains why I've been throwing up. It wasn't a stomach virus or some flu. It was my...baby.* I count back two and a half months and realize I must have gotten pregnant during my time with Xavier in Myrtle Beach.

Before I break down and cry, the hospital phone rings. I clench my teeth together, trying to bear the pain, and reach over and pick up the phone.

"Hello?"

"Hey, baby! The nurse called me and said you're finally awake," Taz says.

"Hey, Taz," I reply in a dry voice.

"Damn. What's wrong with you?"

"What's wrong with me?"

"Yeah."

"What's wrong with me? The fact that you're so called baby-mama and her bum-ass sister jumped me at Zema's shop…or, how about the fact that those hoes stabbed me in the side and left me bleeding on that floor? That's what the hell is wrong with me, Taz!"

"Baby, listen—"

"Naw, Taz, *you* listen! I'm not about to be disrespected by any bitch and for damn sure not Osha's sorry ass, so yo' ass betta tighten yo' shit up. I lost my fucking baby fighting them messy-ass hoes! Tell me what you're gonna do about it!" Tears are sliding down my face. I attempt to calm down, though, because every time I raise my voice, my side throbs.

"I already went over to her cousin's house and beat her ass, so you don't have to worry about her or Asha anymore. Wait a minute…did you say you lost a baby? You were pregnant, Brandy?" he asks after he finally catches on.

"Yes. Two and a half months." I sob, wiping away tears with the back of my hand.

"Damn, baby. I'm so sorry." There's a small amount of silence on the line. "I should've deaded that ho for killing my baby."

I don't say anything because I want him to think the baby was his. I honestly can't tell him it belonged to the guy he murdered; the timing wouldn't even add up.

"I been cut that ho off, and her sister too, baby. I told her she ain't getting shit from me, and if she needs help taking care of her kids, she betta find they daddy and make that nigga pay. Asha's ass better find a way to foot her own bill for college, because this well has run dry! I promise I ain't giving neither of those bitches bitch another dime, and that's on my unborn seed. That ho is dead to me."

"Taz, how did you know I was in the hospital?" I ask, realizing I don't have him listed as an emergency contact or anything like that.

"Osha called me to brag that she murked my bitch. I didn't know what the hell she was talking about until she gave me the rundown about what happened at the shop. She said Zema called her and told her you were there, so she and Asha came up to fight you. After I heard that you'd been stabbed, I called a few hospitals until I located you. While you were in surgery, I called Dan and had him handle Zema for running her fuckin' mouth, and I headed over Osha's cousin's house to handle mine."

"Did she call the police on you?"

He chuckles. "Hell naw! That ho know better than that. If she'da called the cops, I woulda had her whole family wiped out, and she didn't want that. She just took her ass-whooping like a woman."

I smile when I think about her crying and begging for him to stop hitting her.

"Baby, I ain't no woman-beater, but I tried to break her li'l bony ass in half."

I can't stop myself from giggling out loud, because it sounds exactly like something I would have said. My side begins to sting, and I know I'm doing too much yelling and laughing. "I gotta go, Taz. My side is hurting, and I have a headache."

"Okay. I'm on my way up there now. You need me to bring you anything? Are you hungry?"

"No, I'll be okay."

"All right. I'll be up there in a few."

"Okay."

"Oh, and Brandy…"

"Yes?"

"I just wanna let you know I love you, girl. Don't worry. We'll get past all this."

I don't say anything in return and only smile because he sounds so genuine.

"I barely left your side the whole time you've been there."

"I know. The nurse told me. Thanks, Taz. I'll see you when you get here," I reply.

After placing the phone back in its cradle, I sit back and close my eyes. My thoughts drift to visions of motherhood, and before I know it, I'm wailing like a baby. I cry so hard that my shoulders start shaking. It causes my side to ache, but I can't do anything to stop it; it's as if something has taken control of my body. It hurts so bad, but it also feels good to cleanse my soul. I've been keeping so much stuff locked up in my head, and now's the time to let it all come out.

When I hear a noise, I open my eyes in time to see Taz round the corner and enter my room. In one hand is a glass vase, filled with bouquet of beautiful roses, lilies, and Gerbera daisies. The other hand holds a medium-sized brown teddy bear dressed in a lab jacket, with a little medical bag in his hand. Tied tightly around his little paw are a variety of "Get Well Soon" balloons.

His smile fades quickly when he realizes I've been crying. Before I know it, the gifts are placed at the foot of the bed, and he's at my side, holding me as best as he can without hurting me. I slide over to give him enough room to share the bed, as the tears continue to fall. As he holds me, he gently stokes my head with his hand and tells me everything is going to be all right. I attempt to speak, but nothing comes out except for gibberish. The back of my head is hurting so bad that it feels as if it might explode at any given moment, and the crying doesn't make it any better. I don't know how long I lie in his arms crying, but I wake up a while later, with him watching TV beside me.

"Are you feeling better?" he asks.

"A little bit. I still have a headache though."

"Do you want me to call you nurse so she can give you something?"

I nod my head.

He stands up and walks out of the room, heading to the nurses' station.

A few minutes later, Taz reappears with a tall white nurse right behind him. I can't help staring at her in awe, because she truly resembles a Barbie doll. Her blonde hair is pulled back off her pretty face, held together by a small rubber band. She has short bangs that stop just above her slanted blue eyes. Her colorful Baby Phat scrub top fits snugly on her breasts but is loose around her waist and hangs over black pants. They are loose as well, but she has a pretty nice shape for a white girl. She's holding a clipboard in her hand and walks over to the machine to check my vitals before jotting down a few notes. A couple seconds pass before she looks up at me with a warm smile.

"I'm Nurse Simone, and I hear you have a headache."

I don't reply and just nod to let her know it's true.

"Do you want me to get you some Tylenol, or do you think you need something stronger?"

"Tylenol doesn't anything for me. I usually take Imitrex for my migraines, but I ran out not too long ago."

"That's fine. I'll get you something for your IV and make sure you get a fresh prescription for it before you leave," she tells me with another smile. Before she walks out the door, she informs me that it will take her a couple minutes, but she'll be back as soon as she can.

Taz pulls the chair closer to the bed and takes a seat. No words exit his lips. He simply grabs hold of my hand, letting me know he's here for me.

Five minutes pass before Nurse Simone returns with a syringe and a small bottle of clear fluid in her hand. She informs me that it's morphine and that my migraine should be gone in a little while.

"If the pain doesn't subside, page me, and we'll see what

else we can do." After I thank her, she quickly exits the room.

No sooner than she leaves, Taz's phone rings, and he steps out to take the call. When he comes back, he tells me he has to leave, but he'll be back shortly. We say our goodbyes, and he's gone.

About a half-hour later, my headache finally starts to go away; I'm glad about that, because it was killing me. I pick up the remote and flip through the channels, but when I find nothing interesting, I turn it off. Glancing over at the small table beside my bed and see a small black cord hanging from the inside of it. I reach over and open it and see that it's a phone charger, with my cell phone attached. I smile, realizing Taz must have brought it to make sure I'd have a phone. I lean over to get it and wince as the pain shoots through my side. It takes me a while to catch my breath, but when I finally do, I see that my phone is powered on, but the ringer is turned off. The home screen shows that I have fifteen missed calls, all from a long-distance number I don't recognize.

The small envelope in the notification bar lets me know I have a voicemail, so I slide it down and prepare to listen to my messages. Before my phone connects, it begins to ring in my hand with a call from that same unfamiliar long-distance number. I have no clue who it is, but I figure they must want something if they've called sixteen times.

"Hello?" I speak into the receiver after it connects.

"Hi. May I speak to Brandy please?" a proper voice asks.

"This is she," I reply hesitantly.

"You don't know me, but my name is Andrea. I'm Xavier sister."

My heart drops to the pit of my stomach. *How did she get my number?*

CHAPTER FIFTEEN

"**H**i, Andrea. How can I help you?" I ask, wondering why she's calling me in the first place and nervous as hell to find out.

"Well, let me first start off by saying I got your number from Xavier's phone after we cleaned up his house after the, uh...funeral."

I can tell she's trying to stop herself from crying. "It's okay. Take your time. I'm listening," I reassure her, praying like hell she doesn't know anything about *my* involvement. The story she tells me next makes my whole world come crashing down, bringing on tears I didn't even realize I still had in me.

She tells me that the last time she saw Xavier was the day he was murdered. "He flew me and our parents to Ohio because he had some really good news, and he wanted to tell us in person. When we got there, we dropped our luggage off at the hotel, then went to have dinner at The Cheesecake Factory."

As soon as she mentions that, I get lightheaded all over again, but I force myself to listen to the rest of her story.

"While we were there, Xavier kept going on and on about a woman named Brandy and how he'd fallen in love with her."

I can hear the smile in her voice when she tells me how happy and full of life he seemed because of that new woman—because of me.

"During dinner, his cell phone rang, and he excused himself from the table but came back shortly with a huge grin on his face. We joked about this Brandy having his nose wide open, but then he pulled out a small velvet box with a beautiful diamond ring inside. I was so excited when I saw the ring that I picked it up and slipped it on my finger and started screaming. I gave him a hug and told him how happy I was for him and that I couldn't wait to meet the woman who captured my big brother's heart."

Tears stream down my face as she tells the story; unbeknownst to her, I was there, and I saw the whole thing and mistook it for something else. Instead of his sister, I assumed she was another woman and that he was cheating on me, proposing to someone else.

"Before he dropped us back off, we all made plans to have dinner the following day, where he would propose to her." she continues. "When neither of us received a call, I caught a cab to the address that he gave me the day before and found him…found him." No longer able to hold it in, she burst out crying. "I was the one who found him dead."

I join in and cry with her, when I remember how he told me not to make plans the next day. He told me that he wanted to tell me something and he would do it over dinner. Of course I paid him no mind, because I was to upset about what I assumed I saw that the restaurant earlier that day. I can't even breathe as she goes on about how much he loved me and how he planned to move to South Carolina with me the following year, after he made me his wife. I can't believe I'm hearing this. *All this time, I thought his promises were nothing but bullshit!*

Unable to take anymore, I allow the phone to slip out of my hand and land on my lap. I hear Andrea calling my name, but I can't reply because I'm stuck in a state of shock. I start to scream, a high-pitched scream that comes from the bottom of my belly. It hurt my stitches, but I don't care and just keep on screaming and crying hysterically. A few nurses rush into my room, but even they can't get me to calm down. They alert my doctor, who comes in and tries to ask me what's wrong. I say nothing, just I continue to wail. The looks on their faces lets me know they think I've lost it, and they're right with that diagnosis.

Nurse Simone rushes into the room with a syringe in her hand and inserts it into my IV; whatever it is, I instantly get drowsy and pass out.

***

I open my eyes, and it takes me a minute to focus. I'm at home, lying in my own bed. Instinctively, I reach out and touch my side, but there are no stitches. My face is moist from fresh tears, but I don't mind. I'm just happy that it was all a bad dream. I guess instead of dreaming of Pitch day in and day out, my mind decided to play tricks on me and give me something more in the present.

A noise startles me, causing me to get out of bed and walk slowly into the living room, heading toward the kitchen. Once I get close enough, I can see a muscular frame standing at the stove, cooking breakfast, and all I can do is smile. I tiptoe over toward Xavier, place my hands around his waist, and hug him tight. The smell of his cologne and the softness of his skin captivate me and instantly makes my pussy wet; I love this man so much.

"Good morning, baby," I say.

He doesn't reply. Instead, he continues to do what he's doing at the stove, without even acknowledging me in any way.

I remove my hands from around his waist and tap him on the shoulder, but he still doesn't turn around and just keeps cooking. I figure he must pretty busy to ignore me, so I step away and take a seat at the island to wait for him to finish. Minutes pass and still nothing; he doesn't even turn around. He just continues that same movement, almost mechanical.

"Xavier!" I yell, but he doesn't answer. "Why are you ignoring me?" I ask, but he still doesn't move. "Did I do something to you?" I continue to try to get him to say something...hell anything! When he finally turns around, I nearly fall out of the chair.

"Yeah, bitch. You got me killed!" He roars. His face is badly bruised, and it looks as if his eyeball is hanging out of its socket. There's a bullet hole in the middle of his head, with dried blood surrounding it.

I scream, jump up from the chair, and take off running back into my room. Once I make it inside, I close and lock the door, before falling to the floor and crying. What the hell is going on? The door rams into my back when he kicks it and makes a loud sound that scares me so badly that I piss myself. I run over to my bed and try to drag it across the room, but the muthafucka is way too heavy to move by myself. Since that's not going to work, I knock over my chest; it lands right in front of the door, blocking it. I figure I'm safe and that he'll just go away, but he continues to beat on the door. A small hole forms, and with each hit and kick, it begins to get bigger and bigger. I can see his face, and the way he's looking at me creeps me the fuck out.

"Bitch, I'm gonna kill you! Why did you do this to me? All I did was love you, and this is how you repay me? You get me fucking killed?" He asks question after question.

All I can do is say I'm sorry over and over, but he's not trying to hear it, and he's almost inside the room.

I dash into the bathroom and lock the door behind me. There's nowhere for me to go, and if I try to take the window, I'll be dead anyway. I step into the shower, close the curtain, and slide to the floor, where I hunch in the corner. I squeeze my eyes shut. My heart is beating at a mile a minute and I swear it can be heard from the other side of the door. Seconds go by, and in an instant, I open my eyes because I don't hear anything. There's an eerie silence, and I strain my ears to hear something, to hear anything. I close my eyes again, but this time I say a silent prayer that God will get me through this. I sit on the floor for a couple seconds before I open my eyes and bring myself into a standing position. I slowly reach out and grab the edge of the shower curtain, holding my breath as I pull it back.

Before I know what's going on, Xavier grabs hold of my arm and begins to pull me closer to him. I try with all my might to pull myself back, but he just won't let go. Screaming, I beg him to let me loose and tell him how sorry I am, but he won't let up. Once he has me close enough, he grabs my neck and pulls me even closer, till I'm only inches away from his face—a face that suddenly looks normal.

"Why, Brandy?" he asks in a shaky voice, now calm.

"Why what?" I reply, knowing damn well what's he's asking.

He, in turn, applies more pressure on my neck. "Why did you get me killed when all I did was love you?"

"I'm sorry, Xavier. I didn't mean for it to happen," I say, weeping. "I only wanted him to rough you up, to hurt you in some way, but I didn't think he'd kill you. I loved you also, but when I saw you with that girl, I lost it. I thought you were proposing to her at the restaurant, and I wanted you to feel as much pain as I did. You have to believe me when I say I never wanted you dead." I ramble.

He just stares at me and doesn't say anything at all. The look on his face shows hurt and anger at the same time. "I loved you with everything I had, and you repaid me by getting me killed over some jealously shit. All you had to do was ask me about it, stand up and say something, and this could've all be resolved. I lost my life over a fucking misunderstanding?"

"I'm sorry, Xavier, and I'd do anything to have you back in my life. I-I wanted to grow old with you and raise a family, like we talked about."

"It's too late for that, Brandy, because I'm gone, and you're the cause. That's something you'll have to live with for the rest of your life." He releases his hold on my neck.

I fall to the floor, gasping for air. "I-I'm sorry," I stutter as he turns and walks out the bathroom door.

As he rounds the corner, he turns to me. "Our daughter is living in heaven with me. Her name is Brianna, and she's beautiful, Brandy. She knows you're the reason behind her losing her life as well, but she still loves you the same. You have a nice life, and I pray you'll change your ways because you don't have long to make it right."

I don't get a chance to say anything back, because he's gone in a flash.

***

My eyes shoot open at the sound of the beeping monitor once again. *These damn dreams are going to be the death of me.* I guess the doctor must have sedated me after my session of screaming and acting a damn fool, because my head feels groggy, and I'm still a bit shocked by my dream. *What did Xavier mean when he said I don't have long to make it right? Was he trying to tell me I'm gonna die to, or was he just trying to scare me?* Whatever he meant, it freaked me the fuck out, and I know I'm going to drive myself crazy thinking about it. Painfully, I pull myself into a sitting position and place my face in my hands. There's so much on my mind, and it's really hard to process it all. In the past two weeks, I've lost everything that was important to me. I've even almost lost my life. Truthfully, though, I know it's my own fault. The things I've done have led up to this moment, and now I regret it all.

I'm responsible for the death of a man who loved me unconditionally, the man I loved more than any I've ever known. Xavier brought out emotions in me that I didn't even believe were possible anymore. I opened up and told him all about me and my past, and he never once judged me. He was there for me through thick and thin. Even though I thought it wasn't possible, we would've had a daughter, Brianna. I smile when I think about the three of us together. I picture him being the best daddy in the world, treating his daughter like the princess she'd be. Xavier was a wonderful man, *my* wonderful man. He was my future husband, the father of my child, and I got him murdered over jealousy and payback, a bunch of unnecessary shit!

My heart hurts tremendously, but there's nothing I can do about it. Even if I could, I think I would stop it, becaue I deserve this heartache. *This shit is all my fault! All I had to do was ask him, give him a chance to explain his side of the story. I know I wouldn't have believed the shit he would have told me, but after he called his family and proved it, everything would have been okay. But no. Instead, I flew off the loose end and formed a nasty plan in my head that ultimately got him killed by a nigga I don't give two shits about.*

"Taz," I say out loud to myself, "you're responsible for this shit also, and trust me when I tell you that you ain't getting off easy either, nigga."

Just as I finish my sentence, Taz walks in.

"Speak of the devil."

"You must have been thinking about me." He grins.

"Sure was."

"What were you thinkin' about, baby?" He walks over to me and kisses me softly on the cheek. He doesn't notice the facial expression I'm making; otherwise, he'd back the fuck up out of my face.

"Nothing. I'll tell you later," is the only answer he gets out of me, because for the rest of his visit, I'm plotting my payback.

***

Cachet

After staying the hospital for another week, I'm finally discharged and allowed to go home. I'm the happiest muthafucka on the planet, because that hospital is no place for me, and I'm more than ready to go. Taz had my car towed from the shop to his house, so I have to go past there to pick it up before I can head home. We ride in silence, which shouldn't have come as a shocker to him because I've barely said two words to him since I found out about Xavier. As I climb out of his truck, he asks if I want to just stay at his house, but I quickly refuse; I don't feel like being bothered with his ass now. He looks disappointed, but I really don't give a fuck. Before he pulls off, he tells me to call him later. I don't reply and just get in my own vehicle and head home. It takes about fifteen minutes to get there, and I smile as I pull into the parking garage. *Ah! Home sweet home.*

Being inside my apartment feels strange at first, because I haven't been here in three weeks, but I get used to it in no time. My side is still a little sore, but that doesn't stop me from cleaning my shit from top to bottom. I do all my laundry and fold it, then put it in its place. I go in the kitchen and clean out the refrigerator and the top of the stove before sweeping and mopping the floor. Every room is vacuumed and tidied up, even though everything was already in place when I got here. Finally, I head into the bathroom and clean the tub, shower, and the sink. When I'm done with that, I sweep and mop the floor, then go into my room and change the sheets on my bed, even though they're still fresh. After I'm done with everything, I walk around my whole house and light a candle in each room. The smell of vanilla quickly spreads throughout the house, and I make my way into the kitchen to fix something to eat.

I have a taste for something quick, but I really don't feel like cooking. Plus, I already threw everything out after being gone for three weeks. I pick up my phone and call the Chinese place down the street and order a pepper steak meal. The guy on the phone tells me it will be about twenty minutes, so I while I wait, I head into the bathroom to run some bathwater. I pour a capful of bath beads under the stream and light each of the candles surrounding the tub. Next, I pull out my nightgown drawer and find something to put on. I finally settle on a Victoria's Secret long-sleeved flannel slip and lay it out on my bed beside a pair of cotton boy shorts. The doorbell rings, and before I head over to answer it, I reach into my purse to grab my wallet so I can pay for my food. My phone lights up with a call from Taz, but I don't even bother to answer it.

Sitting at the island in my kitchen, deep in thought, I eat my food. I still can't believe everything that's happened in these past few weeks. I don't really have much of any appetite, so it takes me no time to get full. I play with my pepper steak and rice for a minute, not really eating much. Once I convinced that I'm done for good, I wrap the leftovers up and place them in the refrigerator. Back in the bathroom, I turn off the water and walk over to the mirror. Looking at my reflection, I let my ponytail down to fall past my shoulders. It hasn't been done since Zema had her hands in it. I know it's about time for me to find me a new hairdresser; the problem with that is, I don't trust everybody with my hair.

Still standing at the mirror, I undress myself. I want to see what my scar looks like. It's not as bad as it feels, but I can definitely tell it's there. I'm still pissed that the little bitch cut me, and I want to get them back so bad I can taste it. I'm not going to do anything, though, because I don't want any more blood on my hands. Being in the hospital gave me time to think about a lot of things, and I know I've hurt a lot of people. I'm not saying Osha and Asha weren't wrong, because they were. I do know, though, that I'm the cause of all of this. If I had never started fucking with Taz, none of it would have happened in the first place. I befriended Osha knowing damn well I wanted her man, and that just wasn't right at all. I betrayed her, making her believe we were friends, and being stabbed was the price I had to pay for it.

I step into the water and exhale, because it feels so good against my skin. It's a lot different to take a bath at home instead of a shower at the hospital. This is exactly what I've needed, and it feels good to be home. I soak my body for about a half-hour before washing up and getting out. In my bedroom, I lotion up and get into my pajamas, then pull my covers back. My bed feels so good—even better than I expected. I turn on the TV, but I don't get a chance to watch it because I'm asleep in no time.

CHAPTER SIXTEEN

"Yo, Brandy. I don't know what the fuck yo' problem is, but you need to answer your damn phone. You been acting really funky since before you got out the hospital, and I don't know why. I told you I'm sorry about what happened between you and Osha. Damn! What more do you want from me? I shouldn't have to keep calling yo' ass tryin'a get you to answer or even call me back. If you don't wanna be bothered, you oughtta just say that shit, but don't have a nigga blowing yo' shit up daily for nothing!"

I press seven to delete yet another of Taz's messages. It's Friday afternoon, approximately two weeks since I've been out of the hospital. I have yet to answer any of his calls. It's funny, because he said if I didn't want to be bothered, I only have to say so. *Hell, I thought that'd be obvious when I didn't answer for the past few days. I don't see why he doesn't get it. I don't want to talk to his ass. He's left numerous messages on both my phones, but I haven't called him back once.*

The phone rings as I hold it in my hand, and of course it's Taz. I debate on whether to answer it or not, but I know if I don't, he's going to call me until I do.

"Hello?" I answer dryly.

"Where the fuck you been?" he yells in my ear.

"Well hello to yo' ass too, nigga."

"Look, Brandy, I ain't got time for the bullshit. What the fuck is up with you, man?"

185

I do my favorite move and pull the phone away from my ear and just stare at it, because this dude is tripping for real. "What the fuck is up with you?"

"Ain't shit up with me."

"Well, then what the fuck's your problem?"

"First of all, don't talk to me like that. I ain't one of your fucking kids. Second, I'm a grown-ass woman, and I don't have to answer to anybody," I snap, wondering who the hell he thinks he is.

"Fuck all that dumb shit. I've been calling you for days, and yo' ass ain't called me back once. What, you don't wanna fuck wit' a nigga no mo'? If that's what it is, just say that shit."

I don't say anything.

"Look…I said I was sorry about what Osha and her sister did to you, but you tryin'a play me and shit like I did the shit or something. What more do you want me to do?"

"For starters, stop blowing up my fuckin' phone every five minutes," I blurt out by mistake.

"Okay. How about I don't call yo' joint no more, huh?"

"That'll be okay too."

"Take that as done."

Figuring that it's the end of the conversation, I prepare to tell him goodbye but what he asks next throws me off guard.

"All I need to know is where the fuck my money is."

"What you mean?" I ask.

"I mean what the fuck I said. Where's my money?" he asks once again.

"Right where I told you it is. It's in your bank account," I lie, all while praying like hell that he hasn't already checked it.

"Hmm. Well, there's a problem then, 'cause there's only 50 Gs in that account. I'm missing at least 2.5 mill."

"What?" I act shocked. "I'm going to call the bank Monday morning and see what the hell is going on," I lie again.

"Yeah, you do that, but don't play with me, Brandy. You, of all people, know I don't play about my money, and if you're thinking about fucking me over, you'd better think again," he warns. I chuckle, because he really must think I'm scared of him or something.

"What the fuck is so funny?" he snaps.

"Nothing," I say and continue giggling.

"Bitch, you laughing at me now?"

"Bitch? Did you just call me a bitch?" I ask, shocked, as he's never disrespected me like that before.

"Yeah, because you're acting like a bitch right now. You making me wanna put two in your fucking head right now, girl, and that's not a good thing. My money is missing, and I'm not in the mood to be playing and shit. Peep this. You have my money back in my account by Monday, and I'll let you live. If it's not there by, let's say, noon, yo' ass is gonna come up missing."

I laugh once more just to fuck with him a bit more. "You ain't gon' do a muthafucking thing to me, nigga! You might wanna save all those empty-ass threats for somebody else."

"Yeah, I hear ya hollerin'. You just make sure you handle that li'l mama. Yo' life depends on it."

"Fuck you, Taz!" I yell into the receiver, only to find out that he's already hung up.

Dropping my phone into my lap in disbelief, I chuckle because I can't believe he even fixed his lips to come at me all greasy. *Who the hell does he think he is, and who does he think I am? I'm not the least bit worried about him doing a damn thing for me.* Getting up off the couch, I head into the kitchen to grab something to drink. With bottled water in hand, I close the fridge and stare at the calendar hanging from it. The date reads December 15, and I almost drop my water. Today's the day Taz meets up with his connect.

My mind begins to churn as I come up with a plan to teach this muthafucka that I'm not the one to mess with. I walk over to my purse, and fish around inside, until I have exactly what I need. Back over to the couch, I pick up my cell phone, and begin dialing the digits on the card I'm holding. The phone rings about three times before he finally answers.

"Cuyahoga county police department, this is Detective Andres speaking. How may I help you?"

"Hello. I have some information about a drug transaction and an unsolved murder," I say into the phone.

"Okay. Can I have your name, ma'am?" the Detective asks.

"I would rather remain anonymous."

He tells me that he understands and I tell him the location where he can find Taz and Dan. I disclose the color of the truck and mention that they'll have a trunk full of drugs. I give him all the information I know about Xavier's murder and where they can find the murder weapon. I also tell him that I have evidence with the victim's blood on it: Taz's t-shirt that I took out of his bag after he fell asleep. The next morning, when he took the bag out of the house, he didn't even think to check for everything inside, and now he's royally fucked. As soon as I give Detective Andres all the information, I smile.

Mission accomplished!

I just hope that he can get to Taz, just as fast as he got to Angel when I gave him information about him.

***

It's been a week since I saw the story on the news about the biggest drug bust in Ohio history. The police caught up with Taz and Dan the night I reported them. A rookie trooper pulled them over on the freeway, but instead of waiting for backup, he decided to take matters into his own hands. When he first walked up to the truck, he smelled weed and asked to search the vehicle. At that point, all hell broke loose. Dan shot the trooper in the neck and jumped out of the truck, running on foot into a wooded area. About that time, backup arrived, and a few of the officers jumped out of their cars and gave chase. Moments later, gunfire erupted. Two officers died, including the one who was shot in the neck, and three others were injured. Dan was taken to the hospital with bullets in his chest and back.

Taz, on the other hand, put the truck in gear as soon as Dan fled and led the other police on a high-speed chase that ended with him losing control and hitting a telephone pole. Once they had both men in custody, they searched the truck and hit the jackpot. They confiscated 100 kilos of cocaine that was stashed in a built-in metal floorboard of Taz's truck. They found 600 pounds of marijuana packed tightly in suitcases located in the trunk and over a 1,000 ecstasy pills. Both were denied bail and were charged with trafficking of drugs, conspiracy to possess with the intent to distribute cocaine, fleeing and eluding, possession of a firearm, two counts of aggravated murder, and a list of other charges that will pretty much guarantee them both life in prison.

Taz called me the following day to give me the scoop about the whole thing. He said he and Dan were riding on the freeway, after meeting his connect, when a police car pulled behind them and turned on his lights. Dan got nervous and put out the blunt he was smoking, but it was too late because the officer had already smelled it when he rolled down the window. Everything was cool until the officer asked if it was okay for him to search the truck. Taz said everything from then on was in slow motion, and all he saw was Dan reaching for his gun and firing one shot at the police. He panicked and hit the gas as soon as Dan jumped out and started running. "It was so fucked up, Brandy. It was so fucked up," he kept saying, and I kind of feel bad for him because I don't think Dan would actually murder a police officer. I've always viewed that nigga as being way too soft for that, but I guess you really can't judge a book by its cover.

Taz said he just got a few bruises from the accident and

an ass-whooping from the police when they caught up with him, but Dan was another story. After talking to a hysterical Zema, he found out he'll never walk again; one of the bullets he took severed his spinal cord. Not only will Dan spend the rest of his days locked away in prison, but also in a wheelchair. I know he has to feel like shit, but he brought it on himself. Nobody told his dumb ass to fire shots at the police like his ass was invincible or some shit! I listened as Taz when on and on about his fucked-up situation, and I even pretended to be worried about him—until he had the nerve to ask me for his money.

He said he needed it because he needed to hire a real good lawyer to get him out of the jam he was in. He wanted me to withdraw it from the bank for him ASAP. I sat quietly on the phone and didn't respond right away, because I was trying to form the proper words in my head. After a while, he began to call my name over and over again, and that irritated the shit out of me. At that time, I explained to him that he no longer has any money and that it all belongs to me. Of course he became irate and threatened to kill me and everyone I know, which made me even more upset. I spilled out that I'm the one who tipped off the police about them riding dirty.

The real icing on the cake was when I let him know it was me who mailed the police his bloody t-shirt, the one he was wearing the night he and Dan murdered Xavier. I didn't know if the police where listening or not, but I explained to him that Xavier was the love of my life and that he murdered him for nothing. I didn't understand a word that came from his mouth after that because he was yelling so loudly. I ended up shutting him down and letting him know I'm not worried about anything he was screaming because I have all his money, and he's not getting out anytime soon. He yelled a bit more, and when I couldn't take it anymore, I told him I hope he rots in hell and just hung up. All that screaming was giving me a fuckin' headache anyway.

Finally pulling myself out of the slump I'm in, I pick up my phone and call my realtor. I inform him that I want to put my house on the market, because I'm ready to relocate to another state. I don't mention which state, because I'm not even sure my damn self. He tells me it won't be a problem and says he'll put it on the list for first thing Monday morning because everything is closed over Christmas weekend. I thank him and tell him I'd like to have it sold as quickly as possible. Again, he tells me it shouldn't be a problem, and we disconnect our call.

I lie in my bed for a few more minutes, thinking about where I should go and when I should leave. I decide to leave as soon as New Year's is over. Putting my things in storage won't be a problem, and I can just stay in a hotel until I find a house. I know I've already burned enough bridges in Ohio; it's time for me to make a change and get the hell out of this dreadful-ass place. I have more than enough money to do whatever I want.

Excited, I jump out of bed and head into my office. I power on my laptop before I even get a chance to sit down. I pull up the FrontDoor.com site and began searching for real estate in South Carolina. I've fought with myself over and over about whether or not I actually want to go there, and I know that I do. Even though Xavier is no longer with me, I'll always have the memories of the wonderful time we shared while there.

It doesn't take long for me to find a place I like, a four-bedroom condo with three full baths. The place sits right on the beach, and the gourmet kitchen, walk-in closets, two balconies, and pools really catch my eye. The price tag is $495,000, but I don't bat an eye at that, because I've got that and plenty more. I pick up my phone and call the realtor to see if the property is still available, and I'm excited to find out that it is. After I explain to her that I live in Ohio and am interested in relocating, she's more than happy to hold off showing the property until after New Year's. I make a few more calls about other homes, then hang up the phone, really looking forward to getting away.

Back inside my room, I throw on my gray Donna Karan jogging outfit and a pair of Air Max and head for the door on my way to U-Haul to get a bunch of boxes. I plan to come home and pack my shit so I can be out of here in less than a week.

***

Yesterday, while I was out, I stopped and spoke to a storage company about keeping my stuff there until I find a new home. They gave me a wonderful deal and even allowed me to pay beforehand so I can have my belongings shipped to me once I'm settled. I graciously thanked the clerk and told her she'll be hearing from me within the next week or so.

After I picked up the moving boxes, I went to work and packed up almost everything I own, only leaving out the things I plan to use for the next week and the stuff I'll be taking to South Carolina. It took me quite a few hours to get everything boxed up, and after all that hard work, I just sit on the floor. I don't think I've ever been so tired in my entire life!

Today, my body is sore, and I'm still beat, but I've got a huge smile on my face—at least for a minute. I'm just sitting in my dining room, dressed in my panties and bra, pouring shot after shot from a bottle of Jose Cuervo. I rub my hands across my face and sigh. I suddenly realize I've got nobody in this world besides me, myself, and I, and that really sucks. I don't have a bit of family, not one friend, or even a man in my life and it's mostly my fault. Besides my mother, my father, and Rodger, I basically pushed everybody else away. Tears fall from my eyes and land on the glass table in front of me. My shoulders tremble as I cry from deep within. There are so many questions floating around in my head; some I have the answers to, and others I don't. I wish I could get all of my questions answered so I could figure out what my purpose in life is. *What am I destined to be? Will I ever know?*

There are a few questions I've asked myself over the years, questions that could possible reveal why I am the way I am. *Why didn't my mother love me? Why did she feel the need to treat me the way she did? Why couldn't she just love me the way mothers are supposed to love their children? Was I not good enough for her to love?* No matter how many times I ask myself these questions, I will never know the answer to any of them, because my mother is long gone. I still don't know if Pitch was even my real father. All I do know is that he came to the hospital, and they allowed him to take me away. *Did they allow it because he was really my father or simply because I had no one else in this world, so giving me to him was easier than finding proper foster care? If I was his daughter, why didn't he love me? Why'd he put me on the track like I was just some chick off the street?*

"Why!?" I yell out loud. The questions are driving me crazy! Then, suddenly, it finally hits me. I want to blame my parents for how I've turned out, but truthfully, I can't. There are only a few things I can totally blame them for, and one of them is my abusive childhood. They made a lot of bad decisions concerning me, and that's why I grew up never being able to trust anyone. Beyond that, it all falls on my shoulders. I chose to ruin people's lives. Yes, it was partially my parents' fault for screwing me over so bad that I couldn't trust another human being, but I'm the one who tried to make people pay.

I didn't have to do the things I've done to get by; I could've just cut the ones loose who did me wrong and kept it moving, but my vindictive nature wouldn't allow me to. Take Rodger, for instance. Sure, he lied to me, and I truly believe I was entitled to his money. Still, I went so far as to turn him in to the police and ruined his life and his family's lives. I could've easily gotten the money and left him alone, but I didn't.

Then there's poor Sade. I didn't care before, but now I feel really bad for the girl. Yes, she attempted to use me, but that's only because I let her. It started out as just a quick money scheme, but because of me, it turned into something much more. I didn't have to take my payback as far as I did; hell, I killed her baby, for Christ's sake! What makes that even more fucked up is the fact that I knew what the consequences might be, but I did it anyway. I didn't even offer the girl an apology. Now that I've lost a child, I can't even imagine the pain that she went through when her son died. I know it won't make things right, but I'm going to put a nice amount of money on her books before I go, just to make sure she'll be all right while she's incarcerated. I'm also going to contact a lawyer and see if they can either shorten her sentence, or get her released somehow. As a matter of fact, on Monday, I'm gonna call around and make sure her kids are straight. I know it won't make everything right, but I at least owe them that much.

As far as McKenzie, the girl just wanted what I owed her, and I couldn't even do that. I tried to pretend she was obligated to do something for me, when she really didn't owe me shit! Yeah, she was a booster, which is against the law, but who am I to turn someone in? That girl got jail time because of me and lost her baby in the process. I did her real dirty by leaving her daughter in the car like that, but I didn't give a damn at the time because I was all about me. I heard she got shipped off to do the rest of her sentence, so on Monday, I'm going to get a money order for what I owe her, along with a little more, and send it to her. I have no way to find her daughter, but if I give her enough money, she'll be all right once she's released.

Angel was nothing but nice to me, yet I stole his money and got him busted. I can't even blame him for trying to kill me; truth of the matter is, I deserved it. Now he's probably going to sit in jail for the rest of his life because I was being greedy.

I even feel bad for the way I did Osha, and right now I forgive her and Asha for what they did to me; they were both justified. I befriended the girl just so I could fuck with her man. I could've done things so much differently, now that I think about it. Pretending to be her best friend was just my vindictive side showing again, because I could've easily left her out of the equation or found my own damn man. I videotaped her and mailed Taz the tape, which caused them to break up and him to move out. Then, just because she called my phone and flipped out on me, I got her kicked out of her house and had Taz questioning if the kids are even his, even though I know they were.

Then there's Taz, who's sitting in jail because I stole his money and didn't want to suffer the consequences for it. He's also charged with murder because he was trying to protect me, all over a lie.

My heart drops into the pit of my stomach when Xavier crosses my mind. *What the hell have I done?* That was the most unnecessary thing I've ever done in my life, and an innocent man is dead just because I thought he was cheating on me. Why couldn't I have just asked him about it or even cut him loose? Naw, I had to take it a step further and make up some bogus-ass story about him raping me and send Taz over to his house. I didn't expect them to kill him, but I knew they were going to do something, and that's just as bad. That wonderful man is no longer here, and that's because of me. He was my lover, my friend, my protector, and my future all wrapped up in one. I guess it's safe to admit it now: He was my everything. We were supposed to raise our child together, but she's not here either, and that's also my fault.

I push the chair out, slowly stand up, and grab the half-empty bottle of tequila and shot glass. I stagger into my bedroom, not even bothering to turn off any of the lights around the house. In my room, I set the glass and bottle on the nightstand. I climb into my unmade bed, plop down, and continue crying about how pathetic my life is. *My baby! A baby I never knew existed until she was gone, a baby I didn't think I could have because of the illegal abortion I was subjected to as a child, a baby I would've died for if it came down to it. She's gone, in heaven with her father. Xavier took his last breath, and Brianna wasn't even able to take her first—all because of me.* I reach over for another drink and fumble with the bottle, almost dropping it because I can't really see through all the tears in my eyes. When I finally have a good grip on it, I fill my glass to the rim and toss it back, allowing the drink to heat up my throat and chest.

I then close my eyes and say a little prayer, letting my daughter and Xavier know how sorry I am and that I hope I will see them in the future. This is something I'm quite sure will never happen, though, because I know that when I die, I'm going straight to hell for all the things I've done and all the people I've hurt in the process. I'm sure I'll be reunited with my mother and Pitch there, because they did so much unthinkable shit while they walked this Earth. It's crazy, but I'm not scared of going to hell. The part that scares me is seeing either of them ever again. The thought of that unhappy reunion makes my skin crawl and causes my heart to beat a mile a minute. Two more full shots in my glass finishes off the bottle, and before I know it, I'm out like a light!

CHAPTER SEVENTEEN

A noise awakens me from my drunken slumber, and my eyes shoot open. I sit up quickly, but this proves not to be a great idea, because my head is spinning, and there's nothing I can do to stop it. The time on the clock reads 3:24 a.m., and it's Christmas morning. I hold my breath and strain my ears to see if I really heard what I think I just heard or if it's merely my imagination. Satisfied that it was nothing, I lie back down, roll over on my side, and prepare to go back to sleep. No sooner than my head hits the pillow, I hear the noise again, louder this time. I'm not crazy, so I know something's going on, and it's in my fuckin' house!

I climb out of bed as slowly as my body permits me to, but it's hard because I'm unsteady from drinking. My feet hit the floor, and as soon as I stand up, I fall down to my knees, catching myself on the bed. I sluggishly pull myself back up into a standing position before reaching into my drawer and grabbing my gun. Feeling a bit more secure, I make my way over to my door. Nothing is in front of me but darkness, and I don't remember turning out all the lights before I went to bed. I'm not really sure, though, since I was drinking pretty heavily and might have forgotten about it. It is eerily silent in the house as I finally make my way to the door; the only thing I can hear is the thumping of my beating heart, so loud that it sounds like it might come out of my chest at any moment.

Reaching my arm outside my door, I slide my hand up

and down the wall until I feel the light switch. Once I have it between my fingers, I slide it up, but nothing happens. I try it a few more times, but no lights come on. I'm scared and don't know what the hell is going on. Next, I hear a noise again. It sounds like someone is walking toward the back of my apartment. My body freezes in fear, and I'm sober all the sudden—more sober than a muthafucka, thanks to what's going on around me. Someone is inside my house, and I'll be damned if they're going to get a hold of me without a fight.

My office door opens, and I take that as my cue to make a run to the door. I have my gun in hand, but I'm too damn scared to use it. I also don't give a damn that I'm only clad in panties and bra, because I'm ready to get the fuck out of here! I take off running into the living room, but as I try to scurry across it, I trip over the glass coffee table, making a lot of racket. Even though my toe is killing me, I still continue my stride to the front door; whoever is in here surely heard that noise. Limping lightly, I make my way around the table and a chair and head to the door. I see light creeping in below it, and I pray I can make it that far. I'll then have to get on the elevator and make it down to the lobby; only then will I feel safe. My heart beats even more rapidly as I get close enough to reach out and grab the doorknob, but a powerful blow to my head causes everything to go black.

***

When I finally open my eyes, I'm dazed and confused. I look around, trying to figure out where I am, but it's too dark to see anything. It seems like I'm sitting in a chair of some sort. *But...how?* I wonder. Trying to move my arms gets me nowhere, because they seem to be bound tightly by something; the same goes for my legs. Panic shoots through my body when I remember that I am in my own house, and I think someone is still inside with me. I recall making my way to the front door, but just as I reached out to grab the knob, I was hit over the head with something hard; I don't remember anything after that. My mind is racing, I'm trying to figure out what the hell is going on and what whoever is in my house plans to do to me. I kind of figure they must not want me dead, because if they did, they could have already made it so I'd never wake up. *What else could they possibly want?* I'm scared to ask the question and even more scared of the answer.

The back of my head is throbbing, and I smell the stench of blood in the air. Again I try to move my arms and legs, but nothing happens; I'm still stuck. Minutes pass as I'm tied to this chair, and I still don't hear anything—nothing at all. I want to scream for help, but I'm worried that the person who did this to me is still inside. *What will I do then? I guess the same thing I'm gonna do whenever that bastard decides to come back and do whatever he or she has planned to do all along. Fuck it,* I decide. *It ain't like I have anything to lose at this point anyway.* "Help! Help!"" I scream at the top of my lungs.

Suddenly, the lights come back on, causing my eyes to sting a bit. My head instantly begins to pulsate from the pain of being drunk, as well as from the blow I received. I try my best to squint, trying to regain focus in my vision; that's pretty hard to do since I've been in the dark for so long. When I'm finally able to see clearly, I notice that I'm in the center of my master bathroom. Duct tape is around my wrists, and I'm tied to one of my dining room chairs. I'm still dressed in my panties and bra, so I kinda figure I haven't been sexually assaulted. There are small stains of blood on my left breast and my shoulder, but I've got no idea where it came from. I tilt my head toward the mirror over by the sink; my hair has dried blood caked in it, and my it's on my face as well. I cringe at the sight of my reflection. *Who in the hell could've done this? And why?*

"So Sleeping Beauty's finally awake, huh?" a female voice says.

I snap my head in the direction of the voice, which is coming from right outside my door, but I don't see anything.

"You thought you were untouchable, didn't you?"

Still, I can't seem to make out the bitch's voice. "Wh-who the hell is that?" I ask.

"You've done a lot of shit to a lot of people, Miss Lady, and now it's time for you to pay."

"Who the fuck are you? Why don't you show your face, bitch?" I boldly yell, even though I'm scared shitless.

When she rounds the corner and enters the bedroom, I find myself in utter shock. *Wait...what the hell is she doing here?*

"Don't look so surprised, Brandy. Aren't you happy to see me?" she mocks. She's dressed in black leggings, black combat boots, and a black t-shirt under a half-zipped black hoodie.

I just stare at her, still taken aback by her presence.

"Say something, bitch!" she yells as she takes steps closer toward me.

I still don't utter a word.

My silence makes her angry, because before I know what's going on, she reaches back and smacks the shit out of me with the back of her hand. My head snaps back before bouncing back into place. The whole right side of my face stings, but there's nothing I can do about it. At this moment, I wish like hell that I could get up out this chair and beat the brakes off this ho for putting her hands on me, but I don't say anything. I just glare at her, letting her know that if and when I get loose, her ass is surely mine.

She knows it to, but right now she has the upper hand, so she uses it to her advantage. "Aw, did that hurt?" she taunts, then laughs, making me angrier and angrier by the second.

Her smile disappears, and she balls up her fist and hits me in the side with all her might—the side where all the stitches are. This knocks the wind out of me, before the pain starts. It shoots though my body with a feeling so intense that it causes me to throw up all over my chest and legs. A small amount lands on her boots; pissed off about that, she hits me again in the same exact spot. I cry out in pain and beg her to stop, but she hits me twice more with jabs to my side. I can't take it anymore, and it feels like that area is about to explode.

I can't hold my tongue any longer, so I finally break my silence. "How did you know where I live…and why are you doing this to me?"

"Oh! She finally talks." She walks over to my bathtub and stands there a while before taking a seat on the edge; I notice she's put on a small amount of weight since the last time I saw her. "I know where you live because Osha told me not too long ago. We were riding by, and she showed me your apartment building. I figured the rest out because of your parking space. Smart, huh?" She laughs. When I don't reply, she says, "Tell me, Brandy, why do you think I'm doing this to you?"

"Shit, I don't know. You tell me. You broke into my home and tied me up, yet I don't remember ever doing anything to you. I admit I crossed your girl, but that shouldn't have anything to do with you. What the fuck is your beef with me, Zema?"

"You can't really be that stupid, can you?"

When I don't answer, we share a stare-down for a full minute.

"Look, if you ain't gon' tell me what the hell you trippin' on, then let me the fuck go!" I yell.

"You and I both know that's not about to happen, so I guess I'll just tell you why I'm here." She leans back against the wall, stretching her legs across the tub. "First off, my full name is Zema Vines, and I'm the daughter of Roger Vines, your ex-lover."

My eyes nearly pop out of my head. "You…you can't be," I say, unable to believe I've been getting my hair done by his daughter all this time. It makes sense, now that I think about it, because she has the same weird-colored eyes as her father. Now that I know the truth, I can see the resemblance.

"Trust me, I'm his daughter, but that's not even why I'm here. I knew you were fucking my father. I found out right before you enrolled in Life Skills. He asked me to keep an eye on you, and at first, I was going to tell you, but Daddy made an offer I just couldn't refuse. He promised me that if I befriended you and kept you close, not only would he pay for me to get my own shop after I finished cosmetology school, but he'd also give me the money to purchase everything else I needed for it. I had to do what he wanted, for the sake of my future." She leans forward and unzips the hoodie, then removes it and lays it on the floor. "I don't blame you for what you did to my father, because he deserved that and more for the way he did my mother. She gave him everything he needed, and he chose to throw it all away for a girl the same age as his only child."

"Okay, so Roger is your father, but you're not here for him. Why are you here?"

"You ever hear of a little boy named Tyreak?"

"No."

"Well, he was my cousin's son, and you poisoned him just because you didn't want to pay his mother the money you owed her."

What!? This has gotta be a joke. There's no way in hell she can know about that.

"Yeah, Sade had a baby by my oldest cousin on my mother's side, the little boy you poisoned. Now his mother is sitting in jail for some shit she didn't even do."

"You can't put that shit on me. I didn't have anything to do with that."

"Do you remember McKenzie?" she asks, ignoring the hell out of me.

I don't reply and nod my head.

"Well, she's my god-sister. That's why I let her sell her shit in my shop. She told me about your fight in the mall that day, and I put two and two together. My cousin told me that

Sade's cousin ran up on some chick named Brandy and whooped her ass in the mall. I didn't know before that, I didn't have a clue who the chick was he was talking about until that day. Ironic, huh?" She chuckles. "By the way, I know you did McKenzie dirty also."

"I didn't do shit to that girl! She went into the store stealing and got caught. How is that my problem?"

"I'm not stupid, Brandy. You can try to run that innocent game on the next bitch, because I ain't falling for it!" she yells. "The security guards told her a woman called in and gave them an exact description, even described what she was wearing. She wouldn't have gotten caught otherwise. She also told me you'd been bullshitting about paying her the money you owed her. With her in jail, you don't have to pay her a dime, right?"

"That's not what happened," I lie.

"The real fucked-up thing is that you called the cops on her and told them a bogus-ass story about her leaving her daughter in the car. They took her baby from her for neglect, when you were supposed to be watching her. If anything, you should have been locked up for abandoning a child in a hot-ass car in the middle of summer!"

"I didn't just leave her in the car. I stuck around until the police came. What the hell else was I supposed to do, take the little girl home with me?" I ask, irritated.

"What you should have done was pay her the damn money you owed her. Then, none of that shit would've happened."

I don't even have to think about what she's saying, because I know she's right. All of it is my fault. "You're right, Zema, and I'm sorry. I swear I was thinking of ways to make it right last night. I was going to mail off a money order to her with the money I owe her and more. I feel really bad about the way I did her, and I want to apologize to her."

"That's cool, and you can do that, but that's not why I'm here either."

I exhale because I know she's beating around the bush, and I'm losing patience. *Who else does this bitch know?* "Once again, if you're not here for that, then what are you doing in my damn house, tying me up and shit?"

"You've done so much dirt, Brandy. You have no clue how many people you've hurt in the small amount of time you've been around. You played Osha to the left after you pretended to be her friend. What kind of bitch are you? How can you sleep at night knowing that you've hurt so many people for nothing?" When I don't say anything, she continues. "She knows you sent that videotape to the house for Taz to watch, and she also knows you drugged her that night. It took me a while to figure out that Taz was your focus all along. I remember when I did your hair in the shop that day and told you about the party, you couldn't have been less interested." She giggles. "Then I started talking about Taz, and you were all ears, asking me all kinds of questions about the party you didn't seem to give a fuck about just minutes earlier. It didn't hit me at the time, because I was trying to give you a chance. I knew you had it rough growing up."

"What do you mean by that?"

"Daddy wrote me and told me everything after he was sentenced. I know all about how your mother and father made you sell your body. Daddy met you on the track, didn't he?"

I don't reply, but my eyes begin to water from the memories she's drudging up. The bitch knows my deepest, darkest secrets because Roger told her. He promised me he wouldn't tell anyone about the things I'd shared with him. Just like everyone else in my life, he turned out to be a liar. I know I shouldn't be shocked, considering how I did him, but it still hurts because I actually thought he'd hold up his end of the bargain, even if I didn't hold up mine. Secretly, I wonder how many people she may have told. *Did she tell Osha? Did Osha tell Taz everything? Did Dan know? Who*

*the hell else knows about my sordid past, all the shit I went
through as a child?*

"Don't worry. I didn't tell anyone," she says, almost as if
she's reading my mind. "I don't know if you're even aware
of it, but Osha really did like you, and so did I—until I saw
you all up in Taz's face at the barbecue that day. I knew
something wasn't right, and I tried to tell Osha about it, but
she just brushed me off and said you wouldn't do anything
like that to her because you were her friend. I backed off, but
I still kept an eye on you, and look what happened. You took
my best friend's man and made him your own."

"What about Osha? She ain't innocent in this. Her and
her sister jumped me and stabbed me. I was in the hospital
for weeks, and I lost my baby because of it! What about
me?"

"I'm sorry to hear about your baby, as I'd never wish
harm on an innocent child, but you brought this all on
yourself. You're lucky that's all she did to you, because I
would've killed you for doing some shady shit like that to
me."

"So you're paying me this little house call because of
what I did to Osha? That shouldn't even been your problem,
Zema. You're getting in shit that doesn't even concern you.
You already called them up to the shop when I was there.
What more do you want from me?" I ask, because none of it
makes any sense. She says none of these people are why
she's here, and I want to know what the hell she's doing in
my house. For a minute I think Taz sent her, but I quickly
erase that thought from my mind, because I know he
would've just sent Osha instead.

"I'm here because you also took my man from me."

"Dan?" I ask, confused. "I never fucked with Dan, and if
he told you I did, he's a damn liar!"

"You might not have fucked with him, but you sure as
hell fucked him over. You're the reason he's in jail," she tells
me coldly.

"I didn't have shit to do with that," I lie.

"Don't insult my intelligence, Brandy. Taz already told me what happened. You ratted them out to the cops, and you even gave the police evidence to convict Taz for murdering your boyfriend."

The words cut deep, because I know I'll never forgive myself for Xavier's death.

"Now my man is paralyzed from the waist up, all because of some grudge you had with Taz. That beef you had was with him, and Dan had nothing to do with it. Why should he have to suffer for it? On top of that, I'm four months pregnant with his baby, you bitch!" she yells; it now makes sense why she's put on a few extra pounds.

"Dan shot a cop. How the fuck is that my fault? Your baby-daddy is paralyzed because of the dumb shit he did, and you can't possibly blame me for that! I wasn't even in the car, so how can you blame me?"

"Are you fucking kidding me?" she asked, placing her feet firmly on the floor. "Do you even believe the shit that's coming out of your own mouth? Are you telling me Taz lied to me?" She reaches down on the floor and into her jacket, then produces a long army knife.

I'm scared as hell now, because the flicker I just saw in her eyes can't be good for me. All I can think to do is to lie my way out of it and pray that she believes me. "That's what I'm saying. I didn't do any of that stuff, Zema."

I brace myself as she gets closer and closer to me, because I know she's going to hit me at any moment. Instead, she uses the knife to stab me in the shoulder and twists it into my wound. I try to scream, but I can't. The pain is too much for me to handle, and I can't breathe. It feels like it did when Asha stabbed me at the shop, only ten times worst. When she finally pulls the knife out, I can breathe again. This only lasts for a minute, though, because no sooner than I exhale, she's plunging the knife into my other shoulder and doing the same. Blood leaks down my arms and onto the floor, and all I can do is watch helplessly, in a great amount of pain.

"You're gonna pay for the shit you've done to people, and it's gonna cost you your life." Her eyes look empty, and she looks possessed. "Yes, Dan shot the cop, but you called the cops in the first place. Tell me I'm lying." She takes another step toward me.

I'm too scared to lie, so I try to make her pity me instead. "Okay, okay! I did call the police, but only on Taz. He told me he was going to kill me, and I got scared. I had no idea that Dan was in the car. I'm sorry about what happened to him, and if I could take it all back, I would, but I can't. I'll go down to the courthouse and tell them I made a mistake and that they have the wrong guys. I'll do it first thing in the morning. Just please…please don't do this," I plead. I'm still in agonizing pain, but I have to say something, anything to get her to let me go.

"It's too late for that, and all that shit ain't gonna change the fact that he'll be paralyzed and in jail for the rest of his life. You're going to die tonight," she says menacingly with that same empty look in her eyes.

I begin to move my arms and legs as best as I can, trying to release myself from the chair. I have to get out of here because I know if I don't, she's going to kill me. I have no desire to die on Christmas day—or any day thereafter. She bends down in front of me and forces the knife into my side, then pulls it out quickly and does it again, not too far from the first wound. This time, I cry out like an injured animal, and she shuts me up by hitting me in the mouth with a closed fist. My jaws instantly fill with blood, but I continue screaming praying that someone somewhere will hear me and help me. I yell until I can no longer hear myself; it sounds as if I'm gargling because of all the blood in my mouth.

"Take that, you whore!" she yells, stabbing me again, this time in my stomach.

I bend over as much as I can, considering I'm still tied to the chair.

"I'm done playing games with you. Do you have any last words before I send your ratchet ass straight to hell?"

"Fuck you!" Gathering as much saliva and blood as I can muster, I spit it directly into her face, which causes her to scream. I know for a fact that she's going to kill me, and I might as well go out with a bang.

"Naw, fuck you!" She laughs as she wipes the blood and spit off her face with the bottom of her shirt, showing off her small baby bump.

She then walks casually behind me and grabs a bunch of my hair. I grunt when she pulls my hair back roughly and slides the sharp end of the knife across my neck with so much force that I can hear my skin being separated. Blood immediately exits my throat, and the warm liquid slides from my neck down to my chest, landing on my thighs. I make more gargling sounds as I try to speak, I'm bleeding to death. Zema lets my head go, and because I can't really control it, it bobs back and forth with no direction. I try with all my might to reach up and grab my throat, but my hands are still tied down with tape, and all I can do is cry. Using a white washcloth in the bathroom, Zema wipes her face and the knife clean, then slides the blade back in her jacket pocket. She then puts the hoodie back on and begins to exit the bathroom, only turning around to blow me a kiss before leaving.

I can't believe that in one year, I've done enough damage to ruin many lives. Not one thing was minor; everything I've done has practically ruined the rest of their lives. My own choices got me where I am today: drowning in my blood in my own bathroom, killed by a person I never would've thought would have the balls to do it.

It's faint, but I can hear the door open and close in the front of my apartment, and I know Zema is gone. My body starts to convulse, and my eyes roll to the back of my head. I try to suck in air, but nothing seems to work. As I take my final breath and surrender to the inevitable arrival of death, one final thought occurs to me: Being heartless has a way of catching up with you these days, so be careful who you cross. You never know whose lives you might ruin in the process...or who'll come after you for payback!

The End

42241569R00129

Made in the USA
Middletown, DE
05 April 2017